Praise for Patricia Park

4 Stars! "Dead of Winter un_____ _____ people in a race to find a killer before they strike again...The relationship Steve and Kate found was based on trust, equality and finally a love that bound them together. Patricia Parkinson writes an intriguing and highly entertaining story of two people discovering a love that overcomes any obstacle in its way and bringing closure to questions asked. Dead Of Winter is definitely one book that needs to be added to my collection."

~ Sheryl, eCataRomance

4 Angels! "Dead Of Winter by Patricia Parkinson is an exciting, thrilling, and suspenseful novel about a couple trying to apprehend a killer all while dealing with their growing attraction for one another. I applaud Ms. Parkinson on doing an amazing job of withholding the identity of the mysterious killer until the very end. I found myself trying to guess the identity of executioner all thought this splendid murder mystery...If you are a fan of a romantic murder mystery, then pick up Dead Of Winter by Patricia Parkinson. You will not be disappointed!"

~ Contessa, Fallen Angel Reviews

Dead of Winter

By Patricia Parkinson

A Samhain Publishing, Ltd. publication

Samhain Publishing, Ltd.
PO Box 2206
Stow OH 44224

Dead of Winter
Copyright © 2006 by Patricia Parkinson
Cover by Scott Carpenter
Print ISBN: 1-59998-128-9
Digital ISBN: 1-59998-012-6
www.samhainpublishing.com

First Samhain Publishing, Ltd. electronic publication: March 2006
First Samhain Publishing, Ltd. print publication: June 2006

Dead of Winter

By Patricia Parkinson

CHAPTER ONE

The rear end of the four-wheel drive truck did a swift slide to the right. Kate corrected by turning the steering wheel in the opposite direction, easing up on the gas at the same time.

The fact that Harley's driveway wasn't plowed increased her uneasiness, which was growing at a rapid pace. She pressed down hard on the gas pedal again, her Toyota truck fishtailing like a salmon swimming upstream.

"Hold on, girl. We're almost there." Sunny didn't answer and Kate hadn't expected one. Her sixty-pound mutt dog was a strange color of yellow, black and brown, all tossed together.

The Montana sky was a bright and vivid blue. The February sun was a burning yellow ball high in the sky. The snow had floated and tangoed from the sky for thirty-six hours straight, covering the mountains with a heavy blanket of snow. The temperature plummeted during the night. It was a cozy ten above.

The brakes locked and Kate missed the parking area, finally stopping somewhere on Harley's lawn, buried under deep snow. The familiar curl of smoke from the chimney was missing.

Kate shoved her door open, and sunk almost to her knees when she climbed out of her truck. She was dressed for snow in warm, waterproof pants and sturdy winter boots. Sunny vaulted out behind her, burying herself in the deep snow. The dog shook herself off, then started leaping through the snow toward the house.

Apprehension coiled into a tight ball inside her tummy.

Three nights ago when she had visited Harley, he'd been distracted, not his usual self, with something obviously on his mind. Kate hadn't pushed about the issue troubling him, believing Harley would tell her in his own good time. She knew Harley and his ways. He had stepped into the shoes her runaway father had left behind. Over the years Harley became the real father of her heart.

The first signs of unease had inched through her when she'd called him an hour ago and he hadn't answered.

Her palms sweated inside her wool gloves as she trudged through the snow toward the house. Ranger, Harley's dog, was nowhere in sight. The walkway was buried under the fresh snow, too.

Kate bounded up the steps and banged on the door. "Harley!" She didn't wait for him to answer. Kate threw open the door, rushing inside.

The frigid air inside the house slammed her, like a hard slap to her face.

"Harley!" Kate raced through the small two-bedroom, one story house, praying the old man was okay. That he was fine, his bluer than blue eyes twinkling.

Kate stopped at the door of his bedroom and saw that the bed was made. Ten seconds later, she threw open the back door, slipping on the steps covered with snow. She managed to catch herself before she took a tumble. It was a short hike to the garage behind the house, but that walkway hadn't been cleared either. Kate pushed open the door, hitting the light switch.

Harley's vintage nineteen seventy-eight Ford truck, with the straight edged plow attached to the front, sat in the middle of the building, lonely and forlorn. Kate sucked in a couple of deep breaths to fight back the panic attack threatening to erupt inside of her. A moment later, she heard Sunny barking. Kate wheeled around, fear bursting inside of her, struggling to run through the deep snow toward Harley's firewood stacked behind his house.

If something had happened to Harley...

There weren't any papers, or blood, to prove he was her father. It all was in his heart, and hers.

Kate lost traction, slipped, and landed hard on her fanny. "Damn." She scrambled to her feet, not bothering to brush the snow off her pants.

Kate found Sunny behind the stacks of wood, standing next to Ranger. Ranger lay on the ground, his furry head on his front paws, a look of utter helplessness flooding his canine eyes. The half Husky, half Shepherd, with his black eyes and dusky brown and black fur, raised his head. Kate went to the dog, dropped to her knees. She cradled his head in her hands. "Ranger, what is it, boy? Where's Harley?"

Ranger whined. The dog and old man were inseparable. Where Harley went, so did Ranger. Kate scrambled to her feet, every muscle in her body strung tight with fear.

Nothing made sense. Harley was gone. Ranger, out by the woodpile, alone. No answer when she had called him this morning. For a man in his seventies, he was in good shape, with a strong heart. Kate slowly circled around, her eyes scanning the area. The pine trees, their branches drooping under the weight of the recent snow, bordered the large open space around the house. When she turned back, she noticed Sunny digging at the snow, burrowing her brown nose into it. Kate took a step.

Sunny dug at the snow, her paws frantically clawing their way deeper. When faded red flannel surfaced, Kate nearly toppled over. She moved closer to Sunny, forcing air into her lungs.

"Ohmigod." Kate sank to her knees and started digging at the snow beside her dog.

※　※　※

Sheriff Steve Lambert stopped his sheriff's Blazer next to Kate Madison's dark green Toyota. He spotted her sitting on an old rocker on the covered front porch with Harley Wilson's dog resting his head on her lap. The dog was mostly Husky and mean looking. Kate's dog, Sunny—an undetermined breed, but big nonetheless—sat on the porch next to her, ears and eyes alert.

Why did Kate have to be the one to find the old man? From what he understood, Harley Wilson was more than a friend; he was a father, minus the blood genes. Steve got out, feeling the chill of the snow slipping over his uniform trousers into his boots.

Cursing under his breath at the snow soaking his pants' legs, he walked to the porch. "Kate?"

She stopped petting the dog, looked up at him. Kate Madison wasn't a classic beauty. She was early forties with rich brown hair that curled around her face and kissed her shoulders. Laugh lines fanned out from her almond colored eyes. Some might call her face plain, but it was her brown eyes that stole the show. The sorrow pooled deep in her gorgeous eyes forced him to glance away for a moment. He only had a few minutes with her before the ambulance arrived. Ten minutes ago, the dispatcher had called him with the news. "Kate, are you okay?"

She shook her head, bit her bottom lip. In contradiction, she said, "Yeah, I'm okay." Kate glanced away. "Harley was murdered."

Steve's spine tingled. "What makes you think that?"

Kate shifted on the chair and patted the dog's head again. "Because he was healthy."

"Jesus, Kate, he was in his seventies."

"He was still healthy."

"Where is he?"

"Behind the woodpile."

Steve nodded. He took one long look at Kate before he turned and went down the steps. Besides grief, there was a stubborn look in her brown eyes. Kate worked part time at the Pine Branch Café, writing mystery novels in her spare time. He hoped like hell her fiction world hadn't caused her to go over the deep end about Harley's death.

"There's a gash on the back of his head."

Startled, Steve swung around to face her. The dogs flanked her on each side. He didn't want to make any rash judgments or jump to conclusions before he had a look at Harley. "Why don't you go in the house?"

"The house?" Her lower lip trembled. "It's like a walk-in freezer in there. Harley's stiff as a board."

Steve winced at Kate's description of Harley. He wanted to hug her tight to his chest, but Kate Madison wasn't interested in him. She'd never said it outright and he had never made a move. He'd always figured her divorce had soured her on men.

"You'll see I'm right."

Steve ate a curse word, then turned back in the direction of the stacks of firewood. He heard Kate and the dogs at his heels. He was the leader of the mini parade trudging out to view Harley's body. Steve's jaw tightened. He followed the tracks to the back of the neatly stacked rows of lodgepole firewood.

He swallowed another four-letter word, when he saw that Kate had completely uncovered the old man. If there had been foul play, she might have disturbed evidence. But hell, it had snowed a good eighteen inches the last day and a half. The snow on its own would have erased any evidence.

Steve angled over to Harley, crouched down and gently lifted the old man's head. His slate grey hair was thick and wavy. Harley's blue eyes stared up at nothing. Harley was medium height, stout, but not overweight. For a man his age, he had been in good shape. Steve heard one of the dogs whimper, probably Harley's mutt. Ignoring the dog, and Kate, he studied the back of Harley's head. A deep gash, approximately five inches long, was dried and matted with blood. Harley's thick grey hair was tangled, blood frozen to it. A hard coagulated pool of blood was on the snow-packed ground where his head had rested.

Steve fought to keep his expression neutral while lowering Harley's head back to the frozen ground.

"I told you."

Steve glanced up at Kate, noticing how her lower lip still trembled while fire blazed in her eyes. "I can't make any judgments at this point, Kate."

"He's been dead awhile. The snow covered up all the evidence."

He saw that she was struggling to be detached, cool in the face of the death of someone so close to her. "I won't argue the point that he's been dead for awhile." Steve stood, catching Kate staring at Harley's lifeless body. He sidestepped a dog to get to her, putting a hand on her arm, turning her away from Harley's body. She tried looking over her shoulder. "Don't, Kate."

For a split second Steve thought she was going to lose it. The grief on her face wrenched at his heart. He gave her a few moments to compose herself. She stared at the house at least a minute before she looked at him, more under control.

"When was the last time you saw him?"

"Three days ago. I came out and visited with him Monday night."

"How was he?"

"Physically, he was fine. But..."

"But what?"

Kate shrugged. "I don't know. He seemed distracted, like he had something on his mind."

"You have any idea what?"

Kate shook her head.

A siren screeched in the distance. Why in the hell the ambulance ran their siren when someone was already dead, Steve had never figured out. He'd been a cop for over twenty years and for some insane reason, it always irritated him.

"Why don't you go home since the house is cold?"

"I don't want to go home."

Steve decided to shift tactics. "Harley has a daughter somewhere in Washington, doesn't he?"

"Some daughter," Kate snorted.

So much for that idea. "She needs to be notified."

"She hasn't seen Harley in years."

"Doesn't matter, Kate. She's blood kin. She has to be notified." Steve saw her sniff while her eyes grew misty. He shoved aside the urge to comfort her.

"I'll go see if I can find a number or something."

Kate turned toward the house, just as the ambulance roared up the driveway. Chuck, the paramedic, locked up the brakes, then slid past Kate's truck, missing it by inches. Steve knew it was going to be an extra long day.

※　※　※

Kate built a fire in the wood stove because she couldn't handle the frigid, empty air in Harley's house. The dogs immediately staked out their places beside it. She tried to coax

Ranger to eat some dry nuggets. The best he could do was half a dozen bites. Ranger would be coming home with her. She'd try later.

She sat at Harley's circa nineteen fifties blond wood desk, battling back the urge to put her head down and cry. She rifled through the drawers. In the second drawer, under his auto and house insurance policies, she found a stack of newspaper clippings. Harley never saved newspapers. He wasn't sentimental. He hadn't even saved the obituary of his wife, Grace, who had died ten years ago. Kate plucked off the paper clip, glancing through the stack.

Each article from the local newspaper had to do with the illegal shooting of a grizzly sow a year and a half ago. Fish and Wildlife officials had never caught the poacher. A picture on the front page of the slain bear with the thick, cinnamon colored coat had been circled with a red pen. Harley had been a legal and ethical hunter. She was positive they had discussed the grizzly sow at some point, but she couldn't exactly remember when. The grizzly had been shot, left for the scavengers, a couple of months after she'd returned to Windy Creek. The yearling cubs had been rounded up and taken to a local wildlife center to hibernate for the winter.

Frowning, Kate slipped the paper clip back on the articles, setting them on the desk. Three nights ago drifted back to her.

Harley had sat in his comfortable, old recliner near the wood stove, some pressing issue gnawing at him. She had asked him if he was okay. He had told her he was fine, but his eyes had betrayed him. She hadn't pushed, now she wished she would have, but there was no going back. Angry at herself, she yanked her knit hat off, tossing it on the desk.

Although she didn't want to admit it, Steve was right. She needed to find his daughter's address. Kate wondered if Diane would be saddened by the death of her father. She had major doubts about that. She finally unearthed a Christmas card, the postmark five years earlier, with a return address scribbled on it. She had no idea if Diane still lived at that address. Kate pulled out the generic card, opened it. There was one word written on it, Diane's name. Another pot of anger started to simmer inside of her, this time at Harley's daughter. Diane had split Windy Creek the day after high school graduation. She'd last been in town ten years ago for her mother's funeral.

Kate stuffed the card back into the envelope, anger and grief swirling inside of her like a blinding snowstorm. She heard the front door open.

Steve tramped inside, pulling off his gloves. His blue eyes gave nothing away. Steve plucked off the black sheriff's ball cap, raking a hand through his raven colored hair, which looked like it had been recently cut. He settled his hat back on his head. The cheeks of his hard, angled face were burned from the bright sun reflecting off the snow.

"You should wear sun screen."

He walked over to the desk. "I should do a lot of things, Kate."

She shrugged, held the card up to him. "I found an old Christmas card with an address. Who knows if Diane still lives there?"

Steve took the card from her. "It's a place to start." He studied the envelope before looking at Kate. "Was the door unlocked when you got here?"

Kate nodded.

He glanced around. "Has anything been disturbed in the house?"

"Not that I noticed."

"I probably shouldn't have let you come in here."

"So you do believe Harley was murdered."

"I never said that." Steve paused. "Did you go in the garage?"

"Yes. I didn't notice much, except Harley's truck just—just sitting there."

Steve folded the card in half and stuffed it inside his jacket pocket. "Can you walk me through the house and garage to let me know if anything is missing?"

Steve was thinking it was a burglary. Her instincts told her differently. Kate stood up. "Sure." She grabbed her hat off the desk. In the kitchen, she happened to glance out the window, saw Chuck and Jay, the paramedics, carrying the litter with the black body bag. Her stomach lurched. She grabbed onto the counter for support.

Steve's hands settled on her shoulders. "Easy. Take a deep breath."

Kate closed her eyes, did as she was told. She didn't want to see Harley's body loaded into the local ambulance. Her real father had hightailed it out of Windy Creek when she had been two years old, leaving Kate and her mother behind. Kate's mother, Donna, had been best friends with Grace. Harley had stepped up to the plate, filled in for Kate's missing father. He had been father to both her and Diane. But she and Diane had never been close. Harley's daughter was three years older than her. It hadn't been the age difference; it had been the attitude difference.

And when Kate's mother had died six years ago in a senseless car accident, Harley had been her rock. Never mind that she had been married, living in Butte with her husband and son. Harley had been a phone call away.

"Kate?"

She pushed her memories aside, fought to keep herself together. When she turned, Steve dropped his hands to his sides.

"Let's just do it."

"If you're not up to it..."

Kate squared her shoulders. This was just the beginning. She would have to make the funeral arrangements, pack up his belongings, his life, because she knew Diane wouldn't lift a finger to help. When she'd moved back to Windy Creek, Harley had asked her if she would take care of things after he passed.

"Like I said, let's just do it."

CHAPTER TWO

At nine sharp the next morning, Kate stood at the door of Windy Creek's one and only funeral parlor, two blocks off the main street of town. The parlor was a two story older house, flanked by tall grand fir trees. Frank did his embalming in the basement where he kept the caskets on display. Frank lived with his wife, Sheila, above the basement. She'd always thought it was weird to live above dead bodies, but Frank and Sheila were a little on the strange side. It was one thing to be an undertaker, it was another to live where you worked.

Frank was more than an undertaker, he was a coroner, too. Frank and Sheila had moved to Windy Creek five years earlier, leaving the big city of Chicago behind to live a simpler life in the wilds of Montana.

Frank opened the door, dressed in black slacks, white shirt, and light blue tie under a black v-neck sweater. His fifty-something face was pressed with concern, compassion. Frank might be a little different, but he was known for his compassion in times of death.

Kate swallowed hard. "Frank," she managed to squeak out.

"Kate." He reached for her hand, wrapped his hands around hers. "I am so sorry for your loss."

Last night, she'd crept around her house with her lights dimmed, refusing to pick up the phone, letting the answering machine record the condolence messages. Now, in the bright early sunshine, facing Frank with his faded, green sympathetic eyes, she almost lost it and gave into her grief.

She swallowed back her tears, stood straighter. "Thank you, Frank."

"Come in out of the cold." He stepped aside. "Would you like something hot to drink?"

Kate felt like a guest coming to visit with Frank. She didn't see Sheila anywhere, but at any moment the skinny woman might step out of the shadows. "Tea would be good."

A few seconds later, Sheila appeared with a hot steaming mug and handed it to Kate. "I am so deeply sorry for your loss, Kate."

Sheila was too thin, with a lackluster complexion. She had short wispy pale blond hair and the lightest blue eyes Kate had ever seen. "Thanks." She looked down at the steam rising from the mug.

"I understand he had a horrible, horrible gash on the back of his head."

Kate's eyes shot up. She watched Sheila fumble with the fake pearls clasped over her dark grey turtleneck. Steve wouldn't say anything. He was too cool, too professional. Frank must have mentioned it to her. Usually sooner than later, after an accident, the entire town would be repeating the grisly details of a car crash.

"Did you do an autopsy, Frank?" In this remote part of the state, he did the autopsies.

Frank looked taken back for a moment. "Yes. Sheriff Lambert requested one." He turned to his wife. "Sheila, whatever came over you? You know you're not supposed to discuss these things with a loved one."

Sheila's flushed. She fussed with her pearls again. "I'm sorry, Frank. I wasn't thinking. And I'm sorry to you, Kate, too." That said, she turned, disappearing into the shadows again.

Kate cradled the hot mug in her hands. "What did you find?"

Frank clicked his teeth. "I'm sorry, Kate, I can't discuss this with you."

But Steve could. Kate nodded.

"Why don't we go downstairs to my office and start the paperwork?"

She didn't want to descend to the basement, the bowels of the earth. But she didn't have a choice. She had promised Harley she would take care of him. The afternoon of his request, he had waggled a finger at her. No fancy casket.

⚉   ⚉   ⚉

When Steve spotted Kate's truck slowing to a stop in front of the sheriff's office, his gut tightened. He'd just gotten off the phone with Frank. Harley had died from a blow to the head. Frank's opinion was a splitting maul. Steve had figured the same thing when he had checked Harley's head. He finished off his coffee, grimacing at the bitter taste.

Jenny, his secretary, typed furiously at her computer. Jenny was thirty with short, cinnamon colored hair, and ten pounds overweight.

Steve watched Kate angle around her truck. Frank had warned him, Kate would be stopping by. He strode to the door, opening it for her. She looked startled that he was playing doorman.

"Morning, Kate."

"Frank called you."

Steve didn't answer. Instead, he said, "Get inside, it's damn cold again today." Her lips tightened into a thin line as she walked inside.

Jenny stood up, rushed around her desk and gave Kate a big hug. "I'm so sorry about Harley, hon."

"Thanks, I appreciate it, Jenny."

"Want some coffee, Kate?" Steve asked.

"No, thanks."

"Let's go to my office." Steve watched Jenny hug Kate again. He wondered if she had let go and cried yet. Her face was carved in stone, only her beautiful brown eyes gave away her grief. The dark almond color of Kate's eyes had always gotten to him. He'd spent more than one night dreaming about those eyes.

Kate followed him to his office. Steve closed the door behind them. At his desk, he put his empty mug on a stack of papers, then sat down. "Come on, Kate, sit down."

She walked over to his desk. "Harley was murdered. Frank did an autopsy."

Steve scrubbed a hand down his face. He hadn't gotten much sleep last night. Not enough to deal with Kate, anyway. "Can you at least sit down?"

Kate perched on the edge of the chair across from his desk, peeling off her gloves. "Okay, I'm sitting. Now tell me."

"You know I'm under no obligation to tell you anything."

"I know that. But can't you bend the rules just once, Sheriff Lambert?"

He flinched inwardly when she addressed him so formally. "I got a hold of his daughter. She'll be here in a few days."

Kate snorted. "After all the dirty work is done. Now back to what happened to Harley."

Steve leaned back in his chair, noticed how Kate glared at him. "Kate, you're not officially a member of the family." When she started to protest, he held up a hand. "I know you were family. That you were like a daughter to Harley."

She jumped up, started pacing. "Come on, Steve. How official is Windy Creek? It's probably all over town by now. If I were working at the café today, I would be getting an earful." She stopped, pointed her gloves at him. "And you know it."

Steve blew out a frustrated breath. In Salt Lake City, where he had been a cop for twenty years, he had always followed the rules, protocol. It was part of him. He was a rule follower by nature. Against his better judgment, he would bend the rules for Kate. "It appears Harley was murdered."

Kate threw up her hands, sending her gloves in two different directions. "Big surprise."

She settled her hands on her hips. "With what, a maul? An axe?"

"Probably."

"Harley had a collection of mauls and axes."

"You didn't notice any missing yesterday."

"No, but I don't know how many he had for sure."

Steve drummed his fingers on the arm of his chair. "I'll have to go back out there."

"I'll go with you."

"Now wait a minute, Kate. This is an official police investigation. I can't allow you into Harley's house or garage again."

She stomped over to his desk, putting her hands palms down on it. "Yesterday you let me go in. Yesterday you didn't believe Harley had been murdered. This is the first murder since you came to town. It even happens in Windy Creek."

Steve scowled at her. "No can do, Kate."

"I have to get clothes for Harley."

Steve hadn't considered that. "I can get them."

"No, you can't. I'm going to pick out his clothes."

Her eyes brimmed with determination as she stared at him. "Dammit, Kate! You're making this hard."

She straightened up, folding her arms over chest. "It's just something I have to do."

"Okay, okay. But you're not going out there alone. You'll get his clothes, and that's it."

"I have to go through all of his things. He asked me to do that, take care of everything, when he—he died."

She looked ready to cry. He wanted to round the desk and gather her in his arms, but he stayed put. "I'm sorry, but the rest will have to wait until I've conducted a thorough investigation."

When she didn't answer, he said, "Kate."

"Okay, we'll do it your way."

Steve stopped himself from pointing out to her that his way was the official way. "We can go now."

Kate nodded, her lower lip trembling. "Sure." She spun around, bent down and retrieved her gloves off the floor.

A bad feeling settled inside his gut, knowing Kate wouldn't be so easy to pacify in the future if he didn't find Harley's killer soon.

⊰⊱   ⊰⊱   ⊰⊱

Kate walked out of Harley's bedroom, carrying a pair of folded jeans, a new red and black checked flannel shirt, and hiking boots.

Steve frowned at her. "Jeans and hiking boots?"

Kate dropped the clothes on the sofa. "Harley didn't own a suit. He borrowed one when Grace died." She wasn't about to have Harley dressed in some fancy clothes that weren't him. Jeans, a flannel shirt, and his new hiking boots were what he would want to be buried in. She glanced over at Steve. He was looking at her like she had lost her marbles. "Trust me. I know what I'm doing on this."

"Yeah, you probably do know best. I'll help you carry his things out to your truck."

She squared her shoulders. "You're not getting rid of me so fast."

"We agreed, Kate. Remember?"

She ignored him, went to Harley's desk, grabbing the stack of newspaper clippings she'd found yesterday. When she turned back to Steve, she saw irritation flashing in his dark blue eyes. She handed him the clippings. "I came across these yesterday, when I was looking for Diane's address."

Steve took them from her, started glancing through them. After a few minutes, he said, "So?"

"So. Harley wasn't sentimental. He didn't keep old newspapers. He read them and used them as fire starter."

"This poaching must have interested him, or else he wouldn't have kept them." He shuffled through the clippings again. "He circled the picture of the grizzly."

Kate waved a hand in the air. "There's always been poaching around here, for as long as I can remember. The grizzly sow was shot before you moved here."

Brows puckered together, he looked at Kate. "I still don't get it."

"Neither do I. It doesn't make sense. It was out of character for Harley."

Steve scratched the back of his neck, still looking confused. "I'll take these with me."

Kate shifted back on the balls of her feet, hating the fact she had to leave. It was hard being back in Harley's house. It had been even harder to sort through his clothes. She had come too close to losing control of her emotions in Harley's bedroom.

"Okay, Kate, now it's time to go."

Kate set her teeth together. "I can help check the mauls and axes."

Steve shook his head. "I can handle that."

"You're not going to give an inch, are you?"

"Nope."

Still not ready to give up, she said, "I can help. I know everything around here."

A muscle ticked in Steve's jaw. The man had such control. He wore his uniform well. He was tall and rangy with wide shoulders. His black hair was thick with a slight wave to it, grey showing at his temples. Suddenly Kate felt her face color. Why was she having fantasies about Sheriff Steve Lambert while standing in Harley's living room? It must be the life affirmation thing, she decided. After losing someone she loved she wanted to feel alive, needed to feel alive. Kate battled back a crazy urge to rip off his crisp, dark brown uniform and tumble to the floor with him. She hurried over to the sofa, grabbing Harley's clothes.

When she straightened up, Steve took her arm. "Are you okay?"

"Of course," Kate lied, refusing to look at him. She hugged Harley's clothes to her chest. She wasn't even close to okay. She'd just been blind sided by a sudden, powerful urge to jump his bones. "I'll get out of your way." Kate pulled away from his hand, snatching the boots off the couch.

At the door, she stole a glance over her shoulder at him, seeing the confusion etched across his face. She slipped out the door, striding to her truck, her face flaming in spite of the frigid temperature.

※　※　※

"What the hell?" Steve mumbled after Kate scurried out of the house like a frightened mouse. When he heard her truck start, he walked over to the window, pushing the curtain aside. Kate backed up, then peeled down the driveway, the dark green truck fishtailing until it disappeared from view.

Steve scratched the back of his neck again, still confused by Kate's abrupt shift in behavior, plus the look in her eye when she had stared at him. He couldn't ponder the whys and wherefores of women all day. He had work to do.

He walked through the house, his keen eye taking in everything. According to Frank, Harley had been dead for two days when he performed the autopsy. Steve stepped into Harley's bedroom. The bed was made, covered with a cocoa brown, chenille, vintage spread. The room was neat. He went over to the nightstand. The old style wind-up alarm clock had stopped ticking at ten after four. There was a dog-eared paperback next to it. He picked it up, turned it over, read the back. It was a true story of a trapper in Alaska in the early nineteen hundreds.

Steve knew Harley was an avid outdoors man who had hunted, fished, camped, hiked; the whole ten yards.

He laid the book down, checked the window near the bed and saw that it was locked. Steve prowled through the house, quiet, light on his feet like a burglar, noting that nothing was out of order. He ended his search in the kitchen. There was a large coffee mug and spoon sitting in the sink. He noticed the coffee maker on the counter. The glass carafe was half full.

Had Harley known his attacker? The odds were yes, because nothing had been stolen. Harley had been behind his woodpile without a jacket, gloves, hat. Steve supposed he could have gone out there to grab an armload of firewood. Considering the frigid temperatures the past few days, Steve didn't understand why Harley hadn't put on a jacket, or at least gloves. The old man had been tough, a native Montanan.

He shouldered open the back door, tramping through the snow toward the garage. After he found the light switch, he opened the passenger side door of Harley's Ford truck. The truck was an older model, but well maintained. He wandered around the large garage, stopping by a variety of tools hanging on hooks attached to the wall. Beneath the tools were four splitting mauls and three axes. Two of the mauls looked like they were the first ones ever made.

Steve took his time examining each one of the chopping tools. They looked clean to him, but he gathered them up anyway, carrying them to his truck, where he deposited them in the back. He'd ship the whole lot of them down to Kalispell and have them tested for traces of blood.

An uneasy feeling balled inside his gut, figuring the lab wouldn't find a damn thing.

CHAPTER THREE

Like a guilty teenager out past curfew, Kate snuck in the back door of the Pine Branch Café. She pictured the large eating area of the café. The walls constructed of knotty pine wood, the booths dusky red, the Formica tables a lighter shade of red, filled with regulars holding up their mugs for more coffee, talking and laughing, eating too much bacon.

Life went on. People kept doing what they always did. Kate sighed.

After she had fought back her abrupt, unwanted feelings for Steve, she had realized she was starving. She'd barely eaten anything since she'd found Harley. She needed to nourish her body to keep up her strength to get through the coming days.

Pots and pans clanked in the kitchen area while Ace, the cook, muttered curses to himself. Sounds of laughter greeted her as she snaked her way through the storage shelves stacked high with canned and dried goods. She grabbed a clean bowl off a shelf, heading straight for the soup pot.

She barely had the ladle dipping into the hearty beef noodle soup when Clara gasped behind her.

"Kate, what in the world are you doing here?"

Again feeling like a guilty teenager, this time for skipping school, she ladled the hearty soup into the bowl. "I was hungry. I needed to eat."

Clara hurried over to her, wrapped her arms around her. "I am so sorry, sweetie."

Kate didn't want to cry. She wanted to eat. She laid her head on Clara's plump shoulder for a brief moment, then continued filling her bowl with the steaming soup.

"I don't know how many times I called you last night, and you didn't answer. I had a mind to drive out to your place, but Carl talked me out of it. He said you probably needed to be left alone for awhile."

Carl Hanson was mayor of Windy Creek, a retired logger and Clara's special friend. Carl was a paragon of common sense. "He was right. I did need to be alone."

Clara stepped back, adjusted the white apron tied around her thick middle. Clara had eaten too much of her cafe's food over the past twenty years, but her heart was the size of her native state. Kate smiled at her while her stomach wailed in hunger.

Clara waggled her finger at Kate. "I bet you haven't eaten more than a spoonful of anything since you found Har—" Clara stopped, her eyes filling with sorrow. "I'm sorry, Kate."

"Don't apologize. You're right. I haven't eaten enough to keep a chickadee alive."

Clara lifted her apron, dabbed at her eyes. "I'm gonna miss that old man. I've known him for over twenty years. It won't be the same around here without him."

Kate bit her lip, fighting back her own tears.

"You need more than that soup to keep you going." Clara disappeared through the swinging doors.

Kate walked to the small table in the corner of the room where the waitresses took their breaks. She slid her soup bowl on the table. From behind strong arms wrapped around her in a big bear hug.

"Ace," she whispered.

"I'm sorry, Katie."

If Kate turned and let Ace hug she would collapse into a blubbering mass of emotions. "Thanks. You've got a lot of hungry customers out there."

"Hell, they can wait. Besides, they'd all understand."

Ace hugged her tight again before he released her. She sat down on the chair, looked up into his face. Ace was a Vietnam vet from New Hampshire. His lean face had a jagged scar across one cheek, a result of hand-to-hand combat with a North Vietnamese soldier. He'd been passing through Windy Creek fifteen years earlier and had parked his skinny butt here, as he liked to say. He'd done lots of odd jobs around town until Clara hired him nine years ago to cook. He was as much a part of the café as Clara.

Clara appeared with two homemade rolls on a plate and a large banana. Clara might serve chicken fried steak, mashed potatoes and gravy, but she believed in people getting their fruits and veggies.

"Ace, I got people out there on their lunch hour. They need their food."

"No shit, Clara. How long have I been here now?"

She spun him around, giving him a shove. "Too damn long, if you ask me."

The two grousing at each other made Kate smile. She dipped the spoon into her soup.

"I'll talk to you when the rush is over, so don't go running off."

"Are you shorthanded?" She was on the schedule to work today.

"Don't you worry about that. Carol came in. She needs the extra money. Said she'd do your shifts until you were ready to come back." Clara bustled off to wait on customers.

Kate tugged off her knit hat, dropping it on the table. She felt a warm hand on her shoulder.

"I'm sorry, Kate."

She looked up into Carol's hazel eyes. "Thanks. And thanks for taking over my shifts."

Carol slid a steaming mug of coffee in front of Kate. "It's not a problem. I need the money. As usual." She pulled her order pad out of her apron pocket. "When's Harley's funeral?"

Kate paused, the spoon halfway to her mouth. "Uh...I'm not sure." She hadn't asked Frank when the service could be scheduled. But did it matter? Harley was the only one who had died in the past few days. When she delivered Harley's clothes, she'd tell Frank the sooner the better. She wanted it over with. "Probably soon."

Carol laid her hand on Kate's shoulder again. "If you need any help..."

Kate nodded, refusing to give into her emotions. She had to eat. She had to concentrate on that one little task. "Thanks."

After Carol left, Kate took a minute to pull herself together, then finished off her soup and rolls. She peeled the banana and ate that, too. While sipping her coffee, Clara reappeared.

"Steve is out there." Clara sat down across the table from Kate. "I told him you were here. He said I'm supposed to look after you."

Why would he say that to Clara? Probably because of her speedy exit from Harley's house. "I'm okay, Clara." She felt like a parrot, repeating to everyone that she was okay, when in reality, she was far from okay. If Harley had died of natural causes, it would be easier to accept. The image of Harley, abandoned behind his woodpile, was nearly her undoing. Kate paused, fighting to keep herself together.

If Steve was at the café that meant he must be finished at Harley's house. "Is he having lunch?"

Clara nodded.

"When it's ready, I'll take it to him."

"Why?"

"Because I want to talk to him. It sounds like it's thinning out on the floor."

"The rush is over. What's going on, Kate? I get the feeling you're not telling me everything."

Kate drank more coffee. "People aren't talking, speculating?"

Clara folded her hands together in front of her. "Yeah, they're talking. But people are always talking in this town. It's what they do."

"Harley didn't die of natural causes." Clara's eyes betrayed her. It was obvious she'd heard the grisly gossip circulating around town.

"You don't know that for sure."

"Yes. I do. I knew it when I found him."

Clara studied her shiny, red nails.

"Somebody murdered Harley."

Clara reached over, covered Kate's hand with hers. "I know, hon. I just didn't want to believe it."

"Order up," Ace yelled in the background.

Kate jumped up from her chair. "Is that Steve's?"

"Give the man a break," Clara said. "He looks beat."

"I'll give him a break when we finds the s.o.b. that murdered Harley."

Clara dropped her head in her hands. "Uh...oh."

> ⚒ ⚒ ⚒

When Steve saw Kate back through the swinging door from the kitchen, carrying his cheeseburger and fries, he groaned out loud.

Kate slid the plate stacked a mile high with fries in front of him. "I heard that."

"Don't you give a thought to your cholesterol?" She reached under the counter, snagged a ketchup bottle, sliding it next to his coffee mug.

He wondered what happened to the scared little mouse that had scampered out of Harley's house. Now she was determined, with something on her mind. Steve smacked the bottom of the ketchup bottle before he tipped it over the fries.

"You can give the tip to Clara." Kate snatched a fry off his plate.

"I'll do that."

Kate dropped her elbows on the table, leaned toward him. "The whole town knows what happened to Harley."

Steve picked up half of his fat cheeseburger. "The whole town is assuming." He took a bite, suddenly feeling defensive under Kate's intense gaze.

She grabbed a fry. "Did you find anything after I left?"

Steve knew if the café was packed with people Kate wouldn't be grilling him. "I loaded up his axes and mauls, dropped them at the station. We'll get them shipped to Kalispell today."

Kate ate another one of his french fries before she asked, "Did you find any evidence on them?"

"I won't know that until I get the lab results."

"And then you'll let me know."

"Jesus, Kate."

"If you don't agree I'm going to eat every single one of your fries." She slipped another one off his plate, started nibbling on it.

Steve stared at her while he bit into the cheeseburger. After he finished chewing, he said. "That's blackmail. I could lock you up for bribing an officer of the law."

Kate snorted, reached for another fry, but he grabbed her hand. Steve wasn't prepared for the jolt to his system when he touched her soft skin. She stared at him, wide-eyed. He stared back at her before he realized the few people in the café were probably getting an eyeful. Tongues would be flapping. He let go of her hand.

He cleared his throat. "I'll call you."

⁍ ⁍ ⁍

Sheila couldn't hide her displeasure when Kate handed her a brand new pair of blue jeans, a folded flannel shirt, and a pair of brown leather hiking boots. "Kate, oh Kate. These aren't proper burial clothes."

Kate crossed her arms over her chest. "Why not?"

Sheila looked completely dismayed. "It's customary for a man to be dressed in a suit, and a woman in a dress."

"Harley didn't own a suit."

"But," Sheila protested. "His daughter might not approve."

Kate wanted to say screw his daughter, but she kept her anger in check. "I'm not even sure if his daughter will show for the services. When is it?"

Sheila pursed her lips together for a moment. "Frank says we can hold services Monday at one."

Kate nodded, ignoring the lump inching up the back of her throat. "Sounds good. I'll be in touch with Frank." She circled around, so Sheila wouldn't see the tears pooling in her eyes.

⁍ ⁍ ⁍

When Kate got home, she took the dogs for a walk down the county road, hoping Ranger would perk up. Sunny managed to seduce Ranger into a game of canine tag, which raised Kate's mood a notch.

After she finished walking, she went into the spare bedroom she had converted into an office and booted up her computer.

It was her obligation to write Harley's obituary.

First she wandered through the house, feeling like a sleepwalker. She loved to write. Fiction. Not hard, cold reality.

Her mystery writing career teetered on barely making enough money to pay the bills. That's why she worked part time at the café. She wouldn't be recognized if she strolled down Madison Avenue in New York City. She'd dabbled with the craft since grade school, but hadn't gotten serious until the last year of her marriage, before the divorce. Now, three years later, she had two mystery novels published with small presses and a third in the works.

When the phone rang in the living room, she welcomed the diversion, hurrying to answer it.

"Hello."

"Kate, this is Diane."

Kate clammed up, stared down at her snow boots. She noticed she was still wearing her jacket.

"Kate, are you there?"

She started shrugging out of her jacket. "Yeah. I'm here." She transferred the cordless phone to her other ear, dropping her jacket on her plump, maroon couch.

"I'm sorry about Dad."

Funny that Diane would be offering her condolences. She was his birth daughter. "Me, too." She didn't reciprocate.

"Um...when is the funeral?"

"Monday at one."

"I'll be there."

Was she supposed to give Diane a gold star for saying she would be at her father's funeral? "Okay."

"Come on, Kate. You could at least try to be civil to me."

"I am being civil."

"Dad and I never saw eye to eye."

Anger started a slow burn in her system. "So what? He was still your father." She'd never known her father. She had no idea if he was alive or dead, if they would have agreed on anything, or fought like cats and dogs. She had just wanted the chance.

"He had you. He didn't need me."

"What the hell does that mean?"

"It means, he preferred your company over mine."

"That's bull and you know it, Diane."

There was a long pause, before Diane said, "That's water under the bridge now. I'll be there for the funeral." The line went dead.

Kate wanted to hurl the phone at the living room window that looked out at the tall, snow-covered pines dotting her front yard. Instead, she slammed it down on its cradle, on the end table next to the couch. The lamp next to the phone, teetered, started to topple, when Kate caught it.

Why was she so angry? Was there a grain of truth in what Diane had said? At this point, running on bottled up emotions and Clara's hearty soup, she didn't care. Kate marched into her office, sat down at the computer.

Then she started writing Harley's obituary.

꭪ ꭪ ꭪

The next morning when Kate woke up, she felt like she had a supreme case of PMS. But it wasn't her time. Her sour mood had nothing to do with hormones. Anger, sadness, depression; all coiled together inside of her. She had dreamed of Harley. His blue eyes twinkling when he had teased her. Of how he'd taught her to operate a four-wheeler when she was ten, followed by driving lessons at fifteen. Her mother had proved to be too nervous to teach her teenage daughter how to drive.

Kate sat up, tossing the blankets back, realizing the house was freezing. She'd forgotten to bank the wood stove before she had fallen into bed, exhausted. Both dogs were curled up together on Sunny's bed in the corner of her bedroom. "Sorry, guys."

Ranger peeked at her from half closed eyes. Sunny glared outright at her. "I'll get the fire going in a jiff." She knelt down, found her mocassin slippers under her bed. She padded into the bathroom, grabbing her flannel robe off the hook on the wall.

When she opened the back door, she saw that it had snowed three or four inches during the night. She glanced at the thermometer nailed to her house, seeing that the temperature had risen. It was a high twenty-one degrees this morning. Normally that would lift her spirits, but not today. She gathered up an armload of firewood, carrying the wood into the house.

Tossing and turning, dreaming, waking had left her too damn grumpy to rejoice at the elevation in temperature.

After a quick breakfast, an even quicker shower, Kate was outside shoveling her driveway. Harley had ridden her case about getting a four-wheeler with a plow, but she had decided it was too much money. He'd even offered to loan the money to her. When she remembered his offer, her heart grew heavy with sadness.

The dogs romped in the snow while Kate finished scraping snow off her driveway. When she reached the road, she paused a moment to watch three whitetail deer, a doe with twin fawns, ambling down the snow-packed road. This would be the last winter she would have venison in her freezer. The last two years Harley had kept her freezer filled with the wild meat.

Biting back tears, she wheeled around, marched down the driveway. She stomped back into the house, grabbed her purse and keys. Five minutes later, the dogs locked in the house so Ranger wouldn't try to follow her, she steered her truck onto the county road.

×⟨   ×⟨   ×⟨

When Kate turned into Harley's driveway, she immediately hit the brakes, going into a short skid. Someone had plowed Harley's driveway the other day. Probably Sam, his neighbor. There were fresh tire tracks jetting through the new layers of snow. She leaned over the steering wheel, staring at the tire tracks that couldn't be more than a few hours old. Maybe Steve had driven out here again to check for more evidence. But it was only a little after nine. She started down the driveway, apprehension gripping her.

She parked her truck, climbed out, noticing the large footprints in the snow leading up to Harley's front porch. Only a few flakes drifted from the steel grey sky.

She stood by her truck, door still open, her apprehension increasing. She wished she had the dogs with her, but she'd felt Ranger was better off not coming to Harley's place. Ranger searching for Harley would be her undoing. Kate slammed her truck door in warning if anyone was still lurking around. "Hello!" The tire tracks stopped next to her truck.

Lack of sleep and emotional grief had her doubting her sanity. She squared her shoulders, hiked toward the porch, making sure she didn't step in the large footprints.

This time a different kind of fear trickled through her as she walked up the steps. Two days ago fear that something had happened to Harley had her near panic-stricken. The fear that clutched her now was more elemental, like a lone deer sensing danger from a predator.

Kate pulled the house key out of her front jeans pocket. For some reason, she tried the knob first. The knob twisted easily. She took a deep breath, struggling to calm herself. It was one thing to write mysteries. It was another to actually be involved in a real one.

She kicked the door open, heart hammering.

CHAPTER FOUR

Kate stepped inside the house. When she noticed Harley's desk, she froze. After a few seconds, she forced herself to breathe.

Harley's desk had been ransacked. Papers, letters, cancelled checks, magazines, pens and pencils were tossed on the floor around the desk. The three side drawers were pulled out, empty. The top drawer was turned on its side on the floor next to the desk chair.

She figured she might have a heart attack right on the spot. Sitting up late at night, pounding away on her computer, creating crime scenes and ruthless murderers seemed like a walk in the park compared to this. No way did she like the real thing.

Stunned, she stared at the mess on and around Harley's desk. Someone had been looking for something. But she had just rummaged through his desk a few days ago and found nothing out of the ordinary.

Except for the newspaper clippings on the sow grizzly that had been shot.

Kate waged war with the panic mushrooming inside of her and the tiny part of her that was fighting to be rational. There was nothing rational about what someone had done to Harley's desk and private papers.

She forced one foot in front of the other until she ended up in the kitchen, seeing that the kitchen had been ransacked, too.

Drawers and cupboard doors were open. Silverware, pots and pans were scattered on the counters and floor.

With a trembling hand, she reached for the phone, called Steve.

><	><	><

Steve scowled at Kate, who leaned against the wall near the wood stove, arms crossed over her chest, shivering. She'd built a fire. The house was lukewarm at best. Maybe she was trembling from fear. Steve didn't know. He wanted to shake her for coming out here alone.

Steve pulled on a pair of plastic gloves. "You had no damn business coming out here."

She lifted her chin slightly. He was surprised he couldn't hear her teeth chattering.

"Why did you come out here?"

Kate lifted a shoulder.

"Not good enough."

"I don't know why I came out here." She paused. "I just wanted to. I thought maybe I might find something. And I sure as hell did."

"Remember I'm the cop here, Kate. This is my job."

"Were you planning on coming out here today?"

No plans. He'd been waiting to hear from the lab. That had been his plan. "Don't turn this around on me." He shot her a look before angling over to Harley's desk. Since they'd been snared in an Arctic front the past week, he doubted he would find any prints. The perp probably had probably worn gloves the entire time he ripped apart Harley's house.

Judging from the footprints outside, the guy was big. Or he owned an extra large pair of snow boots, which could very well be the case. The perp had bigger feet than his own size eleven's.

Steve didn't wear snow boots on duty; he wore a light weight winter hiker.

He glanced over his shoulder at Kate. He couldn't read her expression. "Add some more wood to the damn fire." Harley had been one of those Montanans that believed wood heat was the only heat.

Glaring at him, she picked up a log from the wood holder next to the stove.

Steve knelt down, ignoring her while he sifted through the mess on the floor.

"What did you do with the newspaper clippings?" Kate asked from behind him.

"They're at my office." He'd read the clippings, but they hadn't made any sense to him. Why Harley saved them, he didn't know. He picked up Harley's checkbook and opened it. "Did Harley keep any cash in the house?"

"You think this was a generic robbery?"

Steve tamped down his irritation. "I'm not assuming anything. You didn't answer my question."

There was a long pause before Kate said, "No. He was a check writer. He'd go into town, cash a check at the bank for whatever he needed, then do his shopping. I think the s.o.b. was looking for those newspaper clippings."

The muscles in Steve's jaws clenched. "I already told you I'm not going to assume anything."

"Why are you so grumpy this morning?"

Steve took his time standing up, turning to face Kate. He wasn't sure himself. Since Jenny had rushed into his office, words tumbling over each other with the report of Kate's call, anger had brewed inside of him, ready to spill over. "I am not grumpy."

"Yes, you are."

He ignored her comment. Brushing past her, he stomped into the kitchen. He heard her following him.

"I guess it's none of my business why you're so grumpy."

Steve held himself in check. Kate looked like she hadn't slept in a week. He knew by just looking at her that her emotions were on overdrive. He felt like punching his fist into a wall. The two of them could probably get into a real brawl if they weren't careful. Steve ignored her again, pawing through the rubble in Harley's kitchen.

A minute later, he heard the toe of her boot tapping on the linoleum floor. He circled around to face her. "I think you should go home, Kate."

"I want to know what's going on here."

Steve counted to ten under his breath. "I'll find out what's going on here."

"Why can't I help?"

"Because this is my job."

"So you're saying I'm in the way?"

He could see it in her eyes. She wanted to fight, probably needed to fight to release the bottled up emotions she'd been toting around since she'd found Harley's body. "Kaaaaate. I'm not going to fight with you."

"I don't want to fight," she snapped.

"Yeah, you do. And it's understandable. I'll get to the bottom of this. You have my word."

The anger vanished from her eyes, replaced by a teary-eyed look. Steve took a step, stopped himself. He wanted to comfort her, he wanted to take her to bed. The woman was literally driving him nuts. "Kate, please go home."

She scrubbed a knuckle across her eye. "I don't want to go home."

He struggled for patience. "Why don't you go to the café, have some coffee or better yet, something to eat?"

"I'm not hungry."

His patience was evaporating fast, but he kept his tone even. "I've got a couple of plastic totes in my truck. I'm going to gather up some of these things, take them to the station to check for prints."

"I can help."

She needed to help him because Kate loved Harley. Hope flashed in her eyes. He knew from past experience it was damned hard on the victims' families to sit back and do nothing. He was about to break a rule for Kate. "You can help." When she started toward him, he held up a hand. "You have to wear gloves. And we only load up what I say." Christ, he had to have some kind of control in this situation.

Kate nodded, relief flooding her eyes.

He should call one of his deputies out here. But he knew he wouldn't.

⚒ ⚒ ⚒

Kate watched Steve close the back hatch of the sheriff's truck. Two large plastic totes were loaded with various articles of Harley's. Papers, cancelled checks, magazines, pots and pans, the top drawer from Harley's desk.

"I'll buy you lunch."

Steve wheeled around to face Kate, his dark brows puckering together. "Excuse me?"

Had she completely slipped over the edge? "Yeah. I mean, you let me help with Harley's things. The least I can do is return the favor."

Steve glanced past her. Why had she been so forward with him? She'd thrown out the invitation without thinking.

He brought his gaze back to her. "Thanks, but I have a lot of work. I'll order in."

Kate was surprised at the disappointment trickling through her. "Suit yourself."

Steve nodded, glanced away from her again.

If her face weren't flushed from the cold air, she would surely be blushing for inserting her foot into her mouth. She started to back away. "You'll let me know if you find any prints?" She watched Steve's jaw tighten.

"Yes, Kate, I will, but I can only give you so much information."

His tone was one of an exhausted parent speaking to a hyperactive child. "Gee thanks. See you."

She hurried to her truck. She had the door halfway open when Steve clamped a hand around her arm.

"People will talk, Kate, if we show up for lunch together at the café."

Kate hid her surprise. "Are you worried about your reputation, Sheriff Lambert?" She angled her head in his direction.

"Dammit, Kate. You've got enough on your plate. You don't need the gossip hounds after you."

She pulled free of his hand. "It was a simple, generic lunch invitation."

He considered that for a moment. "I suppose."

She climbed inside her truck. Annoyance at herself, at Steve, rushed through her. She reached for the door, but he stopped her from closing it, bent down, looking liked he planned to climb into the truck with her.

Her heart started an unexpected swift pounding.

"I thought you weren't interested in me."

Nothing like cutting to the chase. "I'm not." Instant attraction had zapped her when she had first seen Steve walk into the café a year ago. He wasn't a pretty man, in fact, his face was hard and angled. She'd managed to hide her attraction for him. She'd decided after her divorce, she didn't want a man or need one. Recently something had shifted inside of her. She chalked it up to the life-affirming thing again.

"Suddenly I get the feeling you are interested in me."

"Well...you're wrong."

"Maybe you want to get close to the man with all the answers."

"What are you implying?"

Steve didn't answer as his eyes turned stormy. It all happened so fast it made her head spin. His hand wrapped around the back of her neck and then his mouth came down hard on hers. Stunned, she stared at him.

Steve opened his eyes, looked at her. "Close your eyes, Kate."

Her eyes fluttered closed against her will. His lips were cold, slightly chapped from the frigid weather. He really ought to wear Chapstick...

His tongue bullied its way inside her mouth. She didn't resist, heat spiking inside of her body. Kate grabbed his jacket, dragging him closer as his hand slid around her back. Their bodies were twisted at awkward angles, but the kiss deepened, grew hotter and more desperate as their tongues explored each other in a sultry way.

Kate couldn't breathe. She wasn't sure she wanted to breathe.

Steve tore his lips from hers, his breathing heavy. "Shit." He removed his hands from her body, his blue eyes brimming with lust and anger. He straightened up, closed her door, then strode away from her truck.

Kate didn't move, her body tingling with hot sensations. She yanked her knit hat off, throwing it on the passenger seat. She heard Steve's truck start, but he let it idle, didn't drive off. Oh, she supposed he was being a gentleman waiting for her to drive off first. He certainly hadn't been a gentleman when he'd kissed her. Kate turned on her truck, jammed the gear shift into reverse, punched the gas, almost smacking a pine tree behind her.

Get a grip. After she shifted into first, she drove slowly down Harley's driveway. She didn't want to plow into the deep ditch next to the road because then Steve would have to give her a tow. She would have to look into his eyes again.

Kate turned onto the road, saw that Steve was following her at a safe distance.

※　※　※

Twenty minutes later, Kate wandered into the café via the back door again. Somehow her lust made her hungry. She headed straight for the soup pot again, lifted the large metal lid, and sniffed the delicious smell of homemade potato soup.

Suddenly the lid was yanked out of her hand, crashed down on the pot.

"No soup today, lady. You need something that will stick to your ribs."

She made a face at Ace. "I want soup."

"It's cheeseburger and fries day."

"Since when did you become so macho?"

"Since I figure you've been eating next to nothing. Go out and sit at the counter."

She turned, planting her hands on her hips. "You sure are bossy today."

"I'm bossy every day. You need to join the living again, Kate."

Concern showed on his hard, scarred face. She ignored the lump forming in her throat.

Ace gave her a push. "Now get out there. I'll throw the burger on the grill."

Ace was right and she knew it. It didn't mean she had to like it. She stuffed her gloves into her fleece jacket, reached up for her hat, then remembered she had taken it off after...after the kiss. Plowing her hands through her hair, she took her sweet time walking through the kitchen.

"Get the lead out," Ace yelled.

She didn't grace him with an answer. Clara bustled through the swinging door with a tub full of dirty dishes. "Kate." Her face lit up in a smile.

"I'm eating a cheeseburger and fries at the counter."

Clara paused, shifted the tub to her other hip. "Uh oh. Ace bullied you, didn't he?"

"Yeah, he did."

"He's absolutely right. Now you get out there."

"Nothing like being ganged up on," she muttered as she pushed through the swinging door. A few people were scattered here and there in the cafe. She looked at the wooden clock, carved in the shape of black bear cub, across the room. Twelve forty-five. By one fifteen, the café would be empty. Between three and four customers would start piling in again for pie and coffee.

She noticed the twins, Dave and Donny, sitting at the end of the counter, their heads together. They were both married, with two kids each, but the two of them seemed to spend more time with each other than their families. She remembered reading once that twins had some eternal bonding thing going. She grabbed a fresh pot of coffee, heading toward the two men.

"More coffee, guys?"

They both gaped at her in surprise. The only way to tell them apart was that Donny wore wire rim glasses. They were dressed alike, both sporting heavy plaid jackets and ball caps.

"Kate." This was said in unison.

She filled their mugs.

"We're sorry," Donny began.

"Very sorry," Dave ended.

"Thanks, guys. Need anything else?"

"We're fine." Again, in unison.

Kate smiled before she returned the coffeepot to the warming burner. The thirty-something twins always made her smile. The men finished each other sentences. She'd even watched them share a cigarette.

Instead of coffee, she decided on a glass of Coke with tons of ice. She saw that Maggie was working today. Maggie was nineteen, slim, with long golden hair. When she spotted Kate, she raced around the counter, giving her a big hug. Kate almost dropped her glass of Coke.

"Oh, Kate." She patted her back. "I'm so sorry. If anything happened to my dad, I don't know what I would do."

Everybody knew, had always known, that Harley was Kate's adopted father. She hugged Maggie back. "Thanks, sweetie."

"Can I get you something?" Maggie fiddled with her ponytail.

"Ace is making me a cheeseburger."

"I'll bring it out when it's ready."

"I can get it. I see you still have customers."

"No problem." Maggie spun around, disappearing back into the kitchen.

Kate circled around the counter, slid onto the end stool. Over the next five minutes, a half dozen people came over to her, patted her back, squeezing her shoulders and offering their condolences. She managed to get through it without bursting into tears.

Maggie appeared with the cheeseburger basket, dropped it in front of her. "You need anything else, Kate?"

"No thanks."

Maggie smiled, then made her way out to the floor. Kate slathered ketchup over the fries. She concentrated on eating the cheeseburger. When she was almost finished someone slid onto the stool next to her.

"Heard about old Harley."

She immediately bristled when she angled her head to look at Hal Jackson. His husky body and clothes smelled of cheap whiskey. She had never liked the man. She stared at his ruddy complexion, partially covered by his reddish-grey beard. A plain navy blue stocking hat was pulled over his thinning hair. "Did you?" She ignored him, while finishing off her cheeseburger.

"Heard somebody whacked him on the back of his head."

Kate flinched, her appetite vanishing. She dropped the last bite of her burger into the basket. Hal had been drinking and it was only one in the afternoon. That wasn't unusual for Hal. She figured he drank everyday starting with his first cup of morning coffee. "That's the rumor."

Clara came out then, saw Hal sitting next to Kate. She was over to the two of them in a flash. "Now don't go bothering Kate today, Hal. Want some coffee? Maybe you want to sit in your usual booth over in the corner."

Hal usually sat in the corner booth so he could fill his mug from the small flask he always carried in his pocket.

"Just offering Katie my sympathies, Clara."

"Hmmph." Clara reached for a mug and coffee pot. She banged the heavy mug on the counter, filling it with the hot brew. "You want some lunch?"

"I'll have the chicken fried steak."

Clara, clearly unhappy that Hal was planning on eating lunch, frowned at him.

"I'm a paying customer."

"It's okay, Clara," Kate said. "Put in his order."

Her boss lifted a brow. Kate nodded.

Clara scribbled on her order pad, then went to the window, stuck the order on the spool. "Chicken fried," she called a little too loudly to Ace.

"I can hear you," Ace groused back.

"You think our citified sheriff will figure out who killed Harley?"

Kate flinched again at Hal's insensitivity. Steve had been sheriff of Windy Creek for a little over a year now. "I have no doubt that he will." She pushed the basket away, grabbed her Coke, took a big swallow.

"Heard the snow washed away all the evidence." Hal slurped coffee.

Disgusted at the smell, attitude and complete lack of manners, Kate jumped off the stool, still holding the glass. She reached for the burger basket. "There's always evidence, Hal."

His ordinary green eyes turned surly as he stared at her. "You must know since you're a fancy, mystery writer."

"You'd be surprised what I know." Kate headed straight for the kitchen.

Clara was right behind her. "Are you okay? I swear that man is the biggest jackass I've ever known. I should eighty-six him. Or Ace could."

Kate dumped the remains of her lunch into the large trash can near the door. "Don't worry about it. He's a hopeless alcoholic."

"That still doesn't excuse his behavior."

Hal had rattled her more than she wanted to admit. Harley's property bordered Hal's. There had been no love lost between the two of them. She wiped the palms of her hands on her thighs. "I should do some work around here since I'm eating here everyday."

Clara patted her cheek. "You'll do no such thing. You should go home and rest. You look terrible."

"Gosh, Clara, thanks."

"You're not getting enough sleep and it shows."

"I'm going to go load the dishwasher." She heard Clara sigh behind her.

The truth was she didn't want to be alone. Alone with her grief and loss.

And now alone with thoughts of Steve.

⚒ ⚒ ⚒

Harley's things had been clean. No prints except Harley's. Steve leaned back in his chair, a fresh cup of coffee cradled in his hands. The perpetrator had worn gloves like he'd figured.

He had nothing. Frustrated, Steve sipped his black coffee, cursing under his breath when he burned his tongue. Harley's killer was running around loose. The more time that passed, the harder it would be to find the bastard.

Jenny knocked on his office door, then let herself in. "The lab called."

Steve sat up straighter in his chair.

"They didn't find any blood evidence on the axes and mauls."

Scowling, he leaned forward, put his mug on his desk.

"Who do you think did it?" Jenny wrapped her arms around herself.

He could see fear swirling in her eyes. "We'll find out. These things take time."

Jenny's brows puckered together. "Do you think whoever did it will—I mean—do it again?"

Jesus, he hoped not. "No." Steve struggled to sound reassuring. "No, Jenny, I don't."

She gave him a skeptical before she turned to leave.

"Jenny?"

She glanced over her shoulder at him.

"Everything will be okay. I promise." He hoped like hell he wasn't making empty promises to her.

Jenny nodded before she left his office.

✂   ✂   ✂

After Kate finished stacking the lunch dishes in the dishwasher, she went out on the floor, helped Maggie fill ketchup bottles and salt and pepper shakers. The café was empty. Clara and Ace were in the back eating their lunch. Kate had waited until Hal left before coming out into the eating area. Alcoholics were insensitive by nature. Hal wasn't the kind of man who was sensitive to begin with.

A few minutes later, she heard the door open. When she glanced over and saw it was Steve, she dropped the shaker, spilling pepper on the table. Their eyes locked for a moment. Kate looked away first. Damn him. He'd turned down her ridiculous invitation to lunch and must have figured she'd be gone by now. She wiped up the pepper with a damp cloth.

"I'll be right with you, Sheriff," Maggie called from across the room.

"No hurry."

He sounded surly to Kate. That was his problem, she decided as she started toward the kitchen. He stood at the end of the counter, pinching the bridge of his nose. She had to walk past him to get into the kitchen and away from him.

Steve's back was to her as she tried to hurry by him.

"Kate."

She stopped, forcing herself to turn and face him.

"Um...the lab called. They didn't find any evidence on Harley's axes."

Her heart dropped to the floor.

"I didn't find any prints on his things, either."

"Are you sure?"

"Yes. I'm sure."

"There had to be fingerprints on his stuff."

"They were Harley's prints."

Kate frowned, forgetting their tumble in her truck earlier. "Then what are you going to do?" Anger blazed to life in his face. Okay, she had just committed a faux pas. "Sorry," she mumbled.

Steve shrugged out of his jacket. His brown uniform shirt pulled against his chest. She looked away. Damn her hormones for raging at a time like this.

"I intend to find who did this to Harley."

"Of course." She started for the kitchen. Steve was good at his job. She realized she had insulted his expertise.

"Kate."

Now what? She circled around.

"Don't go getting any ideas."

She knew what he meant, but she didn't like his tone. "What kind of ideas, Sheriff?"

"You know damn well what I mean."

"Not really." That said, she spun back around and bullied open the door to the kitchen.

Kate avoided Clara and Ace grousing over their lunch in the corner. She stomped straight to the storage room, started straightening canned and dry goods on the shelves.

Her already overwrought emotions threatened to explode. Anger, grief, a deep sense of loss, irritation at herself for not being able to get grip on her emotions. And now add Steve to the mix. She'd been content with her life back in Windy Creek without a man in it.

Her ex, David, was remarried, still living in Butte. Her son, Jason, lived with his father and his new wife. Jason had yet to forgive her for committing one of the biggest mistakes in her marriage. At least now he would speak to her over the phone.

And he had visited for four days between Christmas and New Year's. Things hadn't been as strained between the two of them. If she drove to Butte, he would meet with her. But it was still in his eyes, the slump of his sixteen year old shoulders, the indifference he made her suffer through. She'd tri—

"What in heaven's name are you doing back here, Kate?"

She arranged gallon jars of pickles on a shelf. "Just tidying up."

"Then you need to write your time down."

She paused, looking over her shoulder at Clara. "This is volunteer work. I'm not taking pay for it. Besides, I left you in a bind this week."

Clara settled her hands on her hips. "Steve is out there. Did you talk to him?"

She turned away, pushing another big jar of pickles into line.

Clara walked over to her. "Your face is flushed. What's going on? Are you coming down with something?"

Kate shook her head.

"If you are, it wouldn't surprise me one bit. There's a bug going around. And you're not taking care of yourself."

Relief washed through her that Clara hadn't hit on the real reason for her pink face. "I've eaten well the last two days."

"Just lunches. You should go home and rest. Then come back for dinner."

Clara was a mother hen. She even griped at some of her customers who she knew had high cholesterol, trying to get them to eat healthier. "Thanks. If I do, I'll be a paying customer."

"You'll do no such thing. Keeping your strength up is on the house."

CHAPTER FIVE

Steve rapped on the door with his knuckles, wondering what the hell he was doing. There was a solitary light on in the back of the house. The sound of two dogs barking could be heard out on the front porch. He raised his hand to knock again when the door swung open.

The two dogs nearly bowled him over. "Hey, guys, take it easy." When they realized he was friend, not foe, they wagged their tails, licking at his gloves.

Kate stood there, dressed in faded black jeans, a blue zip up sweatshirt with her hair clipped on top of her head. The light pink clip was basically useless. Most of her thick brown curls hung down around her cheeks.

"What are you doing here?"

Steve ground his teeth together. "How about hello?" When she crossed her arms over chest and didn't answer, he said, "It's pretty damn cold out here." He waited a beat for her to answer. "You're wasting heat."

"Come on, Sunny and Ranger, get back in here."

Steve followed behind the two big mutts, not sure if he had been invited in or not. Kate closed the door, leaned against it, crossing her arms over her chest again. "Just for the record, Kate. You kissed me back."

"Hmm..."

What had he expected? For her to jump into his arms?

"Is that why you came over here? To point out that fact?"

Steve unzipped his heavy jacket, then peeled off his gloves. He'd gone home, changed into jeans and a warm flannel shirt. He decided not to push about their kiss. "I need to ask you some questions about Harley. And I'd give my right arm for some hot chocolate."

Kate made an unlady like sound, then pushed away from the door, brushing past him. So much for cordial greetings. He started to follow her, but paused in the small, cozy living room. This was the first time he'd been inside her house.

A wood stove placed in the corner pumped out heat. There were wildlife paintings on the wall, one of a grey timber wolf on a mountainside with his head raised high in wolf song. Across the room was a painting of a red golden sunset over St. Mary's Lake in East Glacier Park. Along the wall below the painting was a bookshelf crammed with books, both paperback and hardback.

Steve shrugged out of his jacket, dropped it and his gloves on the inviting plump, maroon couch. He watched the dogs each stake out a side by the wood stove. When he walked into the kitchen, he was struck again by the coziness of the room. There were several more wildlife paintings on the walls. One of a sow grizzly with two cubs. Another of a whitetail doe and her fawn standing in a meadow sprinkled with Montana wildflowers. A fruit bowl sat on the table filled with Granny Smith apples and two over-ripe bananas.

"If you want marshmallows, you're out of luck."

Her house was warmer than she was. He pulled out a chair. "I can live without marshmallows." Steve sat down, waiting for Kate to answer, but she didn't.

He leaned back in his chair, ogling at her butt, which was nice, damn nice. A minute or so later, the teakettle whistled on top of the range. Steve watched her tear open two packages of instant cocoa and dump them into the mugs. After she stirred the boiling water in the mugs, she brought a mug over to Steve, sliding it in front of him. "Thanks."

Kate walked back to the counter, leaning against it as she sipped her cocoa.

"Come on, Kate, sit down."

"I feel like standing."

"Okay, suit yourself." Steve picked up the mug, blew at the steam drifting from it.

"What do you want to ask me about Harley?"

Steve took a small sip, set the mug back on the table so it could cool. "I haven't been here that long, so I don't know everybody's past history. I've learned a few interesting things through the grapevine."

"Everybody liked Harley. He was born here, lived in Windy Creek his entire life."

Steve knew that part. "What about enemies? Somebody from the past. You've known him all your life."

Kate drank some cocoa before she answered. "He was a good guy, a good neighbor, a good father."

Steve wondered if she meant to her or his real daughter back in Spokane. He wished she'd sit down at the table with him.

"This is the first murder in Windy Creek since I was a kid."

"The Hayward murder?"

Kate nodded. "Skip Henderson caught his wife, Cherry, in bed with his best friend, Burt Hayward. Grabbed his shotgun off the wall in the kitchen and shot him. Skip went to prison. Cherry took the kids and moved to Missoula. Burt's wife took off for Wyoming with her kids."

Steve had glanced over the file from over thirty years ago. There had been a couple of hunting accidents, but Windy Creek was free of premeditated murder. Burt Hayward committed a crime of passion. Steve had heard he'd been released ten years ago, never to be seen in Windy Creek again. "So no one had a grudge against Harley?"

Kate glanced out the window. Steve did, too. The clear black sky was dotted with bright stars. When it was clear, it was cold.

"I can't think of anybody," she finally said, still staring out the window.

Steve hooked a finger around the mug handle. "There is a possibility somebody had a score to settle with him, maybe before your time."

Kate finally stopped staring on the window, focused on him. "If somebody carried a grudge that long you'd think they would have acted on it a long time ago or gotten over it."

"Maybe." Steve drank some cocoa. "There's no evidence, Kate."

Her eyes narrowed. "Does that mean you're just going to write it off?"

"Hey, take it easy. No. I'm not going to write it off." He hated admitting his hands were tied. "I need some damned evidence. I need a lead." His fingers gripped the mug tighter.

Kate's expression softened. "I guess it could have been random..."

"I doubt it. According to you, nothing was stolen."

"But somebody came back looking for something."

That was the part that gnawed at him. That fact pointed to a local.

"There's a killer in Windy Creek."

Steve didn't answer. He hoped sooner or later the bastard would screw up. That might be the only way he would catch him.

"It could have something to do with the clippings on the grizzly sow." Kate wandered over to the table, sitting down in the chair across from Steve.

"That's an unsolved case. I checked it out with the Fish and Wildlife guys."

"There have been lots of animals poached and the poachers have gotten away with it. But there had to be a reason why Harley kept those clippings."

"He ever mention anything to you?"

"I had only been back in Windy Creek a few months. Yeah, we talked about it. Harley didn't like poachers. He was a responsible hunter."

"Bob, over at Fish and Wildlife, told me it was a dead end. The bear had been shot with a 30-06 rifle, which is the most common rifle around these parts."

"Yeah," Kate agreed. "Everybody and their dog owns one." She propped her elbows on the table. "Maybe Harley figured out who did it, then confronted the person."

Steve paused, the mug halfway to his lips. "That's too easy."

"How sophisticated are we in Windy Creek?"

Kate made a good point. "Okay, let's suppose somehow Harley figured out who killed the bear. Why didn't he report it to Fish and Wildlife?"

Kate picked up her mug, cradled it in her hands. "I don't know."

"According to Bob, the bear was shot about five miles east of town. An out of state hunter stumbled across it."

"It was on Forest Service land. There aren't any houses near there."

"I know."

A subdued silence settled around them. Kate fiddled with her hair. Steve wanted to reach over and pull out the hair clip. To take his mind off Kate's hair, he glanced down at his mug, saw it was empty.

"The killer might get away with it."

Anger churned inside his gut. "Not if I can help it."

"I don't mean you're not capable of solving the case," Kate paused. "I mean there're lots of unsolved murders. You know that."

Tragic, but true. "The bastard will screw up sooner or later. I'll be waiting."

⁙ ⁙ ⁙

Monday afternoon, Kate sat at the counter, a mug of coffee laced with Black Velvet whiskey in front of her. Compliments of Ace. Harley's service was over. Only a few people lingered at the café. Tables were pushed together in the middle of the room. The potluck dishes had been picked clean by the hungry mourners. Harley's friends had devoured the casseroles, potato and macaroni salads, cakes, pies and brownies.

Harley had been sent out in style.

Sunny and Ranger were meandering around the empty tables looking for scraps. She'd taken the dogs to the service and burial at the cemetery. No one had given it a second thought, except for Diane. Kate glanced over her shoulder. Diane was sitting at a booth across from Steve.

Kate figured she was flirting with him. Her brassy blond hair fell to her shoulders. Compliments of Clairol. Her heavy makeup hid her age well, Kate decided. Was that jealousy sprouting underneath the heavy glove of grief snugged tight around her heart? She took a big sip of the whiskey-laced coffee. For the most part, she had ignored Diane since she'd arrived in town yesterday. She was staying at the only motel in town, the Windy Creek Motel. And she'd be leaving tomorrow.

Diane had called her last night, asked if Kate would take care of Harley's things. When Diane offered to pay her, Kate had slammed the phone down. Hoping to get drunk, she drank more coffee.

Clara came out of the kitchen, a mug in her hand too. Kate figured it was spiced with the same medicine as hers. She skirted around the counter, climbed up on the stool next to Kate.

"Looks like she's trying to get her claws into Steve," Clara said.

Kate glanced over her shoulder again. Diane, her head tilted to one side, listening intently to Steve.

"I wouldn't worry about it." Clara took a sip, scrunched up her face. "I declare that man poured half a bottle in my mug."

Kate skipped over the part about too much whiskey in Clara's mug. "What do you mean, I shouldn't worry about Diane digging her claws into Steve?"

"So it's mutual?"

Kate twisted her stool to face Clara, her knees jamming into Clara's thigh. "What do you mean mutual?"

"If you weren't so anti-men, you would have noticed."

She wasn't sure if she liked the direction this conversation was taking. "Noticed what?"

"Kate," Clara said with infinite patience. "You are a very smart woman. But if you didn't have your head in your books, you might be more open to possibilities."

"It's not like you to talk so eloquently, Clara."

Clara pretended to be hurt by Kate's remark, but Kate knew she wasn't. "Why don't you say what you mean?"

Clara leaned close to her. "Steve has the hots for you."

Kate's face heated without her being able to stop it from happening. She remembered the kiss. Damn that kiss anyway. "Did he tell you that?"

Clara waved her hand in front of her before she sipped more coffee. "Of course not. It's in his eyes, the way he looks at you. He only eats lunch here on the days you work."

She wasn't sure if she liked knowing about Steve's lunch schedule. "Baloney." Not very eloquent, but the best she could do.

"Go ahead, deny it all you want. Someday you're going to have to open up that tightly locked heart of yours. We've all been hurt, Kate. Goodness, my first husband, Walt, broke my heart. I still get a little tinge all these years later when I think of him. But he turned out to be a no good cheater, just like your husband."

Kate's face colored again. The people of Windy Creek didn't know the truth. For some insane reason, they all believed David had cheated on her. She'd never bothered to set anyone straight. Harley had been the only one to know the truth. She took an extra big drink of coffee. Slowly the whiskey snaked through her, relaxing her a bit.

"Diane will be gone tomorrow."

Good riddance.

A few seconds later she felt someone walk up behind her. She didn't have to turn around to know who it was.

"I hope you're not driving," Steve said.

She glanced at him. "Why wouldn't I drive?"

Steve took the mug out of her hand. Their fingers brushed, igniting a spark inside her belly.

He sniffed the mug. "Ace's whiskey."

Clara turned to face him, almost knocking Kate off her stool. "Now how would you know about that, Sheriff?"

Steve's eyes twinkled with amusement. "Ace offered me some." He handed the mug back to Kate.

"There's hardly enough in there to bother a fly," Clara said.

Steve didn't answer, but the amusement lingered in his eyes. Ace's hadn't been the only whisky circulating at Harley's wake. If Steve wanted to go after drinking drivers, he'd have to pull over half the town.

"If you need a ride, Kate, I'll drive you home."

Kate felt Clara's gaze boring into her like a power drill. "I'll be fine, thank you. I'm going to help Clara clean up."

Steve zipped up his uniform jacket. "You know where to reach me. Thanks for everything, Clara." He turned and left the café.

"I told you."

Kate stuck her tongue out at Clara, causing both women to burst into laughter. Kate honestly didn't remember the last time she had laughed.

Kate wiped a tear from her eye when Diane sashayed up to the counter. Clara eyed her with suspicion. Kate merely looked at her, wishing she was still laughing.

"I'm going out to Dad's place." Diane scrutinized Kate for a moment. "Anyway, Clara, do you have any spare boxes I could have?"

Anger rushed through Kate like a rocket ship shooting into space. Diane hadn't given her father the time of day for the past two decades, now she wanted to carpetbag through his things.

Diane must have sensed Kate's anger because she fussed with her hair and avoided Kate's eyes. She glanced at Clara, whose expression seemed to silently ask if it was okay to give Diane a few boxes.

"I want to pack up my mother's china," Diane said to Clara, not Kate.

So Diane wanted something of her mother's, not her father's. "Your mom's china is already packed." Kate swallowed a hiccup. She hadn't drunk that much whiskey. "It's in the back corner of Harley's bedroom closet."

"Okay," Diane said.

"Yup, that's right. There's more of your mom's things in the closet, too." Kate might have noticed a trace of guilt in Diane's eyes.

"Um...thanks. So Clara, could I have a few boxes?"

Kate wanted to tell Diane to drive her rental car down to the supermarket and beg for boxes, but she held her tongue.

Clara gave Kate one more look, before she said, "Sure. Go on back. Ace will find you some."

Diane's cheeks turned a deep shade of pink. Kate figured Diane expected Clara to jump up and get the boxes.

"Well, then, thanks." She turned, carrying her coat and purse, her slim figure dressed in a black turtleneck sweater and black slacks.

Clara watched Diane disappear into the kitchen. "Once she's out of Windy Creek, she'll never be back."

Kate nodded. She tamped down the urge to run after Diane and inform her how much she had hurt her father over the years. Instead, she sat there, finishing off the whiskey-laced coffee and slid back into her own grief.

CHAPTER SIX

When Kate parked her truck next to her house, the dogs immediately went into watchdog mode in the back of the truck. Their loud barks echoed inside the aluminum canopy. She killed the ignition while chills climbed up her spine. Twilight started gathering around her small house. A pinkish hue splashed across the sky with the sturdy mountains in the background.

She studied her house for a minute, listening to the dogs carry on. Something wasn't right. She sensed it before she even climbed out of her truck. Her semi-auto .22 pistol was in the drawer of the night stand next to her bed.

At the back of her truck, she opened the canopy door, lowered the tailgate. Sunny and Ranger nearly knocked her on her fanny in their impatience to leap out of her truck. The dogs made a beeline for the house, barking and snarling. They circled around it with Sunny in the lead.

Heart drumming, she crept over the shoveled path to her front door. She'd left her purse and empty casserole dish on her truck seat. Maybe she should have brought the heavy dish to use as a weapon. Kate padded up the steps, inserted her key into the lock, listening to the sound of her heart pounding in her chest. Any effects of the whiskey had disappeared with the kick starting of her adrenaline.

The door was locked. A good thing. The dogs quieted, trotting up the stairs to flank her on either side. She glanced down, hearing a low, guttural snarl from Sunny. Her teeth were bared. She looked at Ranger; he had his nose pressed to the door, ready to jet inside as soon as she opened it.

She should turn, run, jump into her truck and leave. With a trembling hand she turned the key, swung open the door. Like horses out of the chutes at a race, the dogs raced inside the house.

Kate stepped inside, letting her eyes roam the room.

The living room had been tossed. "Dammit!" Every book she owned had been ripped from the shelves, left in a heap on the dark brown carpet.

The dogs roamed from room to room, their noses pressed to the floor. Kate followed them down the hall to the second bedroom, her office. She would kill if some jerk had destroyed her computer or writing in any way, shape or form. After she flipped the light switch, she studied her computer, which was still intact. At least, the monitor screen hadn't been bashed in.

But her desk and the one bookcase in the room had been ransacked. The lone drawer of the desk had been yanked out, thrown on the floor. Notebooks, papers, pens, and pencils were scattered across the carpet.

The dogs pushed past her, sniffing like certified bloodhounds. She was Mt. St. Helens ready to erupt as she rushed through her house, surveying the damage. She checked the back door and found it unlocked. She couldn't remember if she had locked it before she left for Harley's services. Half the time, she didn't lock her doors.

When she was finally done checking her house, she picked up the phone.

And waited.

⚶ ⚶ ⚶

Steve was still at the station when the 911 call came in from Kate. He was in the sheriff's cruiser, with lights flashing, siren screeching in less than a minute. He tore through town, bullying every vehicle out of his way. Glancing in the rear view, he noticed a couple of curiosity seekers following him.

"Jesus," he muttered. All he needed was to pull up to Kate's with a three-ring circus dogging him. They probably figured it was an accident. He'd never understood why people wanted to view the scene of a car accident. Fatal crashes were ugly and tragic.

Once he left town, he killed the flashing lights, turned off his siren. Kate lived three miles out of Windy Creek. She had two acres, sitting between a ten-acre plot and a four-acre plot. The back of her property bordered state land. He knew these things because he wanted to.

Steve glanced in his rear view again. The accident chasers had slowed; one did a U-turn across the road. He didn't need backup. He needed to make sure Kate was okay.

Steve peeled down Kate's driveway, locked up his brakes barely missing the rear end of her truck. He managed to stop before he plowed into a tall pine tree. He had to push the dogs out of his way to get his door open. They were yapping, snarling and carrying on. "Hey guys, mellow out. I'm the good guy."

Kate whistled from the top porch step. The dogs calmed down, trotting along beside him up to the porch. He grabbed her arms. "Are you certifiably nuts?"

"Is that proper police conduct?"

Steve ignored her sarcasm. "Are you okay?" She tried to yank herself free from his hands, but he tightened his grip. "I said, are you okay?"

"No. I'm not okay. My house is trashed."

Steve set her aside, strode into the house. Kate ran into the back of him when he stopped a few feet into her living room to study the damage. She angled to his side.

"It's the same bastard that trashed Harley's place."

He figured that, too. "We don't know that."

"Oh please," she drawled. "Spare me about assuming things."

He glanced at her from the corner of his eye. Her profile was locked in anger, with good reason. "Did you touch anything?"

"Yeah, I did. I turned on my computer to make sure it was okay. It's practically brand new. Computers aren't cheap."

Steve didn't argue with her, but he knew that was what she wanted. To vent her anger on him.

"And you know he wore gloves."

He scowled at her before he started trolling the house with Kate at his heels. "Maybe."

"Hey, maybe Diane trashed my house to make sure I hadn't taken anything of Harley's."

At Kate's office door, he stopped, wheeling around to face her. "Why would you say that?"

"Because she asked Clara for boxes so she could get some things from Harley's house."

He highly doubted that Diane trashed Kate's house. That wasn't her style. He had learned a lot about Harley's one and only daughter at the wake this afternoon. She was divorced from husband number one, which had produced a very ungrateful daughter, now in college. She was separated from hubby number two, on the rebound. She'd put the moves on him in a very straightforward way at the café.

Diane's makeup had been applied perfectly, her brassy hair from a bottle, her nails done at a salon, but her eyes and words had made her come across like a desperate woman hanging out on a barstool, looking for love.

"You really believe that, Kate?"

"No."

Steve wanted to drag her into his arms, kiss the anger from her eyes and mouth. Then bed her. He abruptly circled back around. "I'm going to take a few things, dust for prints anyway."

"It's pointless."

There was another opening for an argument, but Steve didn't bite. He walked over to the mess of things by her desk. "Any damage?"

"Not that I can see."

He stared down at the papers, notepads and pens. "Anything missing?"

"I don't think so. My gun is still here."

He walked back over to her, his emotions and hormones semi-under control. "As soon as you stepped inside your house, why didn't you call?"

Her chin lifted. "How do you know I didn't?"

"Gut feeling."

She dropped her eyes, seemed to be studying his boots. "I had the dogs here with me. They went crazy." She raised her eyes. "The jerk must have just left, but I didn't pass anybody on the road."

If it was a random burglary, a gun would be the first item to be taken, along with jewelry, spare cash and electronic equipment. The most lucrative things to pawn. "So any spare cash, jewelry taken?" He'd seen that her TV and VCR were where they should be in the living room.

"Number one, I don't have any jewelry worth taking. And I keep my spare cash in my purse. My computer is my newest purchase. Since it's still here, I really doubt it was a burglary."

Steve hated it when she played cop. He ground his back teeth together. "I don't think you should stay here tonight."

Kate crossed her arms over her chest. "And where do you suggest I stay?"

"Remember I'm on your side."

Her face flushed. "Sorry," she mumbled.

He'd take the apology. "You could stay with Clara."

Kate shook her head. "I'm staying right here. The bastard either found or didn't find what he was looking for."

Steve shifted his position so he could look out the window. It was dark outside, night had settled in. He'd get his flashlight from his truck, see if there were any tracks in the snow behind her house. State land was public land. The perp could have come from that direction. If she did come home when the perp was still in the act of trashing her house, he might decide to pay another visit later. He didn't want to know if Kate had already checked. "I'm going to check around outside."

"I'm coming."

That pretty much answered his question. "It's better if I go alone. The two of us will mess things up, not to mention the dogs."

She frowned at him. "The dogs have already run around outside."

"Then please keep them inside while I check things out."

Kate's frown deepened. Before she could protest, Steve brushed past her to get the flashlight from his truck. He expected her to follow him. After he retrieved the flashlight, he glanced at the house. She was standing on the porch, arms crossed over her chest. The two mutts stood behind her. Since she hadn't put on a jacket, he figured for once she might do as he asked.

Steve started out in the opposite direction from the porch, in case Kate changed her mind.

He searched behind her house, weaving his way through the thick pine trees, stumbling occasionally on an old rotted stump buried under the snow. Under the awning of the branches, the night was inky black. The ground was covered with deer, wild turkey, snowshoe hare and what looked like dog tracks.

Frustration clawed at him as he swung around, snaking his way through the trees back to Kate's house. Steve happened to glance to his right when he spotted the tracks. Adrenaline kicking in, he trudged over to the tracks made by a human. He shined the light over the extra large snow boot tracks. They were too big to be Kate's.

Steve pulled his cell phone from his jacket pocket. "Is there a snowmobile trail out here?"

"Where are you?" Kate asked.

"Behind your house." There was a long silence. "Kate?"

"Yeah, there's an old skidder road the neighbors and other people ride their snow cats on."

"How far back?"

"Probably a mile? Where are you? I'm coming out there."

"You stay put." Steve turned off his cell phone. She damn well better not follow him.

Steve followed the tracks at least a quarter of mile. He cursed himself for not changing into his snow pants. But he'd beat feet over to Kate's with fear swelling inside his gut. Snow pushed over his uniform cuffs. His warm socks were damp inside his boots.

"Damn." Half a dozen steps later, he found the old logging road. Most of the logging roads had been closed for years to enable grizzly bear recovery.

He walked out onto the road. There were snowmobile tracks going both ways. He walked north on the road, doubled back, hiked south for a while. He couldn't follow the road tonight, but tomorrow, first thing, he'd be on it.

Steve heard thrashing in the brush. He shined his light in the direction of the noise. Two whitetail does stood as still as statutes, caught in the beam, staring at him. He found where he had come out on the road, following his tracks in the direction of Kate's house.

When he was halfway back, he heard thrashing again. He shined the light in front of him, figuring it was a couple more deer.

"You're blinding me."

"Dammit, Kate!" He picked up his pace. When he reached her, he saw that she had a small flashlight in her left hand, with a weak beam, meaning the batteries were almost dead. "I told you to stay inside the house."

"You know something, Lambert, you just can't order me around. I'm not one of your deputies."

Steve threw out several hearty swear words.

"Boy, you sure got a mouth for an officer of the law."

"That's because I'm pissed."

They were standing in a clearing, the quarter-sliced moon high in the sky, stars scattered around it. The snow-covered ground gave him enough light to see that her expression was angry, too.

"What did you find?"

"Footprints that lead to the logging road."

Steve watched her frown, but he couldn't see what was in her eyes.

Kate was quiet for several moments. "Like I said, the Blackwell's kids use it all the time in the winter. Plus, their friends come over and ride their snow cats. Other people use it, too."

"Do you remember hearing a snowmobile when you got home?"

Kate shook her head. "I don't think so. They don't usually ride at night. The boys are only fifteen and sixteen. I don't think Don and Sue would allow it."

Steve knew Don and Sue Blackwell. Don was a log truck driver for the mill. Sue worked part-time at the post office, clerking. He'd talk to them tomorrow. "Let's go back to the house."

"You think somebody came in on a snow cat?"

If he didn't tell her what he was thinking, he'd probably get his head bitten off. "It's possible." He had a map of the entire area back at the station, showing private, state, and federal land. He'd have to find out how far that road went out into the forest. "Does that old road have a name?" After he asked her that question, Steve took her arm, turned her around. His feet were freezing.

"I doubt it. You can access it from Elk Ridge Road."

"You know how far back it goes?"

"It dead ends about two miles north from here."

That meant somebody had to have come from Elk Ridge. "Hmmm."

They walked back in silence, Steve leading the way. When they reached her steps, he heard the dogs barking inside. "My feet are frozen."

Kate shined her worthless flashlight down at his boots. "You aren't exactly dressed for trekking through the snow."

Kate had changed into a pair of black nylon snow pants, designed for wading through deep snow. "You don't have to rub it in."

"I might have a pair of socks that will fit you." She went up the steps.

Kate had a pair of men's socks? "Whose socks?"

"My son's. He forgot a few things the last time he visited."

He knew that Kate had a teenage son who lived with his father in Butte. The relief of discovering a pair of socks belonged to her son, not another man, made him uneasy.

After Kate had given him a pair of warm men's socks that were about a size too small, he dropped his boots by the fire, laid a wet sock over each boot. He walked to the kitchen seeing that Kate had changed into a pair of extra faded jeans that hugged her behind. Her pale pink turtleneck sweater complimented the rich brown of her hair.

Standing at the counter, she glanced over her shoulder at him. "Sorry, still haven't replenished the marshmallows."

He took that as a good sign that he didn't have to beg for a hot drink. Steve pulled a chair out, had just sat down when Sunny wandered into the kitchen with one of his damp socks hanging from her mouth. "Hey, give me that." Sunny ignored him, padding over to Kate.

She spun around. "Come on, Sunny. Give me the sock." She bent down, grabbed it, then a tug of war followed. Ranger came trotting in, muscled his way into the tug of war of game.

Irritated that his sock was getting ruined, Steve got up and joined the group.

"Come on guys, let go of the sock," Kate ordered.

"Those are brand new socks."

Kate finally managed to yank the sock from both dogs' mouths. She held it up in front of him. It was stretched, hanging like a limp flag in front of her.

Scowling, Steve took his sock from her.

He headed back out to the wood stove when he heard her laughing behind him. Kate's laughter erased his irritation at his new sock being used as a dog toy. When he returned to the kitchen, Kate had two steaming mugs of cocoa sitting on opposite sides of the table.

He parked himself in the chair again. "Thanks."

"You're welcome."

Steve noticed the twinkle of amusement in her eyes. "I'm glad you think it's funny."

"Have you ever had a dog?"

"When I was a kid we had a very well-behaved cocker spaniel."

"Are you implying my dogs aren't well-behaved?"

"I haven't met a well-behaved dog since I moved to Montana."

"I'd say you're exaggerating a little."

"They wander all over town, out in the country, chew on dead deer carcasses on the side of the road. Most of them don't have collars."

"They know where their homes are." Kate shrugged. "So you're not a dog person."

"I never said that." As Steve picked up his mug, Sunny sashayed back into the room carrying his sock again, followed by Ranger with the other sock in his mouth. "Ah...hell."

CHAPTER SEVEN

The next morning, Steve caught Don Blackwell at the café having breakfast. He slid into the booth across from him. "How's it going, Don?" Don was early forties, typical logger, his light brown hair speckled with gray, his middle-aged spread starting to show.

"No complaints, Sheriff." Don lifted his mug along with an eyebrow. "What's up?"

"Kate Madison's house was broken into last night." He was still pissed at her for not locking her back door. There had been no signs of forced entry.

"No shit?" Don almost choked on his coffee. "There's a lot of that going on around here. I don't like it."

"Can't blame you."

"Is Kate okay?"

Steve nodded. "Did you happen to hear a snowmobile last night between six and seven behind your place, on state land?"

"My wife and boys went out for pizza last night. I went over to my sister's place after work. I had to fix a leaky pipe for her. We all got home about the same time, a little after eight."

"Do you know what time your wife left the house?"

"Yeah, she called me about five or five thirty on the way to the pizza parlor. Afterwards, they went and visited her mother for awhile."

It looked like the entire family had been gone while the s.o.b. trashed Kate's house. Steve slid out of the booth.

"Thanks, Don."

"No problem."

As he was leaving, Clara came over to him, holding a coffeepot in her hand.

"You're not having coffee?"

"No thanks, Clara. I stopped in to talk to Don for a minute." He figured Kate hadn't told Clara about the break-in. Since Don Blackwell knew about it word would travel fast. Not that Don was a gossip. It was how small towns operated. The old reliable grapevine. "Kate's place was trashed yesterday."

Clara's face paled, her hand holding the coffeepot started shaking. Steve took the pot from her. "She's okay, Clara. The guy was looking for something, just like at Harley's."

"I need to call her. She shouldn't have stayed there alone last night. Why didn't she call me? She could have stayed with me." Clara finally paused, taking a breath.

"I tried to get her to stay with you, but she wouldn't."

"She's too stubborn for her own good."

No shit. "Yeah."

"I'm going to call her right this minute."

Clara hustled off, leaving Steve holding the coffee pot. He took off after her. The café was almost empty since it was past nine. The breakfast crowd had eaten and headed out to work. He pushed through the swinging door. "Clara, wait."

She paused, the cordless phone in her hand. "I need to talk to you first."

Steve handed her the coffee pot. "About what?"

"Did Harley have any enemies?"

"Goodness, no. Everybody loved Harley. We're really going to miss him."

"He used to come here in a lot, didn't he?"

"Two or three times a week. He'd alternate between breakfast, lunch and dinner."

Clara got rid of the pot on a small table behind her. She slipped the phone into her apron pocket. "Harley's killer is a local, isn't he?"

Steve didn't see any point in holding back what was probably the truth. "It looks that way."

Clara drew in a shaky breath. "I've lived here for over twenty years and nothing like this has ever happened. It's frightening."

"If you think of anybody that may have had it in for Harley, call me. I need to know."

Clara nodded, pulled out the phone. "I have to talk to Kate."

※　※　※

Kate was ready to head out the door when the phone rang. She hesitated, wondering if it was Steve. If he knew she planned to walk the logging road in search of clues, he'd probably have a hissy fit. Deciding she'd better answer it, she hurried into the kitchen and picked up the phone. "Hello."

"Why in the blazes didn't you call me last night? You don't know how upset I am about all this."

Somehow Clara had found out about her house being tossed. That meant the entire town would know soon. "I'm fine, Clara, just ticked off. Who told you?"

"Steve. I caught him when he was leaving. He came in to talk to Don Blackwell."

She was itching to know what information, if any, Don had given Steve. "I'm really okay. Don't worry. I just got my house put back together."

"Was anything stolen?"

"No."

"Steve asked me if Harley had any enemies. And I told him everybody loved Harley. He wants me to call him if I can think of anything. Anything at all."

"That's good, Clara. That's the only way we'll find Harley's killer."

Silence followed. "Clara?"

"I just can't believe there's a killer in our community."

Kate believed it, especially after Harley's and her house had been tossed and trashed. "I know."

"I want you to come down here and spend the day at the café. You can write or read a book."

"Thanks, Clara, but I'll be back to work day after tomorrow."

"You shouldn't be alone."

"I'm okay. I...uh...have to do some work on my novel. I've been neglecting it lately." She hated lying to her good friend.

"Take a break and come for lunch."

Kate glanced at her watch. Nine-fifteen. She didn't want to commit. "If I don't get too involved. You know me, I lose track of track of time when I'm working."

"Well...okay...but..."

"I'm fine and thanks for calling. It means a lot to me."

"What are friends for?"

She was lucky to have a friend like Clara. Maybe the woman was her employer, but they were close. "I'll talk to you later. And don't work too hard."

"Hard work is in my blood. Bye."

Kate replaced the phone, started for the door again when she heard the dogs barking outside. When she opened the door, she saw a Ford Explorer with a Budget Rent-a-car on the plate pull to a stop by her truck.

Diane. Great, that's all she needed, to deal with Diane. Kate went down the steps, tugging on her gloves. Maybe that would give Diane the hint she was in a hurry to leave.

Harley's daughter climbed out of the truck, wearing brand new black jeans and a red turtleneck under a deep brown leather jacket. Dress for success. Kate was wearing her black snow pants, pac boots, and blue fleece jacket. "Easy, guys."

Diane looked at the dogs with total disdain. Kate remembered when they were kids Diane hadn't liked dogs. "The Husky looking dog is Ranger. He was your dad's."

That stopped Diane in her tracks. She glanced down at Ranger, who stood looking up at her, tail still. "My father always liked dogs. Are you going to keep him?"

"Of course I'm going to keep him."

Diane lifted a shoulder, giving the impression she could care less about Ranger's fate. "I'm sure you'll take good care of him." She made her way over to Kate. "I'm on my way to the airport in Kalispell. I found my mother's china and a few other things of hers to take back with me. Anyway, I know you don't want to be paid for taking care of my father's things, but I'll be more than happy to do it."

Kate fought back the urge to bust Diane's bright red-lined chops. "I don't want your money."

Diane finger combed her brassy hair. "Okay...then..."

"I'll probably never see you again."

"Probably."

"Tell me why you didn't want anything to do with your father. He was a damn good man."

Diane actually looked sheepish. Kate figured she had hoped to blow off Windy Creek without anybody confronting her about her estranged relationship with her father.

"Does it matter now?" Diane's voice was tight.

"It does to me."

Diane looked away, stared at Kate's house for a moment, then shrugged. "We just never had anything in common. Dad didn't want me to leave Windy Creek. He wanted me to go to college, then come back when I graduated. But, good Lord, what is there to do here? I always hated this place."

She'd always known, even as a kid, that Diane had hated Windy Creek. She had craved the excitement and continual movement of a big city. That was all fine and well, but Diane could have kept in touch with Harley. "He loved you, Diane."

"If you're trying to lay guilt on me, it's too late for that."

It was Kate's turn to look sheepish, because that's exactly what she'd been trying to do.

"He didn't like it when I got divorced. He was from that generation that believed marriage was 'til death do us part. Things happen."

"You couldn't get past that?"

"I'm surprised Dad didn't confide in you. You two were always so close."

Kate felt the sarcasm in Diane's words. "He really didn't talk about you much the past few years."

"Then how do you know he still loved me?"

"He told me once a couple of years ago. Said he was sorry for all that happened between you two. Or didn't happen."

Diane glanced away again. Kate could have sworn she noticed Diane's bottom lip tremble slightly. Diane hadn't shed a tear yesterday at the service, but then, neither had she.

"We grew farther and farther apart. That's all there is to say. If you don't want money, that's your choice. If you change your mind, let me know." Diane skewered Kate with a look, then turned and walked back to the rental truck.

Kate watched Diane until she disappeared down her driveway. Their conversation left too many unanswered questions. Harley had pretty much suffered in silence over the rift with his daughter. As far as she knew, they'd never had a big blowout about anything in particular. Caught off guard by Diane, Kate had decided to seize the opportunity.

Father and daughter had grown apart. It happened. That was life. So forth and so on.

Kate went back inside her house, locking the back door before she grabbed a bottle of water out of the fridge. On her way out, she double-checked the front door, making sure it was locked, too.

Sunny and Ranger trotted beside her as she hiked through the snow behind her house.

She supposed what little information Diane had volunteered was better than nothing. Her real father had taken off years ago. Kate didn't remember him. She didn't know if he was still alive, if he had fathered other children. That was her problem, had always been her problem with Diane. She hadn't bothered to keep in touch with her father, her real father.

Kate considered herself damned lucky that Harley had stepped into her missing father's shoes.

⌖   ⌖   ⌖

Steve steered his truck into the last driveway on Elk Ridge Road. After this, the land became public. He wasn't sure who lived here. Two big, scruffy, black dogs shot over to his truck, started barking. He just loved dealing with big, unruly mutts.

Steve swore under his breath, opened the door, eyeing the dogs. They were still barking, but their black tails were also wagging. He took that as a good sign. "Hey, guys, nice guys." He climbed out of his truck. The dogs backed up several feet. "You're not gonna bite me, are you?"

Two sets of brown eyes stared up at him like he was slightly off his rocker. He shoved the door closed, started toward the front stoop. He glanced over his shoulder. The dogs had quieted, but he could tell they wanted to get closer to him, sniff his boots and trousers. Steve went up the steps, knocked on the door.

When he didn't get an answer, he knocked louder.

The door was opened by an elderly man with a shock of grey hair. "Howdy." His face weathered by time split into a grin.

"Morning, I'm Sheriff Steve Lambert. I would like to talk to you for a few minutes, if you can spare the time."

"Got all the time in the world, I'm retired. By the way, I know who you are." The man held out his hand. "I'm Gus Lansing."

Steve shook the man's hand. "Did you hear a snowmobile up on state land last night between five and seven?"

Gus tapped his left ear where a hearing aid protruded. "Can't hear anything that far away. Unless I'm outside or looking out the window to see trucks driving by, I don't know who's back there."

"Did you see any trucks go by yesterday?"

Gus scrunched up his face. "Earlier in the day before lunch, I saw one of those fancy new Fords go by."

"Did you notice it come back by?"

"About an hour later. But it didn't have a snowmobile in the back. Bed was empty as far as I could see. There's lots more traffic on the weekends around here."

Dead end. Steve thanked the man for his time and left.

He drove to the end of the main road, found where the old logging road branched off to the east, parked and got out. Since it hadn't snowed for a few days, he didn't know how fresh any of the tire tracks were. Snowmobile, human, and deer tracks were scattered along the road and across it. He walked for a while. After a time, the boot tracks stopped, leaving only snowmobile and deer tracks.

Steve stopped, hoping this wasn't a dead end, too. Just because Gus Lansing hadn't seen a truck with a snowmobile yesterday didn't mean one hadn't been up here. He decided to go back when he heard a couple of dogs barking up ahead. He figured it was a couple of roaming mutts. They'd better be friendly.

When he saw Sunny and Ranger sprinting toward him, a deep scowl creased his face. He heard Kate yelling for them.

Steve crossed his arms over his chest, stood in the middle of the road, and waited for Kate to come around the corner. As the dogs trotted closer, they stopped barking, obviously recognizing him.

Thirty seconds later, Kate rounded the corner. When she spotted him, her eyes widened in surprise.

"Fancy meeting you out here," Steve said.

"Can't a girl and her dogs go for a walk?"

"Is that what you're doing, Kate? Just out for a leisurely stroll?"

Imitating him, she crossed her arms over her chest. "How do you know that's not what I'm doing?"

"Oh, I don't know. Something tells me you're out investigating. Which, by the way, is my job."

Her chin lifted. "I needed a walk. There's no harm in checking things out along the way."

"Uh huh."

"Stop looking at me that way. And for your information, I didn't find anything...out of the ordinary."

As much as it annoyed him that she was wandering in the woods alone, he was hoping she might have noticed something. Anything.

"Have you turned up anything?"

Steve shook his head.

Kate frowned. "He moves around among us. So nobody is noticing him."

"I'll take you home."

"I can walk back."

"It's over two miles."

"So?"

"Come on, Kate, I'll take you home."

"What about the dogs?"

"They can run behind my truck."

"No way." She shook her head. "I don't want them learning bad habits."

Two big, wet dogs in his truck. He supposed they were better than a drunk losing his lunch. "Looks like I don't have a choice."

Kate shot him a smug look. "Nope, Sheriff, you don't."

⚼   ⚼   ⚼

Kate tried to hide a smile as Steve scrutinized the back of his truck where the dogs had ridden. On the drive back to her house, he'd kept glancing in the rear view to make sure Sunny and Ranger didn't chew, pee, or in any way violate his truck. Against her better judgment, she wanted to invite him in for lunch since it was almost noon. Bad idea. Besides, her cupboards were near empty. One of these days, she needed to go grocery shopping.

Steve caught her watching him. She shifted back on her feet. "Thanks, I guess."

That made him frown. "You need to watch your back, Kate."

She knew he was right. Her pistol was strapped on under her bulky jacket. She carried the gun when hiking in the woods in case she encountered a mountain lion, rabid coyote, or temperamental moose. Now there was a possibility of running into a killer. A shiver skated down her spine.

When she didn't answer, Steve asked, "Did you hear me?"

"Of course I heard you. I promise I'll be careful."

Steve's expression said he didn't believe her. "The least you could do is give me the benefit of the doubt."

"Believe me, I'm trying."

She held up two fingers. "Scout's honor."

"Real funny, Kate."

The exasperated expression on his face made her want to laugh, but she kept her laughter to herself.

Steve moved close to her, patted her hip where her gun was holstered. "I assume you know how to use this."

He was so close she could see the tiny cut on his jaw where he had nicked himself shaving this morning. Her instincts told her to step back, but she held her ground. "Do you really think I would own a gun if I didn't know how to use it?" At twelve years old, Harley had taught her to shoot a .22 rifle, shotgun and 30-30 rifle. He was still too close and there was a dangerous look in his eye that had nothing to do with the dangers of a gun. "I'll have you know I'm a damn good shot."

"Then carry it with you at all times."

She didn't like Steve's advice, but knew it was good advice. "Okay."

Steve started to lean in closer when abruptly he stopped, wheeled around and strode to the driver's door of his truck. Her heart pounded a crazy beat when she heard his truck door slam. She caught him staring at her from his inside rear view mirror.

Their eyes locked for a time before Kate skedaddled out of the way of his truck in the direction of her house.

Once inside, Kate watched him from her living room window. He didn't leave right away. She'd heard his truck start when she reached the front porch. A big part of her hoped he'd turn off his truck as her heart did that crazy pounding again.

Disappointment washed through her as Steve backed up his truck and started down her driveway. It took at least five minutes for her heart beat to return to normal.

※　※　※

Out on the road, Steve adjusted his trousers. That's what Kate Madison did to him. He'd almost kissed her, managing to dredge up enough control to stop himself.

His powerful desire for Kate was distracting. He liked routine. It was part of his character. Putting on his uniform five mornings a week was a ritual for him. He could never picture himself not wearing a uniform.

At the edge of town, Steve pulled into The Town Pump, filled up the tank, then went inside to pay. First he filled his commuter cup with hot coffee. At the counter, he noticed Ray Wendell, the owner of the station, cleaning a rifle.

A 30-06 rifle.

Steve slid his cup on the counter, tugged out his wallet.

Ray glanced up from polishing the barrel with a cloth. "How's it going, Sheriff?"

"Ray."

"Need to keep this baby in shape." Ray stood, leaned the rifle against a shelf.

"Why's that?"

Ray ambled up to the counter and took the twenty-dollar bill Steve handed him. "Well, with what's been going around Windy Creek lately, I'd say it's a necessity.

It was common knowledge Harley had been murdered. Then his house trashed, followed by Kate's. "Most store owners keep a shotgun or pistol for protection."

"Oh, I got my shotgun under the counter. The rifle's for home protection."

Steve wanted to say call the cops before using a gun, but out in this rural area a person couldn't always wait for the cops to arrive. Steve took the change Ray handed him, shoved the bills in his wallet, dropped the loose change in his front trousers pocket. "You're a hunter, aren't you?"

"Who isn't around here?"

Steve wasn't. "You hunt the usual?"

He watched Ray's reaction. Ray was probably late thirties, with thinning black hair, that's why he always wore a ball cap. He was a big, husky guy, at least six feet.

"Deer, elk, grouse, lions, black bear." He pointed over Steve's shoulder. "I got that cat back in ninety three."

Steve knew he was talking about the mountain lion's head mounted to the wall above the beer cooler. "You ever get any bear?"

"Yeah, I've gotten a few. I got the hides at home."

"You ever shoot a grizzly accidentally?"

That got Ray's attention. "You interrogating me for any particular reason, Sheriff?"

"Just wondering. I've heard hunters doing it by mistake."

"I don't make mistakes hunting. When I see a bear, I watch it for a helluva long time to make sure it don't have any cubs. And I damn well know the difference between a black and a grizzly."

Steve had just been properly put in his place.

Ray took out a tin can of chewing tobacco from his back pocket, wadded up some chew, shoving it in his mouth. "Why you asking, Sheriff?"

"Curiosity," Steve said. "I saw you cleaning your rife." He lifted a shoulder. "Just wondering. I figured you hunted. Just didn't know what."

He'd never had a problem with Ray Wendell. The guy was friendly, ran a good honest business. When the store had been broken into six months earlier, Ray had pretty much kept his cool. The only things stolen were beer and cigarettes, pointing to kids. "I heard there was a sow grizzly shot a few years ago, before my time." He didn't want Ray getting suspicious and clamming up. When he had the time, he'd stand around and chew the fat with him.

Ray eyed him for a few seconds before he said, "Never caught the s.o.b. that shot that bear. They took the cubs to some recovery center to sleep for the winter. They were too young to make it without their mama." Ray chewed his tobacco for a few seconds. "I got a lot of respect for grizzlies. I'd just as soon not mess with one."

Steve's instincts told him Ray was telling him the truth. He did know this is where Harley used to get gas. "It's a shame about Harley. He was well liked in the community."

"Yeah, Harley was a good old guy." Ray eyed him again. His green eyes hinted at suspicion. "You figured out who killed old Harley yet?"

Steve had known, sooner rather than later, he'd be put on the spot. "Not yet. I'm still investigating."

"When you catch the s.o.b., he should get the death penalty."

Steve nodded. He didn't discuss the pros and cons of the death penalty with John Q. Public. His job was to apprehend the bad guys. It ended there. He didn't sit in judgment of the murderers, rapists and child molesters. He maintained strong feelings about the proper punishment for those kinds of predators, but he kept them to himself.

"Ray, you know, sometimes, people talk. Sometimes people brag. Sometimes they let something slip out without realizing it.

You know just about everybody in town, right? Your gas station is a hot spot."

Ray nodded while his eyes narrowed a fraction. Steve tugged his wallet out again, pulled out a business card, handed it over the counter to him. Ray stared down at it like it was covered with flu germs before he finally took it.

"If you hear anything at all that you think might be related to Harley's death, I'd appreciate it if you gave me a call. Night or day."

Ray's chest puffed out a bit, realizing that Steve had just included him in his investigation.

"Sure, Sheriff. Like I said, I want to see the bastard who killed Harley behind bars just as much as you do."

Steve nodded. "Thanks, I appreciate it, Ray. Talk to you later." Steve picked up his cup, turned and left the store.

Sitting in his truck, he sipped the strong coffee before he inserted the key. If he had some kind of description of the killer, he could circulate it around town. But as it stood, he had nothing. He drove down to the newspaper office, The Windy Creek Times. When he went inside, chimes sounded over his head.

Jim Browning, the editor, glanced up from the counter, half glasses perched on his nose.

"Sheriff, what can I do for you?"

Jim Browning was fifty-something, skinny, almost completely bald and had owned Windy Creek's one and only paper for over twenty years.

"I could use some help."

Jim pulled off his glasses. "Always glad to help out the local law enforcement."

"Can you run something in the next edition about Harley's death?"

"You already gave me an interview, told me what you could, and I ran the obituary Kate wrote."

"I know. I need something else. Can you run a follow-up asking people to report to the sheriff's office if they saw or heard anything suspicious the day of Harley's murder?"

Jim nodded, his face sullen. "I still can't believe somebody actually murdered old Harley." He paused. "You're sure it's murder?"

"Right now all the signs point to that."

"I'll tell you something. It's put the town on edge, including my wife. She's skittish by nature anyway." Jim rubbed his chin. "You don't think it was a drifter passing through?"

"No." Steve figured it was time to let the people of Windy Creek know the truth. There was a killer among them. It would undoubtedly make them more paranoid, but it would also make them more alert. And he was desperate for a lead. He'd take anything he could get.

Jim nodded. "I can get it in this week's edition, front page."

"You can send the bill to the office."

"No charge, Sheriff. I run public service announcements for free. I figure that's what this is."

※　※　※

After Steve left, Kate went straight to her computer, pounded out ten pages on her manuscript in progress. She didn't reread what she had written, figuring it wasn't worth much. But at least she'd done some work. When she went to the kitchen for a glass of water, her stomach grumbled and growled in protest. She rummaged through her cupboards and fridge and knew she couldn't put off grocery shopping any longer. Since she'd be back at work tomorrow, she'd better do it today. She'd stop at the café first for a late lunch and let Clara know she was okay.

As she wiggled into her jacket, she remembered her gun. Steve had told her to carry it with her at all times. Her teeth set, she went to get it.

><   ><   ><

"Order up," Ace called.

Kate devoured a grilled ham and cheese sandwich. The immensity of her hunger never seemed to hit her until she walked into the café. Since it was after one, the café was nearly empty.

Clara appeared with a mug of coffee in her hand and sat down across from Kate. "Steve just walked in."

Kate ignored Clara, concentrating on her sandwich. She ignored the rise in her body temperature, too. It was always warm in the kitchen area. Steve had been so close to kissing her, then wham he just stopped. She wondered if that a good or bad thing.

Clara leaned toward her. "I said, Steve is here."

"I heard you the first time."

"Uh huh."

Kate shoved the last bite in her mouth, drinking some Coke to wash it down.

"Are you sure you're okay?"

Kate peered at Clara over the rim of her glass. She assumed Clara was referring to her house being thrashed, not anything to do with Steve. "Yeah, I'm fine."

"Hey, Clara," Ace called. "Your order is up."

"That would be Steve's. Would you like to deliver it?" There was a devilish twinkle in Clara's eyes.

She considered doing just that. It would definitely put him on the spot. Steve had left her hanging, literally, behind his truck. He didn't know she was here because she was parked out back. Kate stood up. "Why not?"

"It's the cheeseburger and fries."

Kate sashayed over to the cooking area, elbowed Ace out of the way, not responding to his four-letter word, and grabbed the burger basket off the ledge.

She nudged the swinging door open with her shoulder, spotted Steve sitting at the far end of the counter, staring off into space, lost in thought. He didn't notice her until she plopped the basket down in front of him.

"Kate?"

"Yes."

"I didn't know you were here."

"Yeah, I was in the back. Clara's busy. She asked me to bring your lunch."

His blue eyes gave nothing away, but he seemed damned uncomfortable, which was fine with her.

"Ah...thanks."

"You're welcome. You really ought to get more variety in your diet."

Steve held a nice fat french fry in front of his mouth when he paused, frowning at her. "Is that why you brought me my lunch?" He paused. "So you could point out that I eat a crappy diet?" He slathered ketchup on the fries.

Kate shrugged, snagged a fry out of the basket.

Steve ate another fry before he picked up half of the cheeseburger. "What's on your mind?" He didn't look happy as he took a big bite. Clara and Ace were both known for their hamburgers. They were the best in the county.

What was on her mind? "Oh, this and that."

He took another bite, ignoring her. Steve looked like he wished she would disappear. For some insane reason, that made Kate smile.

"What's so damn funny?"

"Nothing."

Irritation flashed in his eyes as he proceeded to eat his burger. She nabbed another fry, nibbling on it. Steve watched her, which started to make her uncomfortable. She swallowed the last half of it whole. Noticing he was low on coffee, she circled around, grabbing the glass carafe off the warmer and refilled his mug, avoiding his gaze.

"See you later," she said.

Irritation was clearly evident on his face.

Kate smiled, turned, sauntered away.

CHAPTER EIGHT

Kate sat on a stump next to the abandoned logging road. The dogs, noses pressed to the ground sniffing the wild critter tracks. She jumped up when she heard the loud whine of snowmobiles approaching. When she spotted the first snowmobile roaring towards her, she waved her arms over her head. The machine immediately started slowing down. The second one coming into view eased up on the gas too.

The dogs trotted out of the trees, started barking. "No," she yelled over the sound of the engines. Both dogs quieted.

The first driver came to a stop ten feet back from her. Kate walked over to him. "Hi."

When the driver pulled off his helmet, she recognized him. It was Josh Wyatt, a young guy that worked at the mill. He came into the café a few times a week for breakfast.

"Hey, Kate. Are you in some kind of trouble?"

She shook her head, watching the second snowmobile stop. "I was wondering if you guys were out this way yesterday." She recognized the other man after he took off his helmet. Tim Bradford, Josh's friend and co-worker. She smiled at him.

"Yeah, we were," Josh said. "We're on the early shift this week."

"Hi, Kate. What's up?" Tim got off his snowmobile, angled over to her, his helmet tucked under his arm.

"Did you hear my house got trashed?" Kate figured it was common knowledge by now.

"Anything stolen?" Tim asked.

"No, just tossed."

"Heard Harley Wilson's house got trashed, too." Josh wedged the helmet between his legs.

Kate nodded. "The creep that did mine must have come down this road on a snowmobile."

"We ran into three guys from Kalispell yesterday, but that was it." Josh plowed his hand through his matted down blond hair. "There are a lot more people out snow-catting on the weekends."

"Wait a minute," Tim said. "I spotted one parked about fifty yards north of here." He pointed his thumb in the direction they had just come from.

Josh glanced at his friend. "I didn't see it."

"That's because you were hauling. He has a death wish." Tim grinned at Kate. "It was parked off the road back in the trees. I figured the guy had to take a leak. Excuse me, Kate. Use the outdoor facilities."

"Was there a truck parked on Elk Ridge Road?"

"That's right. There were three trucks parked when we got here. We figured the guys from Kalispell each brought their own truck. But come to think of it, the one truck had a trailer behind it. So they could have come in two trucks."

"Do you remember the trucks?"

Tim scratched his head. "A couple of newer Fords. The third was a Dodge, older model. I think."

"And it was white," Josh added.

Kate was having a hard time standing still. She knew she was onto something. "Have you seen the truck around town before?"

Tim transferred his helmet to his other arm. "There are a lot of older trucks from the eighties around here."

Unfortunately Tim was right. She might not be onto something after all.

"We were in a hurry to get going," Tim said. "Sorry, but we didn't pay that much attention.

Josh nodded. "You know how that goes."

"Do you remember the snowmobile?"

"Not much," Tim said. "I was going pretty fast myself. It was a newer one. Not an old clunker."

"I appreciate it, guys." Kate said. "I don't want to keep you from your fun."

"No problem, Kate." Josh pulled his helmet back over his head. "Hope we were some help."

"You were a big help. Thanks again."

Kate called the dogs and walked to the side of the road. Both men waved to her as they passed. A few minutes later, she heard them pick up their speed, the sound of the snowmobiles fading in the distance.

Kate took her time hiking back to her house. The dogs sniffed, circled trees, trotting ahead of her.

In her kitchen, she put the kettle on to boil for tea. While she rummaged through the decorative Christmas tin can that contained a various assortment of tea bags, she contemplated calling Steve. They already knew someone on a snowmobile had trashed her house.

Disillusioned, when she realized she really hadn't uncovered any new evidence. Steve didn't take kindly to her doing his job. She heard the kettle whistling on the stove. She plucked a bag of Earl Grey tea out of the tin. She was dunking the tea bag in the steaming water when the phone rang.

Kate picked up the phone. "Hello."

"I wouldn't snoop too much if I were you, Kate."

The line went dead.

Stunned, Kate lowered the phone, stared at it in disbelief. First, her house had been trashed, now a threatening phone call. Kate's hand started to shake so much she almost dropped the mug. She went to the table, set the mug down, then herself.

Perched on the edge of the chair, she kept staring at the phone clutched tightly in her left hand. She hadn't recognized the man's voice because it sounded like he'd disguised it.

With trembling fingers she dialed the Sheriff's office. "Jenny, this is Kate. Is Steve there?"

"As a matter of fact, he's hovering over me, waiting for me to type a report. Which, of course, I could do a lot faster if he wasn't hanging over my shoulder."

Normally, Kate would have laughed at Jenny's humor, but because of the threatening phone call, it was lost on her. "Oh."

"Are you okay, Kate?"

"Um...yeah." Before she could say anymore, Steve's voice came over the line. "What's going on, Kate?"

"I...uh...just got a threatening phone call."

"What the hell?" There was a long pause. "Who was it and what did he say?"

Kate leaned her elbow on the table. "He said, 'I wouldn't snoop too much if I were you, Kate.'"

"Did you recognize his voice?"

Kate shook her head like Steve could actually see her. "No. It sounded like he disguised it somehow."

"I'll be right over. Lock your doors now."

CHAPTER NINE

Steve paced around Kate's small kitchen like an African lion in a zoo cage. Sitting at the table, she studied him. His face was etched in a combination of anger and frustration. "Do you want some coffee or hot cocoa?"

Steve shook his head. "No, thanks. It's not in the budget to tap your phone," he finally said, still pacing. "We operate on a shoestring as it is."

The county was sparsely populated, meaning not a lot of tax dollars for frivolous things like phone tapping. "Maybe he won't call again." Kate didn't believe that, apparently Steve didn't either.

He stopped pacing and looked at Kate. "Get real."

She might have been offended but she knew he was right. The maniac would probably call again.

Steve's eyes narrowed. "What have you been doing to prompt that call?"

Kate's eyes widened. "You're blaming me for this?"

"No. I'm not blaming you, but the bastard seems to believe you've been snooping around. Have you?"

Kate stared at the soggy tea bag still in the mug. A half hour hadn't even passed between the time she'd talked to Tim and Josh and the phone call. "Well..."

"Well what?" Steve demanded. He angled over to her, stood a foot front her chair, shooting her a suspicious look.

"Okay, okay. I wish you'd sit down."

"I don't feel like sitting down."

"When I got home from town, I walked up to the logging road."

"I knew I wasn't going to like this."

Kate could feel the tension vibrating off Steve since he was standing so close to her. All it did was add to her agitated frame of mind. "I flagged down Josh Wyatt and Tim Bradford. You know who they are?" When Steve nodded, she continued. "Anyway, they said they saw an older white Dodge truck parked at Elk Ridge the day before yesterday.

"But they ran into three guys from Kalispell some time when they were out riding. They figured it was one of their trucks. There were three trucks parked there all together. One of the trucks had a trailer. So the three guys from Kalispell could have brought only two trucks." Kate paused, taking a breath. "Tim saw a snowmobile parked off in the trees, but Josh didn't because he was going too fast."

"Could he identify it?"

"I don't think so. He just happened to glance that way. He figured the guy had to relieve himself."

"You know something, Kate?"

His voice was definitely threatening. "What?"

"Never mind," Steve muttered before he started pacing again.

"Just like the rifle," she said, more to herself than Steve. He stopped pacing, stared out the window, settling his hands on his hips. "Everybody and their dog has a snowmobile." Not everybody, but just about. She didn't have one. Harley had sold his five years ago, claiming he was getting too old to ride.

Under his heavy uniform jacket, Steve's back was rigid. "It still doesn't make sense. I know Tim and Josh aren't behind this. It must be a strange coincidence that I got that call so soon. Unless," she paused, suppressing a shudder, "I'm being watched."

Steve wheeled around. "I don't think so. Where would somebody hide around here? Coming by here on the logging road on a snowmobile is the easiest way not to be noticed." Steve adjusted his ball cap. "I'm heading out to Elk Ridge." When Kate stood up, he said, "No. You are not coming with me. You're staying here with your doors locked."

✂ ✂ ✂

When Steve rolled to a stop at the parking area on Elk Ridge Road, the only truck parked there was Tim Bradley's with a small utility trailer sitting next to the Ford four-wheel drive. He'd stopped him a few weeks ago for not having his taillights hooked up on the trailer. It would be dark soon, so hopefully the two men would be heading back.

Steve called the dispatcher, gave her his location. Fifteen minutes later, he heard the roar of the snowmobiles approaching. He climbed out of his truck, took off his hat, raking a hand through his hair. Tim and Josh both squealed to a stop in the parking area.

Steve strode over to the two young men, who were both removing their helmets.

"Hey, Sheriff," Tim said.

"How's it going guys?"

"Had a great ride." Josh climbed off his machine.

"I got my trailer lights fixed, Sheriff," Tim said, a wary look in his eye.

"I figured you would. That's not why I'm here." He noticed how Tim's expression relaxed. "Were there any other vehicles here when you guys got here?"

"Yeah," Josh laid his helmet on his seat, started tugging off his gloves. "A white Subaru Outback."

Another popular car in Windy Creek. "Was anybody here?"

"No." Tim unzipped his snowsuit. "I figured somebody was cross country skiing." He pointed over his shoulder. "There's a Forest Service hiking trail that goes back about four miles."

Steve glanced in the direction Tim pointed. The trail sign was leaning against a fir tree. Somebody must have backed into it. "Was there a carrier on top of the car?"

The two men looked at each other.

"I honestly don't remember," Tim said.

"Me neither," Josh added. "We talked to Kate Madison. We heard her house had been trashed. I told her I noticed a snowmobile parked off the road the other day."

"Do you know what make?"

"It was a newer one. It might have been a Polaris. But I can't say for sure."

Tim and Josh both drove Polaris snowmobiles. Why couldn't the perp drive some unique foreign car or own an old rattletrap snowmobile? Frustration knotted inside his gut. "I appreciate it, guys. If you think of anything else, give me a ring."

"Will do, Sheriff," Josh said.

Steve hiked back to his truck. He wasn't a mile down the road when the dispatcher came over the line, alerting him to a one car rollover two miles east of town. The canyon area where the road stayed frozen under the shadow of the rock wall. "How bad are the injuries?"

"It was Gabe Johnson. According to Kurt, he's drunker than a skunk and spitting mad for rolling his truck."

"Tell Kurt I'm on my way."

"Roger that."

Kurt Maxwell was his youngest deputy, still a little wet behind the ears. Steve turned on his siren and lights. Gabe Johnson was a mean drunk and outweighed his deputy by a good thirty pounds.

He needed to get to the scene and fast. At least it would get his mind of who killed Harley and if Kate could be kept safe.

⚞ ⚞ ⚞

Annoyance rippling through her and tired of pacing her living room, Kate decided to drive to Elk Ridge Road to find out what was up with Steve. It had been almost two hours since he'd left. She was out the door, ready to lock it behind her when the phone rang. She hesitated, fear spiraling through her at the thought of another threatening call. Fighting back a small wave of panic, she hurried back inside to answer it. "Hello?"

"Do you have your doors locked?"

Relief overrode the panic attack at the sound of Steve's voice. She peeked around the corner from the kitchen. Her front door was wide open. Sunny stood in the open doorway. "Of course."

"Why don't I believe you?"

Kate skimmed by his comment. "I was just going to look for you."

"That wasn't part of the plan. The plan was for you to stay home with your doors locked."

Her temper flared. "I'm not going to be a prisoner in my own house, Sheriff."

"Why do you always call me Sheriff when you're ticked off at me?"

That brought her up short. She ignored his question. "Did you find anything at Elk Ridge?"

She heard Steve's frustrated sigh at the other end, waiting for him to answer.

"Not much. Tim and Josh said there was a white Subaru Outback parked there when they first arrived. They figured it was cross country skiers."

How many people owned white Subarus in town? Basically, too many to count. Another dead end. They were no closer to finding Harley's killer than they were the first day she found his body.

"Kate?"

"Yeah."

"Promise me you'll lock your doors."

"I'll keep them locked." She glanced at the open door. Sunny was now looking out across her front yard. Ranger squeezed by her, padding inside the house to the wood stove, dropping down next to it. "Okay, I promise."

"You wouldn't break a promise, now would you?"

Only my wedding vows. Guilt, intertwined with remorse, shot through her.

"I'm waiting," Steve said.

She dragged herself back to the present. "I'll lock my damn doors. Okay?"

"Okay."

⚹   ⚹   ⚹

Kate stuffed the order pad in her apron pocket, weaving her way around tables, bumped her hip on the counter on her way to put the order up. "Two number ones, over easy and a full stack."

Ace grinned at her, grabbing the ticket out of her hand before she could snap it to the rotating wheel. "Good to have you back, Katie."

"It's good to be back."

"Work is good for the soul."

"Point well taken." The morning rush was just winding down since it was almost eight thirty. The working class were either at their jobs or on their way. Kate angled over to the coffee maker and made two fresh pots. It didn't matter what time of day it was, Clara insisted the coffee always had to be hot and fresh.

When she circled around, Hal Jackson plopped his beefy body on a stool directly in front of her. What was up with him? He never sat at the counter. Besides, his corner booth was empty. Carol was clearing the table, swabbing it down with a damp cloth.

She gritted her teeth. "Coffee?"

Hal gave her look like, 'what are you, one shy of six pack'?

Kate snagged the pot that had been sitting there the longest. There was barely enough in it for one cup. While she filled the mug, she hoped she might spot some grounds that had managed to sneak through the filter.

She slid the mug in front of Hal. He eyed her again before he picked up the glass sugar container and poured at least three tablespoons into it. While stirring the sugar into his coffee, Hal peered at her with his bloodshot eyes. From the looks of him he must have really tied one on last night.

"I'll have three eggs, hash browns, and four link sausages."

Let the hardening of the arteries begin. Kate scribbled down his order.

"Extra toast, too, Katie."

She nodded. He'd always called her Katie without her permission. But other people used the nickname, too. The difference was, when she liked someone, Kate was fine with it. She spun around, calling out the order to Ace.

Carol squeezed behind her, laid her hand on her shoulder. "How's it going, Kate? Are you doing okay?"

"I'm doing fine, thanks for asking. Work is good therapy."

"Tell me about it. Some days I wish I was rolling in money, so I could sleep in, get a pedicure and have a chauffeur drive the kids around."

Kate smiled. "I can't picture your boys riding in the back of a limo." Carol's boys were ten and twelve, and mischievous to put it mildly.

Carol giggled. "I'm sure the limo driver would have a hard time keeping his cool."

Since her husband, Joe, had split with Roxie Landford, who had blown into town one day, and started doing hair at the only beauty shop in Windy Creek, Carol now a single mom had her hands full. "You need a man."

Carol rolled her eyes before she reached down to grab clean mugs off the shelf. "I need to win the lottery more."

Kate watched her angle back around the corner. Carol, in her mid-thirties, was slim with long, dark brown hair.

"Order up, Kate."

She plucked the plates off the ledge. Steam swirled around Ace's head. The black ball cap with VFW in bright orange letters bobbed up and down behind the ledge. "You're going to go bald if you wear a cap everyday."

Ace waggled his eyebrows. "Women love bald men."

Kate laughed. Laughter was good. "Who says?"

"My harem around town."

That comment had Kate laughing harder.

"Laugh all you want, lady, but you don't know the real me." She heard the sizzle of bacon hitting the grill.

Kate was still smiling when she carried the plates out to the three men clustered around a table midway across the café. She didn't recognize them. She knew they were snow-catters because she had noticed them pull up in a brand new Dodge four-wheel drive king cab, towing an enclosed utility trailer.

After she delivered their breakfast, she glanced around the table. "Anything else, guys?"

The oldest man, about her age, looked up and winked at her. "We'll let you know, sweetie."

Kate set her teeth together. She'd never figured out why men thought they could get away with calling waitresses all kinds of pet names. "Okay, sugar plum." Before her sarcasm could sink in, she spun around, feeling eyes following her and knowing it was the guy that had called her sweetie.

Kate made a point of not getting offended, letting comments like that roll off her back. Men were good tippers if they liked their waitress. She'd waited tables through college. Twenty years later, she was still asking herself why. Working as a business manager for almost two decades had bored the holy crap out of her.

"Order up, Kate."

She saw that Hal's breakfast was ready so she took her sweet time getting to the window. Hal was a lousy tipper, so who cared? After she dropped his plate in front of him, their eyes locked.

She almost asked, what now? Instead, she said, "More coffee?"

"Damn right, I need more coffee."

After Kate poured his coffee, she leaned over the counter, whispered to Hal, "Keep your flask in your pocket."

His already ruddy complexion turned ruddier. His green eyes blazed, but he kept his mouth shut. Kate walked away, enjoying Hal's discomfort.

CHAPTER TEN

Steve leaned back in his chair, rubbing his eyes. He hated sitting in front of his computer for as long as he had this morning. He'd scanned the Department of Motor Vehicle records for white Subarus and older Dodge trucks. There were twenty-two white Subarus and thirteen older white Dodge trucks in town and the surrounding area. He knew some of the owners of the vehicles.

He pushed back from his desk and stood up, stretching his arms over his head. Steve rotated his neck a few times to work out the kinks. It was a slow morning, which was fine with him. No accidents reported so far. No rural neighbors squabbling with each other over petty shit.

He grabbed his uniform jacket off the back of his chair, shrugging into as he left his office. At Jenny's desk, he stopped and waited until she finished her phone conversation. "I'm going out for a while."

He usually gave her a specific destination. "You know how to reach me." The truth was, he didn't exactly know where he was going. A combination of restlessness and frustration clawed at his nerves. He needed to find Harley's killer.

"Okay." Confusion puckered her brows together.

Steve nodded, pulled his ball cap out of his jacket pocket, and snuggled it over his head, then stepped outside. The temperature was upper twenties. A pretty good day for Montana in the dead of winter.

He dug inside the glove box for the Forest Service map and studied it until he found the road where the grizzly sow had been poached. It was a long shot, about as long as it could get, but maybe he could get a sense of something out there. His jaw tight, Steve pulled away from the curb.

※　※　※

Kate happened to glance up from clearing a table when she spotted Steve cruising by. He looked straight ahead, didn't even glance in the direction of the café. If he had, she might have waved at him. Disappointment kicked at her, which in turn irritated her. She lifted the plastic tote loaded with dirty dishes and started across the café.

For some damn reason, Hal was still hanging out at the counter, his breakfast finished at least twenty minutes ago. She'd kept a sharp eye on him to make sure his flask stayed in his pocket. Clara let him get away with it as long as he behaved. Usually he just came in, ate, and left.

When she backed through the swinging door, Ace sidled up to her. "When's Clara getting back?"

"Should be soon."

"That new clinic they built is slower than old Doc Peterson. When he was the only doc in town, there wasn't much waiting."

The new clinic had been built while she was still in Butte. Dr. Peterson had delivered her and nursed her through measles, mumps, chicken pox, and every other childhood disease. The two young doctors that ran the clinic were definitely competent, but waiting seemed to be the norm at the new clinic.

A few moments later, Clara appeared, unzipping her red fleece jacket.

"You gonna live to be a hundred?" Ace asked.

Clara unwound the black wool scarf wrapped around her neck. "You bet, so I can make sure you keep your nose clean."

Kate laughed. "So how did your checkup go?"

Clara slipped off her jacket. "I'm as healthy as a horse, except for the extra fifteen pounds I'm carrying and have been carrying for the last ten years. I told that young doctor he should own a café and try to stay slim."

Kate hefted the tote to the counter next to the dishwasher. "At least you're healthy, that's what counts." Kate didn't know Clara's age. In fact, nobody in town knew her age. It was one of those mysteries of life.

"Did you manage without me?" Clara sauntered into her office, dumping her things on a chair in the corner.

"The place is still standing, isn't it?" Ace leaned against the doorframe of Clara's small, cramped office.

"No thanks to you. I owe it to Kate and Carol."

Kate grinned while she scraped dishes into the garbage can.

"Kate and Carol don't cook."

"But we could if we wanted to."

Ace glanced over his shoulder at Kate. "You'd be so far backed up, it wouldn't even be funny."

"Try us some time."

Ace pointed a finger at her. "You're on, lady."

Kate laughed again. Working had raised her spirits, lightening the tight band of grief cinched around her heart.

※　※　※

While his truck idled at the end of the Forest Service road, Steve studied the map laid out on the dash. He was near the area where the grizzly sow had been found. He killed the ignition and climbed out, dragging a pair of snowshoes with him. After he buckled on the snowshoes, he started trudging through the deep snow. The branches of the fir trees were bowed under the weight of the heavy snow. Deer tracks crisscrossed the road. Murky clouds hovered in the sky, threatening more snow.

A quarter mile down the section of the road that had been closed for grizzly recovery, he figured he was near the approximate area where the sow had been shot. The sow had been found twenty feet off the road, shot twice in the head, once in the chest. Had it taken that many shots to bring down the animal or had the poacher just been feeling vindictive? He circled around, knowing he was on a wild goose chase. The poacher hadn't been too worried about being caught if the bear had been found that close to the road.

Steve stared at the killing ground of the sow grizzly. He wasn't psychic so he questioned his motives for being out in the primeval forest on an ass freezing day.

Frustration chewed at him like a mutt gnawing on a bone. The first murder since he'd been sheriff of Windy Creek and he didn't have one friggin' clue as to who had killed Harley. He knew it was a local. There would be no reason to trash Kate's house, or Harley's, for that matter. Add the threatening phone call to the basic equation.

A local with a 30-06 rife and a score to settle with Harley. He supposed it was possible Harley had discovered who poached the grizzly. But, Christ, a hefty fine and loss of hunting privileges for a couple of years versus murdering a man in cold blood. Steve rubbed his jaw, cursing himself again for even being out in the middle of nowhere.

He started back, decided to drive to Harley's place.

≍　≍　≍

When Kate got off work at one o'clock, she headed straight for Harley's house. The back of her truck was loaded with empty boxes from the café. Packing up Harley's things, his life, would be hard, but it had to be done.

Ten minutes later when she turned into his driveway, she saw fresh tire tracks. Her heart drummed as she reached under her seat and pulled out her .22 semi-auto pistol. She wished she had the dogs with her. When Harley's house came into view, a lump tickled the back of her throat. Harley's small, cozy house looked so empty, forlorn, and lonely.

She spotted Steve's truck parked in the driveway. Relief mixed with anticipation swept through her, but the damn lump stayed lodged in her throat. She parked next to his truck, caught him looking out the window. As she grabbed the boxes inside of the canopy, Steve walked over to her.

"What the hell are you doing out here all alone?"

She spun around, shoving a stack of boxes at his chest. He had no choice but to take them from her. "For your information, I have to start packing up Harley's things."

"Then you need to bring someone with you, Kate."

Kate tamped down her irritation. She no longer felt like crying. She felt like beaning Steve for being so overprotective and macho. Less than a minute ago, anticipation swept through her, now his presence annoyed her. "I just got off work. I figured I'd come out here for a few hours."

"Where's your gun?"

"In my truck, Sheriff."

"Dammit, Kate."

"I don't need to carry it since you're here." She snatched the last stack of boxes out of her truck, circled around to face him. "What are you doing here?"

He scowled at her. "Looking for evidence."

"Find anything?"

"I just got here a few minutes ago."

Helplessness flowed through her. Steve was competent. But if no incriminating evidence had been left behind, his hands were basically tied. She hoped with all her heart Harley's murder would be solved. The killer needed to be brought to justice and pay for taking away a man she loved.

"I'm going to start a fire. You might as well look for evidence in a warm house." She angled around her truck. "I think I might have to plow, too. The snow is getting deep on the driveway. On the walkway too, for that matter." Snow slipped over her boots, dampening the legs of her jeans. "I need to shovel, too. Maybe I'll do that after I start a fire." For some idiotic reason, she was rambling. She wasn't a rambler by nature, but Steve stirred things up in her. She chalked it up to annoyance at his overprotectiveness.

Steve was silent behind her as she went up the steps, opened the door. She was immediately hit by the frigid air inside Harley's house. She dumped the boxes in the middle of the living room, walked over to the pile of wood behind the stove.

While she crumbled up newspapers from the stack, she glanced over her shoulder. Steve still held the stack of boxes, staring hard at her. "Is there something on your mind?"

"I don't like you being out here alone."

"I'm not alone, you're here." She turned back to the stove, stacking kindling over the newspapers.

"I could get called away if there's an emergency."

"And the sky could fall."

"Can the sarcasm, Kate."

Kate piled a few pieces of wood over the kindling, her annoyance returning. Talk about a man with an attitude. She struck a match, held it to the newspapers, watching the yellow flames spring to life inside the stove. After she was satisfied the fire would catch, she shut the door. She stood up, turning to face Steve.

"Is there any particular reason you're on my case?" She crossed her arms over her chest.

Steve dropped the boxes, took off his ball cap, ran a hand through his hair. She liked his hair, the natural thickness and wave to it, the shining black color, even the sprinkling of grey at his temples. "Well?"

"Sorry. This case is frustrating." He glanced away from her.

She did feel sympathy for him. If Harley's murder did go unsolved, it wouldn't be because Steve hadn't given it his all. "Something's bound to pop up."

Steve brought his gaze back to her. "The longer it goes unsolved, the colder the trail gets."

Kate listened to the stove pop and crackle, felt the heat radiating to her backside. "Harley's place is pretty remote. He had a few old buddies that would come out and visit him, besides me."

"Wasn't he pretty good friends with Louis Reynolds?'

Kate nodded. Louis had enveloped her in a big hug at the funeral, tears glistening in his old eyes. Harley and Louis had been friends for at least thirty years. It hadn't even occurred to her to talk to Louis. "I never thought about talking to Louis. I did at the funeral, but we reminisced about old times."

Steve took a small pad and pencil out of his jacket pocket. "Who else?"

"Tommy Brown. They were both widowers. They did a lot of fishing in the summer. Hunted together in the fall." She watched Steve scribble on his pad. "Those two were probably his closest buddies."

Steve nodded. "Maybe he confided something in them."

"Don't you think they would have said something by now?"

Steve shrugged, tucking his pad and pencil back into this pocket. "Hard to say. Maybe they forgot because they were upset over Harley."

Kate supposed that was possible. She unzipped her fleece jacket, tossing it on the back of the couch. "I need to get started." The lump in her throat started to inch up her throat again, but she swallowed it back.

"I'll help." Steve unzipped his jacket, too, and shrugged out of it, throwing it on top of Kate's. "Let's start with his desk."

The two of them basically tore apart Harley's desk, but they didn't find anything out of the ordinary. Kate flopped back in the chair, frustration eating at her. "Do you think this is pointless?"

Steve leaned one hip against the desk, sorting through some papers. "Nothing is ever pointless in an ongoing investigation. Sometimes the tiniest thing turns out to be the best lead."

Kate nodded, studied Steve as he kept glancing at the stack of papers. The crow's feet around his eyes seemed to have deepened over the past couple of days, making him more attractive. She quickly looked away, dropped the stack of old bills into a box next to her feet. "Why did you leave Salt Lake?" She noticed how his hands stilled before he looked at her.

He shrugged. "Needed a change."

"But Windy Creek?"

"You moved back here."

This time it was Kate's turn to feel uncomfortable. "Yeah, well, I'm originally from here."

He put down the papers and picked up another stack, but didn't elaborate on his move to Windy Creek.

"You've been married, haven't you?"

He narrowed his eyes. "Yeah, divorced. The usual story of a cop's life."

He didn't seem too eager to open up to her. "Kids?"

"A daughter, Andrea. She graduated from college last spring. She's a business consultant in Salt Lake."

"Hmmm...I have a son."

"I know. You loaned me his socks."

Their eyes caught. Kate wasn't sure she liked the way her heart fluttered when she looked into his eyes. But on the other hand, it made her feel alive. The only thing that had assured her that she wasn't an endless vacuum inside had been her writing. She picked up a stack of cancelled checks with a rubber band twined around them, seeing they were as old as the hills. She felt Steve's eyes on her.

"Are you over your husband?"

She hated that question. Balls of tension formed in her stomach. "Yeah," she said, avoiding his gaze. She tossed the checks into the box.

"You didn't say it like you meant it."

Kate bit her bottom lip. She glanced at him briefly. "Well, I am."

Steve looked skeptical. "If you say so."

As always, her defensives popped up like dandelions invading a lush, spring lawn. "I don't think there's anything in the desk, just old checks, stuff like that."

Steve was quiet for minute before he agreed. "You're probably right." He straightened away from the desk. "Where else would Harley keep important papers?"

Relieved the subject had been changed, Kate said, "This is it."

Steve scratched the back of his neck. "What do you remember about the poaching?"

At the time, she had been too consumed with guilt, remorse and sadness to have paid much attention to the incident. "Not much really. These things happen. Most people thought it was a shame, but then they shrugged their shoulders and went about their business."

"It would have been in the paper as soon as the bear's body was found."

Kate was able to look him full in the eye now. "True."

"That means Harley saved the papers from the beginning. He must have had an idea who did it from the start."

Kate hadn't given that theory any thought. She leaned forward in the chair. "That's a good point. I remember talking with Harley about it."

"Did he throw out any names?"

Kate shook her head. "Not that I remember."

"Harley knew everybody, and everybody knew him."

"I imagine there are some people in town that didn't know him."

Steve started pacing. "Harley was pretty straightforward. When you get to be his age, I think you gain unexpected courage."

"So you're thinking Harley did confront the killer?"

"Anything is possible." Steve stopped, raking a hand through his hair. "But Harley died here, which means the killer came to Harley."

Kate struggled for objectivity. "Which means Harley confronted the killer sometime earlier."

Steve nodded. "When you last saw him, did he mention anybody else that had dropped by?"

"He told me Tommy Brown had stopped by for coffee Sunday morning."

"I need to talk to Tommy Brown."

"Wait a minute, you don't think Tommy did it?"

"No. I don't think Tommy Brown did it. But he might know something we don't."

"I'd like to go with you."

"K-a-a-a-a-te."

"What, for Pete's sake?"

"Remember we've been over this."

Kate slumped back in her chair. "I thought it was worth a shot."

CHAPTER ELEVEN

Steve had gotten cornered into coffee and a big slice of apple spice cake that Tommy Brown's daughter had baked. Not that he minded. It wasn't often he was offered the pleasure of homebaked goods. Occasionally Jenny brought cookies or banana bread in for the staff.

Tommy slid a plate and fork in front of him. Steve scooted his chair closer to the table. "Thanks."

"Christine is a damned good cook, just like her mother was." Tommy sat down across from Steve at the large, dark walnut antique table. "She keeps me supplied with goodies."

Steve nodded, forked a chunk off the slab of cake. While he chewed, he studied the older man. Tommy was a good six feet, a large boned man in good health for his age. He wasn't overweight, but his hair had disappeared somewhere over the years, because only a few strands of grey were combed to the side.

Tommy paused from eating his cake. "I can't believe Harley's gone. We've been, I mean, we were, friends for over thirty years."

Steve picked up his mug. "I know this is hard, Tommy, but can you think of anyone who might have killed him?" He noticed the old man wince, sorry he hadn't worded the question in a better way.

Tommy shook his head, while his brown eyes grew misty. "No. I can't. Harley was a good guy. He would be the first one to help somebody if they needed it. Hell, he practically raised Kate after her old man ran out on her mama."

Steve drank some coffee, reminded himself he needed to be tactful. Tommy was an old friend, he was grieving, too. "Did you and Harley ever talk about that sow grizzly that was shot a few years ago?"

"Hell, yes. We both wanted to find the s.o.b. and beat the crap out of him. Not that we could have done it at our age." Tommy finished off his cake, pushed his plate away. "We were responsible hunters. We brought down some big bulls and bucks in our time." Tommy pointed over Steve's shoulder. "That black bear hide. I shot the bear and Harley helped me carry it out."

Steve turned in his chair, studied the huge black bear hide hanging on the far wall of the living room. Harley and Tommy must have worked up a real sweat lugging that big animal out of the woods.

"Harley wasn't much into bear hunting, but he'd come along with me," Tommy continued. "He didn't like the meat, too fatty, he always said. I gave up bear hunting years ago, once we were better off financially. When the kids were little we needed the meat."

Steve shifted on his chair. "Do you think Harley figured out who shot that sow?"

Tommy leaned back in his chair, cradling his mug in his hand. He studied Steve for several moments. "I think he had some idea. You think that's who killed Harley?"

His first fragile lead. Steve's adrenaline raced, or maybe it was the strong coffee. Tommy knew how to make coffee. "Did Harley tell you who he thought did it?"

"Damn. No, he didn't. We talked about it in passing and that was about it, but about a month ago Harley brought it up again when I was over at his house having coffee one morning."

"And?"

"I had a doctor's appointment later that day and I was worrying about that. When you get to be my age, you get nervous about your annual checkup."

Steve struggled to sit still. Now he had the jitters. Tommy's coffee resembled rocket fuel. "So," he paused. "You were at Harley's place about a month ago. Harley brought up the subject of the sow grizzly."

Tommy nodded.

"What exactly did he say?" Steve took another swallow of coffee, figuring he might as well get wired.

Tommy rubbed his chin. "Said he thought he might know who shot the sow."

"Did he give you a name?"

"Jack Daniel."

"Jack Daniel?"

"You know Jack Danielson. He's a transplant from Canada. He's been here, let's see now, probably fifteen years."

Steve tried to place the guy. "Does he have red kinky hair, real slim, about forty?"

"That would be him."

"Why did you call him Jack Daniel?"

Tommy stood up, went to the counter, snagged the coffee pot, lumbered back over to Steve. Tommy didn't ask him if he wanted more, he just refilled his mug.

While Tommy was pouring rocket fuel into his mug, he said, "Because when he first came to town, he used to get sloshed every Friday night at Buck's Bar. And all he ever drank was Jack Daniels, straight up." Tommy returned the coffeepot to the stovetop before he came back and sat down.

Maybe that was why the coffee was so strong. Tommy still used an old percolator pot on the stove. "I've seen him around town a few times. At the café occasionally."

"He's not a real social guy. I always thought he was on the strange side."

Steve wasn't sure if he should drink more of the rocket fuel. He was already wired from the coffee and information Tommy was giving him. "What do you mean strange?"

"Keeps to himself. Never had a woman, not that I ever knew about."

"What does he do for a living?"

"Cuts firewood, odd jobs. I hear he's a decent handyman."

"Does he live in town?"

"No. He has twenty acres, east of town."

Steve finished off his cake, figuring that might even out the rocket fuel in his system. "Did Harley say why he thought Jack Daniel did it?"

"Not that I remember." Tommy pointed a finger at Steve. "A sow grizzly was found shot about three months after Jack Daniel moved here. Everybody joked that he did it, 'cause he was the new guy in town, an outsider."

"And they never found who did it?"

"No, sir."

※　※　※

When Steve returned to the station, he nodded at Jenny, who had the phone pressed to her ear while she typed at her computer. He didn't even take his jacket or hat off, just dropped down on his desk chair, calling up Montana Motor Vehicles on his computer.

Jack John Danielson. Birth date: June 10, 1961. Height: 5' 9", weight: 170. Red hair, green eyes. Steve grabbed a pen, jotting down his address on a note pad. He pocketed the piece of paper, then headed out again.

In the hall, he ran head first into Jenny. "Whoa." Steve grabbed her shoulders.

"A deer hit, one mile south of town. You need to respond."

"Where's Ron?"

"At a domestic disturbance. Kyle and Tammy Cheney."

Steve swore under his breath. "Not again."

"Ever since he got laid off from the mill, he's been drinking more."

Kyle Cheney hadn't been laid off because of cutbacks, he'd been laid off for being irresponsible. "Tell Ron to haul his butt in here."

Jenny's brows furrowed together. "Tammy won't press charges."

"Doesn't matter, we can keep him here until he sobers up."

"You sure?"

"Positive."

"Okay, then." Jenny spun around, hurrying back to her desk.

He'd have to put Jack Daniel on hold. If somebody hit a deer a mile out of town that meant the driver had probably been speeding. The limit was fortyfive miles per hour. He couldn't believe the amount of deer and car hits around here. The area was crawling with whitetail deer.

You'd think people would learn.

※　※　※

Kate stopped at the café on her way home from Harley's. She and Steve had come up empty-handed. She needed something to chase away her blues. Company or a piece of Clara's apple pie might do it. It wasn't that she was hungry, she just felt empty. Empty because Harley was gone, empty because they couldn't find one piddly clue as to who killed Harley.

She'd done her homework on enough police cases since she'd starting writing mystery novels. The colder a case got, the more difficult it was to catch the killer. Steve had also mentioned that. And he would know much better than she would. He was the real McCoy. A real cop. She swung her truck into the parking lot. It was after four, so there were only a few trucks in the lot. Dinner customers started trickling in about five, then the real rush started at six, continuing until seven thirty.

Kate entered the café from the front entrance. No more sneaking in the back door like she had done right after Harley died.

She tugged off her gloves and hat, pushing open the swinging door. Clara, Ace, and Ann, the night shift waitress, were clustered around the small table, eating fries and drinking Cokes.

"Pull up a seat," Ace said when he spotted her.

Kate decided fries were as good as apple pie. "Let me get a Coke."

Back in the kitchen area, she tossed her jacket, gloves and hat on a shelf, crowding around the table with the others.

"What are you doing back here?" Clara asked.

"She needs a man," Ace said.

Kate made a face at him before she snagged a fry off the big platter in the center of the table.

"She can have mine." Ann sipped her Coke. "He's got the flu and he's a big, big, baby. I wish he'd get well so he can go back to work. Don's worse than the kids when he gets sick."

Clara agreed. "Men are always like that when they're sick. It's enough to drive a woman to drink."

Ace laid his hand on his chest. "I take offense. I'm not like that when I get sick."

The three women booed and hissed at him.

"Hey, give me a break. I'm outnumbered here."

Kate laughed. Her little extended family could usually cheer her up. Maybe she'd call Josh tonight. Her unforgiving son might even be in a talkative mood.

Ann cocked her head in Kate's direction. "So what's up?"

Kate shrugged. "Not much. I needed a snack and company."

Clara's expression turned serious. "Did you go out to Harley's?"

"Yeah. Steve was there. We looked for clues."

"Anything?" Ace asked.

"Nada."

"I still can't believe it," Ann wiped her hands on a napkin. "Something that terrible happened to Harley in our little town."

"Shit happens." Ace slurped Coke down.

The mood grew somber around the table. "I didn't mean to come here and bring everybody down."

Ace put his arm around her shoulder. "You didn't. We were talking about Harley before you got here."

"You know, remembering," Clara said. "And asking why. And who?"

Anne picked up a fry, inspected it for a moment. "Harley was such a sweet old man. He reminded me of my dad."

Kate looked at Anne. She was early thirties, a few pounds overweight, with shining long blonde hair that kissed her shoulders. She and Don had decided they needed to raise their kids in a small town, so they had moved here five years ago from Spokane. Kate remembered Ann had mentioned her father had died a few years ago of cancer.

"Harley liked you, too. He said you were damn cute." That made Ann smile.

"I can certainly use a compliment, since I went off my diet today by eating these fries."

"You look just fine," Ace said. "I like women with meat on their bones. Kate could use some fattening up."

Ace had mentioned that before. She'd lost a few pounds recently because eating had been the last thing on her mind, but she wasn't skinny. She had large bones, had always made a point of watching her weight. "Am not."

"Are too."

Everybody laughed. Kate's mood lightened a bit.

"I think we should make a list of possible suspects."

Kate glanced at Ann. "That's Steve's job."

"You know I'm a mystery buff. I read your books and every other mystery I can get my hands on. If we make a list, we could start eliminating suspects one by one."

"That's the whole damn town."

"I agree with Ace," Clara said. She reached for a fry. "It is the entire town."

Ann stood up. "I better check on my people. Think about it. You know that, Kate. You're the mystery writer." She disappeared out to the café.

Ace adjusted his ball cap. "She might have a point. Annie's pretty smart."

"Hello," Clara waved her hand in his direction. "Remember it's the entire town."

"Not necessarily." Kate was positive Steve had made a list.

"It's process of elimination," Ace said. "Some people knew Harley better than others. We've got newcomers here that probably didn't know him at all."

"I know everybody in town," Clara said. "And I can't think of one person that is capable of murder. Oh, they're capable of cheating on their wives or husbands, fudging on their income taxes, maybe shooting a deer out of season because they need the meat to feed their family. But murder?"

"There's always a rotten apple in the barrel who's hiding something," Ace cautioned.

Clara frowned at him.

Fear settled inside of Kate, realizing Ace was right.

⌗   ⌗   ⌗

It was after six by the time Steve stopped his truck in Jack Danielson's driveway. A mean looking mutt leaped off the porch, beelining straight for his truck. He killed the ignition, glared out his window down at the dog. The large dog was scruffy looking with black and grey fur. The mutt's teeth were bared. Steve couldn't hear the snarl, but he felt it.

Shit, another mean dog to deal with. He glanced back at the house, or rather the older single wide mobile home, with an addition built onto it that ran the length of the mobile. Smoke billowed out of the chimney. The roof was galvanized metal. No fancy colors for Jack Daniel.

He scanned the area. There were several storage sheds, all roofed with the same dull, grey metal. A pole building was right angled from the mobile. Two trucks sat under the pole building. An old, rusted battered Ford truck and a white Dodge truck, mid-eighties. Danielson's name had popped up when he'd run a vehicle search. At the time, he hadn't given it much thought.

He hoped Jack Daniel would come out, call off his watchdog. Steve peered down at the dog again. The mutt was still snarling. He shouldered open the door, hard and fast. He knew he nipped the mutt in the mouth because it backed off. After he climbed out, he scowled at the mutt. The canine backed up a few more feet.

This was the little dance they performed all the way to the porch where the mutt planted his butt next to the door. Steve was still in uniform, had driven the sheriff's truck out to

Danielson's place. So he was either hiding, wishing like hell Steve would go away, passed out, or hard of hearing.

"Get out of the way." Steve shot the dog a mean look. Then he leaned forward and banged on the door. The mutt stood, snarling up at him.

After a time, the door opened a crack. "Mr. Danielson, I'm Sheriff Steve Lambert. I'd like to talk to you for a few minutes."

"I know who you are. Why do you want to talk to me?" Jack Daniel cracked the door wider.

Steve could see his kinky red hair, light green eyes, and that his matching beard needed a trim. "I'm conducting an investigation into Harley Wilson's death. May I come in?"

"What's that got to do with me?"

Steve picked up on the fact Jack Daniel wouldn't look him in the eye. A real hard time criminal or psychopath could look you straight in the eye and lie right to your face. "I'm talking to a lot of people around here."

The mutt snarled again.

"Bozo, knock it off."

The dog immediately laid down, dropping his head on his paws. At least something positive was coming of this, Steve realized. Jack Daniel opened the door wider. He had on dirty, faded jeans and an even dirtier white undershirt. And the man's hand was resting on something near the inside of the door.

Steve instinctively put his hands on his hips. His right hand over his gun holster. With his luck, Danielson probably had a sawed off shotgun. "So you're saying you didn't know Harley Wilson at all?"

Jack Daniel shrugged. "I knew who he was."

"Do you know where he lives?"

His jaw worked extra hard. "I don't recall."

"I see. Do you hunt?"

"What the hell does that have to do with anything?"

"Just curious."

"Long ways for a cop to come, for just being curious."

"Cops are curious by nature."

Jack Daniel grunted.

"You must remember that sow grizzly that was shot a year and half ago."

Steve couldn't see much of Danielson's face because it was covered with a heavy beard and mustache. But he could have sworn the skin beneath paled.

"Do you remember?"

"What's that got to do with old Harley?"

"The bear was shot with a 30-06. Do you own a 30-06 rifle, Mr. Danielson?"

His green eyes flooded with rage. Steve glanced at Jack's hand near the door. He knew he had a rifle or shotgun leaning against the wall by the doorframe. He struggled to not let his own hand twitch over his gun holster. "Do you, Mr. Danielson?"

The man's lips curled back, reminding him of Bozo, now docile on the porch.

"You got a warrant?"

"No. I don't."

"Then the way I see it, we're done talking."

The door closed in Steve's face. He heard the snarl, didn't bother looking down at the mangy mutt, just wheeled around, bounding down the steps and back to his truck. But he felt the dog tailing him. He also felt eyes boring into the back of his head as he climbed into his truck.

Jack Daniel was hiding something

Frustration riding him, he started his truck, shoved it in reverse. The man had been in Windy Creek for fifteen years. Didn't mean there wasn't an open warrant back in Canada for him. He cruised down the plowed driveway, itching to know more about the man they called Jack Daniel.

※　※　※

An hour and a half later, his belly filled with a peanut butter and strawberry jam sandwich, Steve knocked on Ace's door. When Ace opened his front door, surprise spread across his face, then he grinned. "What's up, Sheriff?"

Steve heard the TV in the background. "You busy, Ace?"

"Nope. Just resting my feet and watching the tube. Come on in?"

Steve followed Ace into his house. It was an older one-story house with a living room and kitchen combined into one large room. An American flag was tacked to the wall across from where Steve stood. A wood stove popped and crackled in the corner of the living room area. Ace had a secret. There were large framed photographs of wildlife scattered across the walls. A black bear cub, peeking from behind a tree; a seven point bulk elk grazing in a spring meadow. A close up of a mountain goat that stared directly into the camera with his gentle eyes.

"I didn't know you were a photographer."

Ace shrugged. "Just a hobby."

Steve angled over to a large photograph of a bald eagle perched on the branch of lodge pole pine tree. "You're pretty damn good."

"Hey, Sheriff, you're going to embarrass me."

Steve circled around. "Wouldn't want to do that."

"How about a beer? You're out of uniform."

"Sounds good."

Steve walked to the kitchen area. It was neat and tidy. Smaller photos of squirrels, wild birds, and whitetail deer were grouped together on one wall of the kitchen. A fat grey cat wandered into the kitchen, twined himself around Ace's ankles while he snagged two beers out of the fridge.

A friendly cat. Beat snarly dogs any day.

"Okay, Mick, get out of my way before I trip," Ace said to the cat as he carried the two long necked bottles of Miller over to the table in the center of the kitchen.

Steve shrugged out of his jacket, sat down. "Mick, as in Jagger?"

Ace handed a bottle to Steve. "That would be correct."

Steve grinned, watching the big cat jump up on Ace's lap as soon as he sat down across the table from Steve. He took a long, slow swallow. Even though it was twenty degrees outside, the beer hit the spot. And Ace's house was cozy and warm. "I need to pick your brain, if you don't mind."

Ace scratched behind the cat's ear. "Go ahead. We'll see if it's a subject I'm familiar with."

"How well do you know Jack Daniel?"

Ace snorted. "Probably as well as anybody around here. The guy's worse than some Vietnam vets. Pretty much a total recluse, except when he does his handyman jobs around town."

"Does he hunt?"

Ace leaned back, took a swig. "Oh yeah. Probably poaches out of season, too."

Steve's radar perked up. "What does he poach?"

"I don't know for a fact he poaches. But if he does, probably deer like everybody else, to make it through the winter."

Steve had heard that the game wardens looked the other way if somebody needed food. Poaching was illegal, but Montana ranked near the bottom for medium income. That didn't include the wealthy out-of-staters moving in and gobbling up land to build fancy houses.

"Why are you curious about Jack Daniel, if you don't mind my asking?"

Steve drank more beer before he answered. "His name came up in my investigation into Harley's death. Since I'm still relatively new here, I don't everything there is to know about everybody."

Ace nodded. "Harley and J.D. weren't pals."

"Yeah, I know that. Do you know anything about his past? I know he moved here about fifteen years ago from Canada." He had a call out to the Canadian authorities.

The cat jumped off of Ace's lap, sat next to his chair, starting an intensive bath. "He's been here a few years longer than me." Ace scratched his balding head. "I do recall one night about twelve, thirteen years ago when he struck up a conversation with me at Buck's Bar.

"That was a while back. Do you remember what you guys talked about?"

"Some of it," Ace said. "It was a Friday night, and we were both intent on getting shit-faced."

Steve chuckled.

Ace drank more beer, lost in thought for a minute. "What I do remember is Jack Daniel going on and on about some gal named Sandy. Kept saying it was a waste, she died too young. That she was the love of his life."

"How did she die?"

"Afraid that's the part I don't remember. The Wild Turkey had caught up to me by then."

"Did you two ever talk about Sandy again?"

Ace shook his head. "We were only buddies that one night, both making a supreme effort to drown our sorrows."

It was common knowledge Ace was a Vietnam vet.

"He pretty much ignored me after that." Ace drained his bottle, slapped it on the table. "I always figured he remembered more than I did. He must have regretted he flapped his mouth too much with me. I staggered out of the bar and managed to make it home without falling in the snow and passing out. I lived two blocks behind the bar back then. I bought this place seven years ago."

Ace now lived at the northern edge of Windy Creek. He probably had an acre at least. It was a dead end road, so he had plenty of privacy. "Do you know where in Canada he's from?"

"Cardston, Alberta. That's just north of the border off the Blackfeet Reservation."

Steve had driven through Cardston last summer on a mini vacation to Alberta.

"You think Jack Daniel killed Harley?" Ace asked.

Steve shook his head. "I wish I knew."

CHAPTER TWELVE

After Kate built a fire in the wood stove, she put on a pot of coffee, then started boxing up Harley's things. She hadn't brought the dogs because she wasn't sure Ranger could handle it yet. She figured it was better if Harley's dog never returned to his home. She didn't know how long a dog's memory was.

What she did know was the contents of Harley's will. He'd given her a copy when she'd moved back to Windy Creek. The house and property were to be sold, divided equally between Diane and her. A mixture of anger and grief burned inside of her. In her opinion, Diane didn't deserve squat, but maybe she didn't either. Kate filled a mug with coffee, sipping on it while she loaded dishes, pots and pans into boxes.

The thick silence in Harley's house wrapped itself around her like a shroud. Her heart still ached for Harley and would for a long time. Unable to bear the silence any longer, she walked into the living room and turned on the TV, extra loud. It wasn't like her to need noise. She cherished her peace and quiet, always keeping her house quiet when she wrote her novels.

A half hour later, Kate was in Harley's bedroom, boxing up his clothes to take to the local Salvation Army. Wired on caffeine, she worked at a frenzied pace. She knelt next to a box, fighting with the cardboard flaps to get them closed.

Suddenly a hand clamped tight over her mouth. Frozen with shock that someone was in the house with her, Kate didn't react. Her heart beat so hard and fast with fear it felt like it was going to burst out of her chest. Panic sailed through her. Fear like she had never known rushed through her body. She struggled against her attacker. He was strong. He started dragging her backwards. She was being hauled on her butt out of the bedroom. When he hoisted her to her feet and pressed her against his body, she managed to jab him hard in the ribs with her elbow.

"Dammit!"

His voice. She knew that voice. Kate managed to come down hard on his ankle with her boot. He cursed again, but he had her in a powerful hold. The bastard smelled dirty, like he hadn't bathed in a week. The foul smell of day-old alcohol spewed from his mouth.

A wave of nausea swept through her. She shoved it back and tried kicking him with the heel of her boot. Kate managed to connect with his leg somewhere. It wasn't hard enough to break his hold on her. The bastard's hand was dirty, adding to her nausea.

She bit down hard on his ring finger, fighting back another wave of nausea.

His hand dropped from her mouth. "Goddamn bitch!"

Kate wrenched herself free, wheeling around to face him. He wore a black ski mask with only his eyes showing. He was dressed completely in black. Why did thugs and murderers always wear black? He grabbed for her again, but she scampered backwards. Harley's 20 gauge shotgun was in the closet. She had moved it minutes before to get to his clothes. Her instincts told her it was loaded. Harley hadn't lived out in the middle of nowhere not knowing how to protect himself.

When he came at her again, Kate managed to punch him in the jaw, feeling as if she'd broken every bone in her hand. He bent over, cursing like a mad man. Kate scrambled to the closet, her left hand wrapping around the barrel of the shotgun.

The son of a bitch came at her again. She yanked the gun from the closet, got it hip level. When he saw the gun, he froze and so did Kate for a moment. She hadn't fired a shotgun in years. Safety. She needed to find the safety. She didn't dare look down. Kate knew without a doubt there was a shell in the barrel, all she had to do was hit the safety.

She raised it to her shoulder as her forefinger landed on the safety switch.

She pushed forward, pressing her finger against the trigger when suddenly the bastard turned and ran like a jackrabbit. Two seconds later, Kate raced after him. The kitchen door was open. She bounded down the steps, saw him disappearing behind the garage into the dense trees. She raised the shotgun and fired.

The recoil and loud bang almost knocked her on her butt again. She pumped another shell into chamber, then fired again, this time bracing herself and gritting her teeth. Branches flew off the pine trees.

Kate trudged through the snow, following his tracks. When she came to branches scattered on top of the snow, she started looking for blood. Not seeing any, she knew she had missed him.

In the distance she heard the whine of a snowmobile.

"Damn! Damn! Damn!" Kate screamed. The gunshots and her scream silenced the forest.

Anger, swift and potent, lunged through her, causing her to feel weak kneed. She leaned against a lodgepole pine tree. The tree she which she had shot all the lower branches off.

Her breathing labored, Kate fought to calm herself. After a few minutes, her breathing slowly returned to normal. The bastard had made a clean getaway.

Kate couldn't identify him, but she knew his voice. If she heard it again, she would know. By God, she would know.

⋊⋉ ⋊⋉ ⋊⋉

"Dammit, Kate. What the hell were you thinking?"

Kate sat on Harley's couch, drinking a cup of hot tea sweetened with honey. There were no lemons in the house. Her throat was sore from screaming and being gagged by a grubby, filthy hand. Steve paced back and forth in front of her. His face was red, his jaw resembling a steal beam. His cursing had mellowed to tolerable. After she had gotten a grip on her emotions, she'd hurried back to the house and called the sheriff's office. "You cuss too much."

Steve angled over to her, so close, his boots pushed against the toes of hers. "I cuss too much, do I? Well let me tell you something."

He loomed over in his dark brown uniform, his ball cap pulled low over his eyes, anger vibrating off every muscle in his body.

"How many damn times have I told you not to come out here by yourself? And where are those damn mutts of yours?" He balled his hands into fists at his sides.

"My dogs, not mutts, are at my place. I don't think Ranger should come here anymore so he'll forget about Harley and his home."

"You could have at least brought Sunny."

Kate shook her head. "Then Ranger would be left all alone."

"Shit, Kate."

"You're still cussing."

Steve's jaw worked hard for a moment, but he didn't say anything. His cell phone beeped. Kate watched him dig it out of his pocket.

"Yeah."

She took another swallow of tea, listening to Steve's side of the conversation. He was still looming over her, staring down hard at her. His answers were one or two words. Her eyes locked with his stormy blue eyes. Heat, swift and unexpected, radiated through her. Sexual heat.

Kate had the notion to reach up, grab Steve's uniform jacket and drag him down on top of her. The life-affirming thing, she told herself. She could have died. That bastard could have killed her, that had probably been his intention.

Definitely not a warning, like her house being thrashed, or the threatening phone call.

Steve lowered the phone, still staring hard at her. "Fish and Wildlife are going out on snowmobiles to see if they can find anything. But Bob said there's an old logging road that connects about two miles north of here. He said a lot of locals use it for snowmobiling."

Kate already knew that because Harley used to snowshoe back there. He'd told her he was always running into somebody to shoot the bull with.

Still feeling the heat for Steve, she took another sip of tea.

"You're going to the doctor to get checked."

Kate shook her head. "No. I don't need to."

Steve leaned down, picked up her right hand. "Your hand is swollen."

Steve smelled good, like piney aftershave and strong coffee, unlike the filthy smell of the bastard that had attacked her. "I just need to ice it." Steve scowled at her. He held her hand gingerly, turning it over.

"You must have gotten in a helluva punch."

"As a matter of fact I did."

Kate felt the same heat radiating off Steve. The same heat she was struggling to keep at bay. Maybe his heat was from anger. She didn't think so. Desire was banked deep in his eyes. One of Steve's deputies was on his way out here. Steve lifted her hand like he intended to kiss it.

"He was dirty, Steve." Her voice was breathless. Damn, she was breathless.

He frowned, still holding up her hand. "Dirty?"

"The bastard that attacked me."

Steve's frowned deepened, then he gently lowered her hand, let go. He stepped back.

The moment was gone.

"Dirty, like he didn't bathe very often?"

Kate nodded. "That's exactly how he smelled. Even his hand was grubby."

"He didn't have on gloves?"

"Not when he grabbed me."

"That means we've got prints."

Kate prayed Steve was right, but she didn't want to get her hopes up too high. "He could have worn gloves when he opened the door.

Steve's jaw tightened again. "The damn doors weren't locked."

Kate glanced down at her mug. Steve hadn't taken the time to check the house or grounds. Once he had realized that she was okay, he had gone into curse mode. "No."

That set Steve off on another cursing and pacing tirade. The man usually had such control. Kate finished her tea, letting him vent.

When he finished, he was over by the wood stove, staring at it like he wanted to pull out his gun and shoot it. Better the stove than her, Kate figured.

"Do you even have your gun with you?"

His words came out clipped, like a military march. "Um...yeah, it's in my truck." She held up a hand before he could go off the deep end again. "There's no point in cussing at me anymore. I know I screwed up. Okay? And," she paused, "I'm not going to the hospital and I'm driving myself home."

Steve wheeled around, turned his back to her. She heard the sound of a siren. The deputy was here. Thank God for small favors.

※　※　※

Kate drove herself home.

In the shower, she let the spray of hot water wash away the filth of the bastard that had attacked her. She shampooed her hair, scrubbing every inch of her body. After she dressed, she checked the doors, both still locked. Great, now she was paranoid.

She had basically refused to dwell too much on what could have happened. She'd wanted to bring home Harley's shotgun, but according to Steve it was evidence. So she had grabbed Harley's 30-30 deer rifle. Either way, she had a bigger gun to protect herself.

The rifle was propped up in the corner of her kitchen. Kate stared at it for several seconds. What she didn't like was the fact she had to have a gun. She'd always considered her pistol enough protection. Now she wanted to stockpile in the heavy artillery.

When Kate's stomach wailed out its hunger, she figured she'd better eat something. She didn't feel like eating, but common sense kicked in, cautioning her she needed to keep her strength up, just in case...she wouldn't allow herself to finish that thought.

She plucked a can of ham and bean soup off the cupboard shelf. Glancing out the window above the sink, she saw that the clouds had moved in. It would snow tonight. Ranger whined at the door, while Sunny stood a foot back from him. She went to the door, flipped on the porch light, unlocked it, blocking the dogs' path while she looked in all directions.

"Damn." She hated being paranoid.

She didn't see any point in keeping the dogs prisoner, so she let them out. They trotted down the steps and into the snow. Ranger lifted his leg on the nearest pine tree. Sunny squatted in the deep snow. Ranger followed Sunny sniffing around the yard.

Nothing unusual, Kate reassured herself. The two were just doing their dog thing. She shut the door and locked it. After she emptied the soup into a pot, the phone rang. The empty can clattered to the floor.

She was worse than she thought.

Kate bent and retrieved the can off the floor, but she let the phone ring. It might be Steve. She took a step, hesitated.

Or it could be Harley's killer. Kate let the answering machine take the call.

Steve's voice bellowed into the small kitchen. "Where the hell are you, Kate?"

She ran over to the table against the far wall that held the phone and answering machine. "I'm right here."

There was a long pause. "Why didn't you answer sooner?"

Her nerves hovered at the snapping point. "Give me a break. I wasn't standing right next to the phone."

Another pause. "Are your doors locked?"

Kate wanted to slam the phone down. He was worse than a big brother, a father. "Yes. They're locked."

"I'll be over later."

Kate started to protest, but the line went dead. She made a face at the phone before she slammed it back on its cradle. Steve had morphed into a macho man cop. Kate went back to the stove, stirred her soup, glancing out the window. Sunny and Ranger were playing dog tag in the snow. If anybody was out there, the dogs would let her know.

While the soup simmered, she checked her cupboards. She had instant cocoa and a brand new bag of marshmallows. Kate banged the cupboard door closed and muttered curses under her breath. Now she was making sure she had Steve's favorite hot drink.

Admit it, Kate. You want Steve in a big way.

Kate told herself she only wanted him when death lurked too close to her. Other than that, she didn't want him or need him.

The image of Michael Crawford flashed through her brain. Blonde hair, a lean runner's body and so totally full of himself it was disgusting. Why had she hopped into bed with him?

One time.

Her guilt had been such a burden to her that she had confessed to her husband, who the very next day had found a lawyer and started divorce proceedings. Kate shook her head, tossing away those bitter memories of her one infidelity in eighteen years of marriage. John had pounced on the chance to divorce her like a cat on a mouse. There had been no forgiveness, no understanding, not even anger.

Her mood soured the exact instant the soup boiled.

※　※　※

An hour later, Kate pounded away at her computer. She had managed to lose herself in her work which had helped her forget, for a short while anyway, all the bad things going on in her life. Leaning back in her chair, she raised her arms over her head and stretched.

Several seconds later, the dogs started a ruckus in the living room where they had both sacked out an hour ago. Heart pounding, she hit the save button on her computer. On her way out of the room, she grabbed the rifle leaning against the wall.

Kate eased her way into the living room, her finger on the safety of the rifle. The dogs barked while the hair on their backs raised.

Someone pounded on her door. "Kate!"

She couldn't quite make out the sound of the man's voice. She crept over to the window, pushing back the curtain only an inch so she could see outside.

Steve. She'd gotten so immersed in her work she'd forgotten he was coming over.

"Kate! Are you in there?" He pounded harder.

"Sunny, Ranger, cool it." The dogs quieted. She hurried to the door, fumbled with the lock and opened it.

She held herself back from launching herself at him. And then she questioned herself as to why she would want to throw herself at a man who had a deep scowl etched across his face and angry fire in his eyes.

"What took you so long to answer?" Steve groused as he walked inside.

The dogs rushed past him and out into the night. Ranger would pee on one of Steve's tires while Sunny would relieve herself close enough to his truck.

Steve walked inside, taking the rifle out of her hand, checking the safety, then leaning it near the door. "At least you're armed."

Kate stared at him, still wanting to launch herself at him. She cleared her throat. "I'm watching myself." She sounded breathless.

"Are you okay?"

"Yes. I'm okay." There was an edge to her voice.

"What were you doing?"

"Working."

Steve nodded. "Is the back door locked?"

"Stop it, Steve. You're overdoing it."

He planted his hands on his hips. "Am I?"

She crossed her arms over her chest, not answering.

"You could have been killed today, Kate."

She flinched when he said that.

"You might as well know from the get go, I'm spending the night here." He glanced over at her couch. "The couch looks comfortable enough." But he didn't say it like he meant it.

"It's a hide-a-bed. Your feet shouldn't hang over the edge, but maybe they will." She had no intention of fighting him about spending the night. Relief pooled inside of her. For one night she would be safe. "How about some hot cocoa?"

Steve's face relaxed when she offered him his sweet treat. "I could use some."

Fatigue showed in his face and his eyes. She started toward the kitchen. "I even have marshmallows."

"Must be might lucky day," Steve said behind her.

She put the kettle on to boil and spun around to face him. He draped his jacket over the back of the chair. He was wearing a black and white checked flannel shirt tucked into black jeans. The sight of him sent electric sparks sailing through her. "What did you find out?"

Steve took off his sheriff's ball cap, dumping it at the edge of the table, then ran his hands through his hair. He had nice, strong, manly hands.

"Well?"

He pulled a chair out, sat down, lacing his hands together in front of him on the table. "I was able to lift prints off the back door, but no match."

"Damn." She'd been swearing a lot today, she realized, but really didn't care. Kate circled back around, got the instant cocoa and marshmallows out of the cupboard, along with two mugs.

"Fish and Game found fresh snowmobile tracks leading to a small parking area about a mile from Harley's house. They're logging up that road. I talked to some of the crew out there."

Kate glanced over her shoulder, hoping for good news.

Steve sighed in frustration. "They were too far off the main road, their equipment is too loud, and nobody really noticed a truck or snowmobile, or horse and carriage for that matter."

Disappointment oozed through Kate like hot, sticky slime. When she heard the kettle whistling, she busied herself making the cocoa. One of the dogs scratched at the back door. She abandoned the cocoa to let the dogs inside. They rushed over to Steve, tails wagging.

Kate watched him pat both dogs on the head while she carried the mugs over to the table. "Okay, you two, go lay down in the living room."

Two heads swung in her direction. She pointed toward the living room. "Go lay down."

Both dogs eyed her before they padded out of the kitchen.

"I thought you were supposed to use short commands with dogs."

Kate sat down across from Steve. "You really aren't a dog person, are you? Animals are smarter than you think."

"Suppose."

Kate smiled.

"What's so damn funny?"

"You and dogs." She was teasing him so she could get her mind off the lack of evidence. "Good thing you didn't become a mailman."

"Very funny."

Kate noticed how he sighed in appreciation when he sipped the hot cocoa, making her feel warm, which of course bothered her.

"I might have to spend more than one night here."

That thought was both soothing and unsettling at the same time. She wasn't sure how long she could have him in her house without something happening. She noticed Steve's expression was neutral, but his eyes were a different story. She shrugged. "We'll see."

"Don't take it so lightly, Kate."

"For your information, I'm not."

This time Steve shrugged.

"How did the jerk know I was even at Harley's? You can't see cars parked out in front of Harley's house from the road."

Steve's brows knitted together. "He could be following you."

Kate shivered. "I never thought of that. In fact, I never gave it much thought as to how the psycho knew I was there." She hadn't dwelled on the attack because it was too unnerving, and too frightening.

"Do you remember anybody following you?"

Kate hooked her fingers around the mug handle. "Not really. There was traffic leaving town. Then when I turned onto Harley's road, there wasn't a soul behind me."

Steve nodded, drinking more cocoa. "Do you know Jack Danielson?"

Kate lowered her mug. "Jack Daniel? Why?"

"Just wondering."

"Come on, Steve. There's a reason why you asked me about him."

"Tell me if you know him first."

"I know who is. He comes into the café every once in awhile for breakfast or lunch. He keeps to himself. Personally, I think he's sort of odd."

"You know why he's nicknamed Jack Daniel?"

"Yeah, I've heard the story." Kate leaned forward. "Okay, give."

Steve frowned at her. "I don't know if I should tell you or not. First, you have to promise me you won't go off the deep end and do something careless."

"You think Jack Daniel killed Harley?"

"I never said that, Kate."

"You must think it, though. Or else you wouldn't have brought it up."

Kate put her mug down, sat back. The voice. Was the voice she heard today Jack Daniel's? She hadn't seen him in awhile.

"What's going on in that head of yours?"

"I was trying to remember the last time I talked to him. I think when he came into the café about a week or so ago, Carol waited on him. I know I didn't. And as far as I know he hasn't been in since Harley died."

"Did he have a set schedule, like every Monday or Sunday morning?"

Kate shook her head. "Not really." Jack Daniel had lost his Canadian accent some where along the way. She was positive of that. The man who had attacked her today didn't have a noticeable accent. She skewered Steve with a look. "You still haven't told me why you think it's Jack Daniel."

"I never said I thought it was Jack Daniel. He may be a suspect though."

Kate threw he hands up. "Stop dancing around the issue, Sheriff."

Steve scowled at her for reasons unknown to her. Impatience dug at her nerves, but she decided to let him tell her why in his own time.

"Tommy mentioned him."

"No kidding? Did Harley say something to him?"

"Harley told Tommy he thought maybe Jack Daniel shot the grizzly."

"Why didn't Tommy say something sooner?"

"He was too upset over Harley, didn't really think about it. Before you ask, I've already questioned Jack Daniel."

Kate leaned forward again. "What did he say?"

"Not much."

Kate glanced out the window, saw that it was snowing. White flakes drifted from the dark sky. "Can't you get a warrant?"

"I don't have enough evidence. All I have is hearsay at this point."

Kate knew enough about the law to know he was right. Jack Daniel? He was a strange cat, that was for sure.

"We still don't know if the two are connected. The grizzly and Harley?"

"It's the only logical reason for someone to kill Harley. If Harley did confront Jack Daniel. The guy is strange. There's no denying that."

"After talking to him, I agree. There are lots of strange cats in the world, but it doesn't make them killers."

Steve's logic annoyed her. The next time Jack Daniel came into the café when she was on duty, she would insist on waiting on him. "If I could talk to Jack Daniel, I would know if it was him."

Steve shot her a skeptical look.

"I heard his voice. I would know that voice anywhere. That I am one hundred per cent certain about."

"Maybe so. But without a positive I.D., the voice alone is not good enough."

"I need to talk to him."

"Kate," Steve warned.

"What?"

"You know damn well what."

Kate had the urge to scream, but she fought it back. "Isn't there some way we could set it up so I could talk to him?"

Steve shook his head. "I knew it would be a major mistake telling you about Jack Daniel. You stay away from him, Kate. I mean it."

This time she had the urge to stick her tongue out at him, because she knew he was right. There would be no plausible reason for her to talk to Jack Daniel unless he came into the café. "Why can't you say you need to talk to him at the café?"

"Kate." Steve finished off his cocoa, stood up, then went to the sink and rinsed his mug.

He stared outside at the snow floating down before he turned to face her. "For starters, he wouldn't meet me at the café for a friendly chat and coffee. He wasn't very friendly when I went to his place."

No. Jack Daniel was not a friendly guy. "Okay, dumb idea."

"Very dumb."

"You don't have to rub it in."

Steve glanced at his watch. "It's been a long day. I say we turn in for the night."

Once Steve pointed out that it had been a long day, as if on cue fatigue rolled through her. She'd been running on adrenaline since the attack at Harley's house. She was safe. Steve was here. She could sleep soundly. Kate looked at him. Her tummy fluttered when she saw the fire in his eyes.

She stood up abruptly. "I'll get some blankets."

⚬ ⚬ ⚬

It wasn't the hide-a-bed that was keeping him awake. The mattress was reasonably comfortable, and his feet only hung over a couple of inches.

It was Kate down the hallway in her bed. Steve propped himself on an elbow, then punched the pillow to soften it up. He dropped back down, staring up at the ceiling. The more time he spent with Kate, the more he wanted her. He had fantasized about spending the night with her, but not on her couch.

"Shit." He needed to get some sleep because he had to get up extra early so he could go back to his place, shower and dress in his uniform.

Sometime later when Steve had finally drifted off to sleep, Kate's dogs burst out in an uproar of loud barking and snarling. He sat up, struggling to orient himself from sleep to being alert. He fumbled for his gun on the end table next to the couch.

CHAPTER THIRTEEN

"Ranger, Sunny, what is it?" Kate yelled over the dogs. A light came on over Steve's head.

"Shut the damn light off."

"What?"

"Kill the light."

The light went off. Steve scrambled out of bed. The dogs were trotting around inside the house from room to room. "Where's a flashlight?" His big beamer was out in his truck.

"I've got one in the kitchen." His eyes finally adjusted to the darkness. He saw Kate's shadow jogging toward the kitchen. "Keep low, for God's sakes."

Steve put his gun down long enough to pull on his jeans, boots, and flannel shirt. When he stood up, the handle of a flashlight thumped him in the chest. He heard Kate mumble sorry.

He took the flashlight from her, turning it on. It was the same wimpy flashlight she'd had that night out in the woods. At least she had added new batteries; the beam was stronger, somewhat brighter. He heard the dogs at the kitchen door, snarling, barking, begging to be let outside.

"I'm going outside. Keep the dogs in here." He should have brought the Sheriff's truck instead of his own Chevy truck.

Kate's hands wrapped around his arm. "You have to be careful."

"I'll be careful. Where's your rifle?"

"Next to my bed. I jumped up in such a hurry, I forgot to grab it."

"Go in the bedroom, stay there."

"Steve."

"Don't argue."

Suddenly her arms twined around his neck. Then she dragged his head down for a hard, swift kiss. Her arms slipped away. Steve watched her shadow disappear from view. He shook his head; he didn't have time to dwell on her unexpected kiss.

In the kitchen, he grabbed his jacket and wrestled with the dogs to get out the door, they wanted out that badly. They would probably lead him to the bastard, but he didn't want one of them hurt for Kate's sake.

With the wimpy flashlight held over his gun, Steve moved his arms back and forth, performing a sweep of the back yard. He immediately noticed fresh boot tracks in the snow. A couple of inches of new snow covered the ground, enough for him to follow the tracks. It was still snowing but only lightly. Damn, he had forgotten his hat. The flakes felt like filmy ice sticking to his face.

He wasn't more than a hundred yards from the house into the trees when he heard the snowmobile start up. The loud whine of the engine breaking the silence of the pitch-dark night.

Steve stopped, listening to the direction the snowmobile headed. The snow machine headed south, not toward the old logging road. "Dammit!"

He couldn't chase it on foot. He had no idea where it would come out since the bastard was going in the opposite direction of the parking area. The problem was a snowmobile could go about anywhere if the driver was experienced.

Anger churning inside his gut, Steve turned back, cursing a blue streak under his breath.

He circled the house, following the boot tracks. The late night caller had circled the house too, had seen his truck parked next to Kate's. By then the dogs smelled him, started barking, which in turn had chased the bastard off.

Steve walked up the back steps, opened the door. This time he didn't have a chance to stop the dogs. They shot outside like two furry rocket ships. He turned and whistled for them. Both dogs stopped at the edge of the trees, didn't go any further.

Steve strode inside and down to Kate's bedroom. Her door was shut. He wrapped his hand around the knob. "Don't shoot, Kate. It's me."

The door swung open, followed by the overhead light coming on.

Kate held the rifle, barrel pointed at the floor. Her dark hair was tangled, her face white, and her eyes wide with fear.

"Well?" she said.

"The bastard was on his snowmobile again. By the time, I got outside he was just taking off in the opposite direction of the skidder road."

Kate's shoulders slumped, then she began to tremble. The dogs had finally quieted down outside. "Here." He tucked his gun into the waistband of his jeans, taking the rifle out of her hand. "Go back to bed."

She plowed a hand through her hair. "No. I wouldn't be able to sleep. I need to get the dogs."

Steve considered dragging her to the bed, but he figured it was pointless. Kate Madison was too damn stubborn for her own good. He stepped out of her way, following her down the hallway into the kitchen.

She filled the kettle, set it to boiling. Steve sank down in a chair at the table, still holding the rifle. While Kate went to the door to call the dogs, he glanced at the clock above the range. It was after four in the morning. He felt like he'd slept maybe two hours, if that long.

The dogs trotted inside, snowflakes sticking to their coats. Once inside, both shook the snow off their backs.

Kate went back to the range. "Coffee, tea, or cocoa?"

He figured coffee since he wouldn't be going back to bed, either.

"Coffee," he grumbled.

CHAPTER FOURTEEN

Kate eyed, listened, scrutinized each and every male customer that walked, sauntered, or swaggered into the café the next morning. When she waited on a man, she paid extra attention to his voice. But not one sounded like the jerk that had attacked her and killed Harley.

When the morning rush was over, Clara came over to her as she stacked dirty dishes in the dishwasher.

"You're going to sit down, have a coffee or Coke, and tell me what's going on with you. You're driving me nuts, I know there's something wrong."

Clara didn't know about her attack yesterday at Harley's, about what happened last night. "Clara," Kate paused. "Sometimes it's better to not know everything."

"Hogwash. I'm your friend. And I'm worried about you. I have been ever since Harley died. So what's it going to be? Coffee or Coke?"

Kate knew her friend too well. There was no point in trying to hedge around the issue. She could give her a censored edition. "Coffee."

Clara nodded, then disappeared. Kate finished stacking the dishes. She saw Clara carrying two mugs toward their little table. She walked to the table, sat down while Clara parked herself across from her.

Kate wrapped her hands around the heavy mug.

She stared at the steam drifting under her nose. "Oh hell. You might as well know everything, but I'm okay so you don't have to worry."

Clara's expression said she didn't believe her.

"Yesterday when I was packing up Harley's things, I was attacked."

Clara gasped so loud Kate figured the few stragglers out in the café probably heard her.

"Come again?"

"You heard me, Clara."

"Are you all right? No wonder you look so pale. My God, you shouldn't have come in today. Did you go to emergency?"

"I'm okay. And no, I didn't go to emergency." Her hand was still sore, slightly swollen because she had never gotten around to icing it. "Besides, work keeps my mind off things."

Clara didn't look convinced. "Did you call Steve? Does he know about this?"

Kate nodded. "Yes, Clara, I called 911. Steve was there faster than a speeding bullet."

"I don't understand why I haven't heard a peep from anybody."

Kate shrugged. "Steve must be keeping a lid on it. I really don't know."

"You can't stay alone. You're moving in with me."

Kate watched Clara sip her coffee, her dear friend's face pressed with worry and concern. "Steve is taking care of things."

Clara eyed her over the rim of her mug. "Meaning?"

She wasn't about to tell Clara about the early morning intruder. She didn't want to worry her anymore than she already had. "Steve slept on my hide-a-bed last night."

Clara's eyes widened. "He did?"

"Hmmm..." Kate drank her first sip of coffee. It had cooled to just the right temperature.

"Is he going to sleep there tonight, too?"

After what happened last night, he'd probably be the one moving in with her. Without thinking, she had kissed him last night. She reasoned she'd been overwrought with fear. That's why she had laid a lipper on him.

"Kate?"

"Uh...yeah?"

"Is Steve staying with you tonight?"

She knew the answer without having to ask him. "Yeah."

⁂   ⁂   ⁂

Steve cruised to a stop on Jack Daniel's recently plowed driveway while his eyes roamed in search of J.D. and his snarly mutt. He'd sweet talked Fish and Wildlife into checking behind Kate's house. They knew how to ride snowmobiles, he didn't. At least not through rough terrain. Since six inches of new snow had dropped overnight, he figured all tracks would be covered.

Jack Daniel appeared at the door of one of the metal buildings on his property. When he spotted Steve, he scowled while his dog trotted straight at him, the snarl set in place.

"Call your dog off," Steve ordered.

Jack Daniel waited a beat before he whistled. The mangy mutt stopped, eyeing Steve for a second before he turned back. He strode over to the workshop. "Good morning, Jack."

Jack leaned against the open doorframe. Wood smoke curled up from the chimney of the building. Steve decided he'd play good cop. "We got a fair amount of snow last night."

Jack nodded, suspicion written across his face.

"I know some people like to go snow catting at night. Did you last night?"

Jack's eyes narrowed to slits. "Why you asking?"

Steve didn't even know if Jack Daniel owned a snowmobile. Since Jack was blocking the door, he couldn't see inside the building. "Just curious."

"Just curious isn't good enough, Sheriff."

"So you didn't ride your snowmobile last night?"

"I don't have to answer your questions. You'd best be on your way."

Steve stood a little straighter, fisted his hands on his hips. So much for good cop. "You can either answer my questions here or I'm going to have to ask you to come to the station for questioning."

Jack straightened away from the doorframe. "You don't have any right to be snooping around here and asking me questions unless you got a warrant."

Steve wished like hell he did have a warrant. "I'm investigating the murder of Harley Wilson. I believe you are a person of interest."

A flush crept up Jack's cheeks. "Why the hell do you think I'm a suspect?"

"Because Harley believed you shot that grizzly sow."

The flush on Jack's face deepened. "That old fart came banging on my door accusing me of the same damn thing."

Steve's adrenaline pumped. Was Jack Daniel going to confess right here on the spot? He knew he was chasing rainbows. Murderers didn't just up and confess, unless pressured into it. "When was Harley out here?"

Jack took two steps closer to Steve. The mutt at his side bared his teeth.

"Hell, I don't remember. A month ago. I told the old man to get the hell off my property."

"Did you go to his house and confront him?"

"You mean, did I kill old Harley?"

"Yes."

Jack shook his head in disgust. "You think if I killed him, I'd tell you? I heard you were some big city cop. I figured you for smarter than that."

Steve ignored the insult, letting it slide off his back. "Did you kill Harley?"

"Hell no!"

Steve studied Jack Daniel. He was royally pissed off. Angry because Steve had asked him point blank if he had killed Harley and he was guilty of the murder? Or angry because he was an innocent man being accused of murder? Steve didn't have squat to go on. He didn't have enough evidence to get a warrant. Anger burned inside his gut. If Jack Daniel did kill Harley, he had nothing to prove it, nothing to pin on the man.

"By the by, Sheriff, I don't ride my snow cat at night. I sure as hell didn't ride it last night."

"You got an alibi the day of Harley's murder? The fourteenth of February?"

Jack Daniel's jaw worked. "I don't remember. I was probably home, maybe I was in town. Maybe I was shoveling somebody's walkway in town. One of my regular customers."

"You don't keep records?"

"Not if they pay me in cash."

So Jack did some of his work under the table. He knew a lot of people did in these parts. "Whose walkway would you have shoveled?"

Jack's face flushed again. "Mary Stone's. She's a widow with a bad back. Henry Tennison. The old guy is over eighty. I run his snow blower for him since he's not in good enough shape anymore. I shovel Mary Stone's driveway and walkway because she can't afford to hire a plowman." Steve memorized the names. Mary Stone was the local librarian. And he'd heard of Henry Tennison.

Jack Daniel was almost coming across as human. Steve wasn't sure if that was a good or a bad thing.

※　※　※

First Steve stopped by the city library where Mary Stone worked. The town's library was one large room next to the only insurance company in town, flanked on the other side by the only real estate office. One building housed the two businesses and library. Mary Stone was alone, returning books to the shelves. A metal cart stacked with books stood behind her.

"Morning, Mrs. Stone."

Mary turned from the high shelf. She was late forties, slightly overweight, with short blonde and grey hair. "Sheriff Lambert." She smiled, walking toward him. "What do I owe this unexpected visit to?"

"I'm sorry to bother you, but I need to ask you some questions."

"Questions?" Alarm spread across her face.

"No reason to worry," Steve assured her. "The questions are about Jack Danielson."

Mary frowned. "Is he okay? He hasn't been hurt, has he? I worry about him living out of town by himself."

It was clear Mary liked Jack Daniel. "I understand he shovels snow for you."

"Oh, yes. My back is not the best. After Jim, my husband, died, I needed help around my place. Jack has been helping me for almost three years now."

Steve nodded. "Did he shovel for you on February fourteenth?"

Mary's thin brows furrowed. "Probably. If it snowed the night before or during the day then he did."

"You're not certain?"

"I call Jack when it snows. If I'm going to be here at work or gone for the day, I just leave the money under the front door mat. He always charges me the same, six inches or two feet."

Once again Jack Daniel was racking up points in the human department. "Does he do a lot of odd jobs for you?"

"If something needs fixing, I call him. The library is only open five hours a day, five days a week. I'm afraid I don't earn that much money working here. Jack is very reasonable for his labor."

Steve nodded.

"I don't understand, Sheriff. Why all the questions about Jack?"

"I'm asking questions about a lot of people in town." Steve paused, cleared his throat. "In regards to Harley Wilson's death."

Mary Stone gasped. "Oh my, you don't think Jack is responsible? Do you?"

"Like I said before, there's no need to worry. I'm asking questions. That's part of my job."

She leveled a skeptical look on him. "I can vouch for Jack. He's a good man. I know he's different, somewhat of a hermit, but a decent man."

"I appreciate your time, Mrs. Stone."

"For goodness sake call me Mary, Sheriff."

Steve nodded. "Mary, thanks again."

Mary still looked skeptical when Steve turned to go.

Next stop, Henry Tennison's house. He had to call Jenny on his cell for directions. Turned out Jenny lived down the street from Henry. Henry Tennison lived in a one story rancher, stained a deep redwood. Tall pine trees bordered the large yard.

Steve knocked on the door, waited for Henry Tennison to answer. There was a separate garage with the double doors down, so he had no way of knowing if Tennison was home. A minute later, the door opened and a small black poodle, yipping and yapping, shot out the door, biting at Steve's boots. Steve glanced down at the little black fur ball, knowing the dog's mouth wasn't big enough to even penetrate his leather boots. A small dog was a welcome change.

"Sheriff."

"Mr. Tennison."

Steve had seen Henry around town. He was average build with a shiny, bald head, and wire rim glasses. His green eyes were alert while his weathered face looked like he could be a hundred, not eighty something. He wore old, faded jeans and a brown pullover sweater.

"Mind if I ask you a few questions?"

"Come on in. When you're my age, all you got is time. Get your butt in here, Pepper."

The poodle stopped gnawing at Steve's boots, pranced inside. Mr. Tennison shut the door behind Steve.

"Want some coffee, Sheriff?"

Henry Tennison probably could use some company and Steve definitely needed some hot coffee. "Yeah, thanks."

"Just made a fresh pot." He ambled toward the kitchen, the dog at his heels.

In the kitchen, Steve took a seat at the table.

"I'm out of cream, have to go shopping later. Hope you like it black."

"Black is fine."

"My taxes are paid. So is my mortgage." Henry carried two mugs over to the table. "I haven't broken any laws since I was a young, rowdy teenager, which was a helluva long time ago."

Henry handed Steve a mug, then lowered himself to the chair directly across from Steve. "Why the visit?"

Steve lips twitched at the corners. Henry was a straight shooter. "I'd like to ask you a few questions about Jack Danielson."

"Jack Daniels, huh?"

"Yeah."

Henry slurped some coffee down before he put his mug on the table. "Jack Daniels keeps to himself. Doesn't bother anyone, far as I know. He snowblows for me in the winter. Damn arthritis in my hands keeps me from doing it anymore."

"Did he snow blow for you on the fourteenth of this month?"

Henry scratched his chin. "Don't recall. If it snowed, he did."

"Do you call him or does he just automatically come by?"

"No. He waits for me to call him. Probably because he wants to be sure he gets paid. He's an honest worker, does a good job, but he don't work for free. Why the interest in Jack Daniel?"

"I'm investigating Harley Wilson's death."

Henry shook his head. "Crying shame. Harley was one of the good guys. We weren't buddies or anything. But we were friends, had known each other for years."

"Can you think of anyone who would want him dead?"

Henry picked up his mug, took another noisy slurp. "If you're pointing your finger at Jack Daniel, I can't see why. He's a strange one. There's no denying that. But he's harmless." Henry paused. "As far as anyone wanting to kill Harley, I can't think of a soul. But then you never know about people." He shook his head again.

Jack Daniel still didn't have a concrete alibi. He might have shoveled snow, he might not have. No one remembered. "How long does it take him to run the snow blower?"

"Depends on how deep the snow. He clears the driveway, blows a path to both doors, one out to my bird feeders in the back. Then he cleans the blower, checks it, and gasses it up. He's usually not here more than an hour, hour and a half maybe."

Steve nodded, drank the good strong coffee. "Do you remember that sow grizzly that was poached a year and a half ago?"

"Course, I remember. I used to hunt bear back in the old days. I hunted grizzlies before they were endangered. Let me tell you something, if you want a thrill, hunt a grizzly."

"So how do you feel about poaching?"

"Totally against it. The bears are protected now. Leave 'em alone. I don't like poachers. Unless you need the meat to survive. But there's plenty of deer and elk around here to fill the freezer if you're hungry."

Henry was an interesting old character and if Steve didn't have a murder to solve and had the time, he wouldn't mind shooting the bull with him for awhile. "Did you pay Jack with cash or a check?"

"Cash. Cash for the little jobs. That way he doesn't have to declare it. He roofed my garage two summers ago. He'll take a check for a big job like that."

No paper trail to prove that Jack Daniels was in town working the day Harley was murdered. Steve drained his mug, stood up. "Thanks, Mr. Tennison."

"We've shared coffee. It's Henry. And you're welcome, Sheriff."

⚯   ⚯   ⚯

By the time her shift at the café was finished, exhaustion had invaded every single muscle of her body. Her ears hurt from straining to eavesdrop on any and all conversations a man had in the café. Maybe she was kidding herself. Maybe if she heard the attacker's voice again, she wouldn't remember it. He'd only said a couple of words.

Kate sat at the little table in the back, letting her coffee grow cold, stifling a yawn. She still had a ton of work to do at Harley's place, but wasn't about to go out there by herself. Steve might believe she had air for brains, but after yesterday and last night, she planned on keeping herself safe.

"Hal Jackson is out there, sitting at the counter again." Clara flopped down in the chair across from Kate, fussed with her hair.

"I wonder why he switched."

"I liked it better when he sat in his corner booth. Then you couldn't smell the booze or have to look at him."

Hal usually only came in three or four days a week for breakfast or lunch. He worked road construction in the summer, collected unemployment during the winter.

"He asked if you were here," Clara said. "Said he was concerned about your welfare."

Kate frowned, sat up straighter. "He did? That's odd."

"He didn't like Harley. Harley didn't like him."

"I know all about them. What are you getting at?"

This time Clara frowned. "I'm not sure. It just seems like he's changed his habits since Harley died."

Kate considered that. "Yeah, he has, but if Hal was going to do anything to Harley, you'd think he'd have done it along time ago. There were neighbors for ten years."

"Hal never got over the property boundary dispute. After Harley had his property surveyed, Hal was fit to be tied."

Kate had been in Butte at the time that controversy had arisen. She did remember talking to Harley about it over the phone. Hal had claimed he owned thirty yards straight across Harley's property. Since the pin markers couldn't be found,

Harley hired a land surveyor to settle the dispute. Hal had harbored a grudge ever since.

"That was ten years ago." Kate looked down at her cold coffee. "Besides once Harley had it surveyed, there was nothing Hal could do about it."

Clara sighed, rested her chin in her hands. "Guess it's a stretch. But he's never been married."

"What's that got to do with anything, Clara? Besides, look at him. What woman would want to be married to him? He's a forty something alcoholic with no manners."

"Order up," Ace hollered.

"That would be the man with his ears burning." Clara stood up.

"Try to be nice, Clara. He is a paying customer."

Clara rolled her eyes before she went to get Hal's order.

Somehow the thought of Hal murdering Harley didn't work for Kate. A drunken rage? For the most part, Hal was a mellow drunk. He wasn't the brawling type when he was liquored up. Kate stood up, took her mug over to the sink.

She knew Hal's voice. His voice wasn't the one she'd heard yesterday. She was sure of that.

※　※　※

Steve rolled into Kate's driveway, killed the ignition and sat there. He'd crossed a line with Kate. The first time in his career. He should order her to stay with Clara until Harley's killer was behind bars. The porch light came on, followed by the dogs bounding down the steps toward his truck. He climbed out, muscling the dogs out of the way, patting each one on the head. When he walked up the steps, Kate leaned against the doorframe, arms crossed over her chest.

She wore faded black jeans and a man's plaid flannel shirt that was way too big on her. He wondered if it was her ex-husband's. Jealousy wasn't his style. Steve stopped as close to her as he could get. He smelled her citrus shampoo, maybe her perfume. Then he put his hands on her hips, pushed her inside, kicked the door shut behind him.

They looked into each other eyes for a long time as heat swelled inside his veins. Kate's lips parted slightly. Steve pulled her against him and gave the French a run for their money with his kiss. Kate's arms circled around his neck, returning his kiss with a willing passion. When the kiss ended, Steve nipped at her neck, sucked on her earlobe. Just as he raised his head to look at her, her mouth closed over his.

Her sweet hot lips made his head spin as Kate did erotic things with her tongue. His hand cupped her breast as she moaned into his mouth. Steve started backing her across the living room. Kate ripped his jacket off, started on his shirt buttons. Down the hallway, Kate's shirt came off, followed by his. They kept kissing, only stopping to rip at each other's clothes.

By the time they reached Kate's bedroom, Steve was bare-chested. Kate's pale pink bra came off just before they fell backwards onto her bed.

Steve bent his head to her breasts. He licked and sucked savoring her hard nipples. Kate fumbled with the zipper on his jeans. Once they had freed themselves of their clothes, Steve laid himself on top of her.

"Kate." His voice came out rusty sounding.

She framed his face with her hands. "No talking," she whispered.

He kissed her, his tongue mating wildy with hers. Her sighs and moans electrifying his powerful need for her.

Losing his balance, Steve clutched Kate tight as they rolled to the floor. He palmed her plump breast, listening to her womanly moans as his leg pushed between her legs. Steve rolled again, positioning Kate on top of him, loving the sight of her face flushed with desire.

Grasping her hips, he thrust inside of her.

Kate came as he fondled her breasts. Seconds later, he was lost in wild, powerful sensations.

CHAPTER FIFTEEN

Kate felt Steve's heart beating hard against her breast. Her head was tucked against his shoulder. Emotions exploded inside of her. Steve was the first man she had been with since Michael, her one night stand. Her husband had moved into the spare bedroom after her confession

Their coming together had been powerful, hot and raw. But regret had been woven in the mix, too.

Steve lifted her chin with his fingers, then kissed her. Without speaking, they got up. Steve climbed on the bed, dragging Kate with him. She ended up on top of him again.

"Kate."

"Um...yeah."

"Any regrets?"

Steve was a strong man, an experienced cop, but she noticed a glimmer of insecurity in his eyes. "No."

Dozens of doubts plagued her, but she didn't regret making love with Steve. She couldn't even explain to herself how it had made her feel, how she felt now.

Kate laid her head on his shoulder while his arms tightened around her. They fell asleep cuddled up together.

※　※　※

Kate woke up two hours later. At some point she and Steve had managed to burrow under the blankets. Seconds from falling back asleep, she heard the dogs barking in the front yard.

She'd completely forgotten about the dogs once Steve had kissed her. She slid out of bed, grabbing her flannel robe on the way out of her room. On the way to the front door, she gathered up their clothes in the hallway. At the door, she whistled for the dogs.

They raced into the house, nearly knocking her over. Once inside, they both curled up next to the wood stove. Kate locked the door. "Sorry, guys."

Sunny thumped her tail once. Ranger shot her a look. "I said I'm sorry." Still holding their clothes, she went to the kitchen, filled a glass with water. She stood at the sink drinking it, gazing out at the clear night. No snow tonight.

She wondered what the dogs had been barking at. She figured a deer or two, wandering through her yard. An uneasy feeling rippled through her as she finished her water and stared outside.

Kate put the glass in the sink, backed away from the window, telling herself she was just being paranoid. The front door had been unlocked. She and Steve had both let their guard down. Ripping off each other's clothes and having wild sex had been the only thing on both of their minds. Kate hurried over to the door, checked to make sure it was locked.

She carried the jumble of clothes back to her room, refusing to glance out a window as she passed.

⚒ ⚒ ⚒

The next morning, Kate woke with Steve on top of her, kissing her awake. Erotic sensations spiraled through her. She had planned to be out of bed, showered and in the kitchen by the time Steve even opened his eyes. She didn't want any awkward moments between them. Last night he had asked her if she had any regrets. She wished now she would have asked him the same question. Kate glanced at her digital alarm clock on the nightstand.

Steve did the same. "Shit. I'm going to be late." He rolled off of her, scrambled out of bed.

Disappointment filled her when she watched Steve stand up and shimmy into his jeans. Although the view was worth savoring. Ignoring her disappointment, she scrambled out of bed too, reaching for her robe. When she turned around, Steve was facing her, zipping up his jeans. His chest was just the right width, with just the right amount of black hair. He kept himself in shape.

"Don't look at me that way, Kate. I have to go home, then to work."

She cinched the sash on her robe. "What way?"

Steve cursed.

Steve was at the door in minutes, his jacket zipped up, hand on the knob when he turned to look at her. Kate stood at the end of the hallway, leaning against the wall, refusing to follow him to the door. He stomped back over to her, hauled her up against him and proceeded to kiss her with as much, if not more, passion than last night.

Feeling slightly off balance, she watched him leave. She had never admitted the attraction she felt for him. And she certainly hadn't shown him until after Harley died. She'd always known he was attracted to her. A woman sensed those things.

Last night on the floor by her bed, they had consummated their attraction for each other. Now what? Kate didn't know, wasn't sure she wanted to know.

꙯ ꙯ ꙯

Steve read the fax from the Alberta, Canada authorities on Jack Daniel. The man was clean as far as crimes against humans went. He'd already checked him out here. One speeding ticket six years ago. Unless he was living under an airtight alias, Jack Daniel was on the good side of the law in both countries.

Steve turned, stared out the window. He had a lousy view. Across the narrow alley was the brick building that housed the only hardware store in town. He was in a mood this morning. And it was all because of Kate. He'd had a thing for her since he first met her a little over a year ago. Now he'd had her and he wasn't sure what to do with her.

He'd been divorced for five years. He supposed Tess was happy with her husband. He hadn't seen it coming.

"Got a minute?"

Steve wheeled around, watching Jenny walk into his office. "Yeah, what's up?"

She sat down in the chair across from his desk, pulled down her bright red turtleneck, then crossed her legs. Steve sat down, too.

"Are you okay?"

Was his mood that obvious? "Yeah." Steve cleared his throat. "I overslept, was running late this morning."

Jenny nodded. "Well...here goes. Have you checked out Hal Jackson?"

Jackson had been the first person he had questioned after Harley's body had been found by Kate. His property bordered Harley's. Besides being on the good side of a bottle of cheap whiskey, Hal appeared innocent and way too unconcerned about Harley's death.

Jackson worked road construction in the summer, collected unemployment in the winter, and drank twelve months out of the year. Since Steve had been in Windy Creek, Jackson had been on the good side of the law.

"Anyway," Jenny said. "I don't want to be a gossip, but Harley and Hal didn't like each other."

That was something he didn't know. "Why not?"

"They had a falling out over their property border about ten years ago or so. When Hal first bought the place he thought he owned more land. Somehow the pin markers had been pulled out or lost or something. So Harley had his property surveyed. Hal was fit to be tied when he found out he owned about a half acre less than he thought he did."

"Everybody in town knows about this?" Steve picked up pen, started tapping it on the Canadian fax.

Jenny nodded. "I know more of the details because my mom worked for the county at the time."

From what he knew of Harley he couldn't picture him feuding with Hal Jackson. "So how did Harley handle it?"

"It was clear he didn't like Hal, but he never bad mouthed him. Hal, on the other hand, shot off his mouth about Harley for years after that."

Kate hadn't mentioned a word about the bad blood between the two men. Irritation threaded through him.

"I mean, I don't want to point fingers or anything. Hal is basically a hopeless alcoholic. Since you've only been here a little over a year I didn't know if you knew about Hal and Harley."

"No. I didn't. Thanks for telling me. I'll check into it today."

Jenny stood up. "You're not going to mention my name, are you?" Worry knitted her brows together.

"No. What you just told me stays in this room. Don't give it a second thought. Okay?"

"Okay."

Steve stood up. "I'm going down to the café for breakfast."

Jenny nodded. "I'll know where to find you if I need you."

⊁ ⊁ ⊁

Steve sat in the back booth of Kate's section. He knew the section she worked for breakfast. He faced the wall, hidden by the high booth. A couple of minutes later when Kate came over to his table, with a glass of water and coffeepot in her hands, her eyes widened.

"I missed breakfast, thanks to you."

She stared at him while she set the glass on the table, filled the heavy café mug with hot coffee. "I could say the same, you know."

Steve shrugged. "I'll have a short stack, bacon, and OJ."

Kate didn't pull her order pad out of her apron pocket, just circled around and left.

Irritation at Kate for not mentioning Hal Jackson and irritation for making love to her like a wild man last night gnawed at his guts. He'd gotten what he wanted. To bed Kate. Why in the hell was he in such a nasty mood?

Kate returned with his orange juice and a bottle of maple syrup. He reached for the glass, pressing his fingers against her knuckles. Whoa, boy. She skewered him with a look before she glanced around the room. It was close to nine, so the café was nearly empty. Steve took the glass from her hand, set it down. Kate disappeared just as fast as before.

When she dumped the plate of pancakes and bacon in front of him five minutes later, she was ready to make another fast getaway. "Why didn't you tell me about Hal Jackson?"

"What about Hal Jackson?"

"He's Harley's neighbor. They had a dispute over property borders."

"Sorry, I should have mentioned that."

Steve poured syrup on his pancakes. "Yeah, you should have."

"I said I'm sorry."

"Sit down, Kate, it's not busy. Clara won't care."

Kate hesitated a moment before she sat down, started drumming her fingers on the red Formica tabletop.

Steve ate a couple bites of pancakes, washing it down with the orange juice. "How did Harley feel about Hal?"

Kate continued tapping her fingers on the table. "He didn't like him." She shrugged. "But he didn't lose any sleep over Hal. He figured it wasn't worth it."

"Was that his voice yesterday?"

"No."

"Not so fast. He only said a couple of words to you."

"I know, but, I'm almost positive it wasn't Hal. I didn't smell booze. You can always smell liquor on Hal."

"Maybe he takes a day off from drinking now and again."

Kate snorted. "I doubt it. The man was dirty. His hands were filthy, grubby." She shuddered.

Steve finished off the bacon. "What about size? You said the guy was big."

Kate was quiet for a moment. "Maybe. The guy was big. Hal is big." She didn't sound convincing.

"Bigger than Jack Daniel?"

Kate dropped her hands into her lap. "Yeah, I would say bigger than him. Jack isn't husky like Hal. He doesn't have a beer belly." She paused. "But he is dirty. That's one thing I've always noticed about Jack."

Both times Steve had seen the guy, he'd been grubby, wearing even grubbier clothes. Steve exhaled in an attempt to get a handle on his irritation before polishing off his breakfast. He felt Kate watching him as he shoveled in his food. "When was the last time you talked to Jackson?"

"Whenever he comes in if I have to wait on him. Yesterday, Clara waited on him, so I didn't talk to him."

"No talking to him, Kate, unless it's here at the café. I'll handle this."

"Don't worry, Sheriff. I won't."

Shit, he hated it when she called him sheriff. His mood turned nastier. "Good. Remember that."

CHAPTER SIXTEEN

Thirty minutes later, Steve slid to a stop in front of Hal Jackson's house. The guy didn't own a plow or didn't care if the snow piled up. A Rottweiler mix ran out to meet Steve. The dog was big, mean looking, and had a bark that could rival Tarzan's yell. Scowling, Steve turned off his truck, studied the dog that studied him back with canine teeth bared.

Steve wondered if there was one person in the state of Montana that didn't own a big mean dog. Jackson's house was a plain, a one story wood sided house with a high pitched tin roof. Smoke drifted from the chimney. There were a couple of outbuildings behind the house. Steve didn't see Jackson's Ford four-wheel drive truck anywhere.

Steve climbed out, eyeing the dog. "Easy there, boy." The dog's ruff was sticking straight up. Steve took a couple of steps toward the dog. It backed up, still barking, still pissed at Steve for interrupting his solitude.

"Back off Bosco!"

Steve glanced at the porch. Hal Jackson stood there looking about as mean as his dog, wearing old jeans, a white underwear shirt that barely stretched over his beer belly. "Morning," Steve said as he brushed past the dog, hoping like hell he didn't take a bite out of his recently cleaned uniform trousers. The dog moved out of Steve's path as he angled over to the porch.

"I'd like to ask you a few questions, Hal." First name basis, hopefully it would wipe the snarl off Jackson's face.

"What about?"

"Harley Wilson." As Steve went up the porch steps, he noticed that Jackson's eyes were bloodshot. Day old stubble peppered his cheeks. Every time he'd seen Jackson he'd been wearing a hat. Today he was without the usual ball cap. The man was nearly bald, his dark brown hair almost nonexistent.

"You already talked to me about Wilson."

Steve felt the dog nosing around his back ankles. "Heard you had a dispute over your property border some years back."

"So what if we did?"

Steve watched him cross his arms over his husky chest, narrow his eyes. He doubted Hal would fall for the good cop routine. He was already defensive, maybe already boozed up for the day. "I understand that you weren't very happy that you didn't own as much property as you originally thought you did."

"Hell. Who wouldn't be? The realtor had me believing I owned more. He told me just because we couldn't find the pin markers didn't mean shit."

"You had it in for Harley then?"

Hal dropped his arms, took a step toward Steve. "If you're accusing me of knocking off Harley, you're way off base, Sheriff."

"Did you kill Harley?"

Hal's ruddy cheeks turned ruddier. "Hell no, I didn't kill the old s.o.b.. I didn't like his holier than thou attitude. Hell, I never liked him after he surveyed his property, but I sure as hell didn't whack him on the head. He wasn't worth going to the slammer."

Hal had moved within smelling distant and Steve didn't detect any booze on his breath. He looked sober enough, just damned hung over. "Where were you on February fourteenth?"

Hal smirked. "Probably here or in town or visiting with my buddy, Paul."

Steve pulled out his pad and pen. "Paul who?"

"Reeves. We work construction together."

The name sounded vaguely familiar to Steve. Jenny or one of his deputies probably knew him or of him. "You just can't remember?"

"Nope."

"Where were you yesterday afternoon around three?"

Hal flushed. "Right here, working on my four wheeler."

Hal could have made an easy getaway back to his place if he was the one that had attacked Kate. "What's wrong with it?"

"Had to change the oil."

"You hear a shotgun go off yesterday?"

"Not that I remember."

"You own a snow mobile?"

"Who doesn't?"

Steve had a feeling Jackson didn't remember a lot of days because of his drinking problem. "I'll be in touch." Steve turned, went down the steps. He didn't feel the mutt behind him.

After Steve climbed inside his cruiser, he glanced back at the house. Jackson was still standing on the porch with what looked like a glare while Bosco mimicked his owner's expression. Steve left, went in search of Paul Reeves, wondering what Hal had really been up to yesterday afternoon.

※　※　※

While Kate filled out her time card for the week, she considered going back out to Harley's. There were so many things to take care of at his house. She wanted the dirty deed done and over with so she could get on with her life. She had her gun in her truck. She could drive home, get Sunny, leave Ranger locked in the house.

Kate gathered up her jacket, gloves, hat and purse, walked back into the kitchen area. "Hey," she called. "I'm out of here." She slipped on her jacket, then buttoned it up.

"See you tomorrow, Katie," Ace said from over by the door of the walk-in freezer.

"Okay, see you. Say good-bye to Clara and Carol for me."

"Will do."

Kate walked out the back way, angled around Ace's Jeep Cherokee, Clara's Subaru outback, and Carol's Ford Ranger. When she opened the door of her truck, there was a folded sheet of lined notebook paper on the driver's seat.

Fear invaded her body. With shaky hands she tugged on her gloves, dropping her purse and hat on the plowed snow by her truck door. Gulping in a breath of chilly air, she reached for the note. Hands shaking even more, she unfolded it and read it.

"Harley deserved what he got. Back off."

Kate leaned back against her opened truck door. The note wasn't written. Letters had been cut from magazines and pasted to the paper. The letters were various colors: black, navy and red. Capital letters were placed in the middle of words. It looked like the work of a small child. Still trembling she refolded it, tossing it on the passenger seat, retrieved her hat and purse, climbed inside her truck.

Before she inserted the key, she stared at the note for several seconds, her heart pounding. Then she drove straight to the sheriff's office.

When she opened the office door, Jenny was talking on the phone. Jenny smiled. Kate nodded and headed straight back to Steve's office. He was on the phone, too, when she walked inside.

She dropped down on the chair across from his desk. He must have noticed something was wrong because he cut his call short, strode around the desk.

"Kate, what is it? What's wrong? You're white as a sheet."

"Somebody," she paused, drawing in a calming breath. "Somebody left a threatening note in my truck while I was at work."

"What the hell?" Steve leaned toward her, touched her cheek. "Where is it?"

"In my truck."

He pushed a lock of hair back from her cheek. "Did you touch it?"

"I put on my gloves." She held up her hands, which still shook.

Steve wrapped his hands around hers. "Where's your truck?"

"Behind yours."

He squeezed her hands. "I'll be right back."

Kate sat there, staring across Steve's desk, fighting to calm herself. To imagine she had planned on going out to Harley's this afternoon. Some jerk had left the note while she'd been at work, right in front of God and everybody.

A few minutes later, Steve returned with the note, wearing a pair of white plastic gloves. He stood by his desk, reading the note, a scowl etched across his face.

Kate felt a gentle tap on her shoulder. She glanced up. Jenny was holding a Styrofoam cup with a Lipton tea bag in it.

"Drink this, Kate. It will help."

Kate took the cup. "Thanks."

Jenny patted her shoulder, looked at Steve for a moment before she left the office.

Steve sat on the edge of his desk, facing Kate. "Your truck obviously wasn't locked."

Kate dunked the tea bag in the cup. "No. I never lock it at work. Nobody does. Damn, I forgot about my gun. It was under my seat." She started to get up.

Steve reached out, gently pushed her back down. "I already checked. It's still there. So it was left in the cab of your truck."

"On the driver's seat."

"Was your truck locked at home last night?"

"Yeah." Kate took a sip of tea. "I usually don't lock it, but I have been lately."

Steve nodded, glancing down at the note again. "No hope for handwriting analysis. I'll check it for prints. I'm glad you put your gloves on."

Kate stared at the steam rising from the cup. "He did it right in front of everybody. I mean the back of the café doesn't see a lot of traffic, but..."

Steve reached behind him, hit the intercom button. "Jenny, see if you can locate Ron. He's patrolling in town, isn't he?"

"Give me a sec, Steve."

"Okay."

Steve plowed a hand through his short hair, studying her. Kate finally shook herself like a dog after a dip in the river, sitting up straighter on the chair. "Now I'm getting pissed."

"Take it easy, Kate."

Before Kate could say anything, the phone on Steve's desk rang. He turned, picked it up. Kate listened to him give instructions to his deputy to check out the back of the café, and to talk to people in the area. When he was finished, he faced her again.

"Ron's going to check things out around the café. Sit here while I check for prints. Then I'll follow you home."

Kate shook her head. "I'm not going home."

"Maybe you shouldn't. You could stay at the café or Clara's house."

"I'm going out to Harley's." The strong black tea had calmed her, buoyed up her courage.

"What the hell?" That started Steve on his usual four-letter word tirade. He paced back and forth in front of her, every once in a while bumping her leg, not seeming to care.

Kate kept drinking her tea, waiting for him to blow off steam.

He stopped in front of her, hands on his hips. "Are you nuts or just too damn stubborn for your own good?"

"No." She squared her shoulders. "I'd planned on going out to Harley's after my shift. I'm not going to let this bastard intimidate me any longer." She would have stood up, but there wasn't enough room with Steve practically in her face and his desk behind him.

His angry eyes grew darker. "You are not going out to Harley's place," he said through clenched teeth.

"It's a free country, Sheriff."

"Don't call me Sheriff. It irritates the hell out of me."

"You're already irritated. You're downright pissed."

"Damn right I am. And well I should be. I can get a court order and close off Harley's house to you and everybody in this town." He paused. "I should have done that in the beginning."

"You wouldn't."

"Watch me, Kate."

Kate stood up, then got in his face. "Why are you doing this to me? I want to take care of Harley's things and be done with it." By the time she finished, her voice bordered on hysteria.

"I'm doing it to keep you safe. Since you won't be reasonable, somebody has to."

"I am being reasonable. The bastard is trying to intimidate me. He already killed Harley." Tears stung her eyes.

"Kate." Steve put his hands on her shoulders.

She shook his hands off, scooted away from him.

"Dammit, Kate. You've got to listen to reason here. You have to be careful."

Kate dumped the empty cup into the trashcan next to Steve's desk. She spun around to face him. "Maybe I don't feel like being reasonable. Harley is dead, murdered, gone forever. Forever." She choked back tears. "I want to mourn him and get on with my life."

Steve scrubbed a hand down his face. "I understand that. But he didn't die of natural causes. If that had been the case, you could take care of his things and move on. The killer is stalking you, trying to get you to back off, just like he said in his note."

Steve was right. She was the one that was being unreasonable. But she felt so helpless, so scared, if she let her guard down. She stomped over to the window, staring outside. Steve had a lousy view. The brick side of the hardware building didn't soothe her. She felt Steve come up behind her.

"Please, Kate. Don't do anything irrational or careless. If you really need to take care of Harley's things, we'll do it this weekend when I'm off. Two of us can get a lot accomplished."

Now Kate really wanted to cry. Steve's offer touched her, raced straight to her heart. "You'd really do that?"

"Yeah. I'd really do that. You shouldn't do it alone anyway. I'm sure Clara has offered to help."

Kate turned to face him, then. "Clara, Ace, Carol. All of them have offered."

"Can you wait 'til this weekend?"

Kate wanted to bury her head against Steve's chest, have him wrap his arms around her, but they were at the Sheriff's office, a public place. "I can wait."

CHAPTER SEVENTEEN

Kate pushed through the front door of the café after she left the Sheriff's office. Steve planned on coming down to the café after he checked the note for prints. She decided to tell Clara and Ace herself. Plus, she needed company after the threatening note. The threats on her life were stacking up at a rapid pace.

She found Ace and Clara in the kitchen eating a late lunch. As she angled over to them Ace leaned back and patted his flat belly. "Hi, guys."

"Kate." Clara lowered her coffee mug, a suspicious look in her eye. "What are you doing back here?"

"Hey, Katie," Ace said.

Kate unbuttoned her jacket, sat down at the table. She took her time peeling off her gloves. As she stuffed her gloves in her pocket, she caught Clara and Ace watching her like she was an alien creature.

"Okay, here goes." She crossed her hands together on the table edge. "Somebody left a threatening note in my truck this morning."

"What?" Clara looked like she'd just seen a ghost.

Ace frowned. "When we were all working?"

Kate nodded.

"What did it say?" Ace asked.

"Harley deserved what he got. Back off."

"Ohmigod..." Clara covered her mouth with her hand.

"Holy shit." Ace shook his head.

"I know. It's freaky. Everything will be okay, Clara, don't worry." Her friend's face had drained of color. Kate reached across the table, taking Clara's hand. "Are you okay?"

Clara squeezed Kate's hand. "You bet I am. This no good s.o.b. isn't going to scare me. Or you, for that matter. None of us." Color slowly returned to her face as she vented her anger.

She let go of Clara's hand. "Steve is on his way over here, after he checks for prints. He'll be asking everybody questions."

Ace picked up his mug. "I don't think anybody went out back this morning. I know I didn't. I never saw Carol go outside. Hell, there was no reason to. The garbage was emptied last night."

Kate and Clara both agreed they hadn't went outside.

"You recognize the handwriting, Katie? A lot of people write checks here."

"It wasn't written. The words were cut out of magazines and pasted on the paper."

"Sneaky bastard," Ace groused.

The three of them sat in silence for a while, each lost in their own thoughts. Their silence was interrupted by Steve walking into the kitchen area.

He joined them at the table. "Hope you don't mind me just walking back here, Clara."

"You can come back here any time you want to, Steve. How about some coffee?"

"Don't go to any trouble."

Kate jumped up. "I'll get it."

She carried the coffeepot and two mugs back to the table with her. After everybody's mug was filled, she put the pot in middle of the table.

Ace blew steam away before he took a drink of coffee. "I already told Katie and Clara none of us went out back during the morning shift."

"I'm calling Carol." Clara disappeared into her office.

Steve picked up his mug. "And nobody usually locks their doors?"

"Nope," Ace said. "No reason to. I've never had a damn thing stolen from my truck all the years I've worked here."

Kate wasn't sure she needed more caffeine but she took a tiny sip of coffee anyway. She glanced at Steve. "Did you find any prints?" She noticed how Steve looked like he wanted to bust his fist through a wall, any wall.

"No."

"The bastard's good. Hell, I didn't think there was anybody in Windy Creek with that much smarts." Ace looked first at Kate, then at Steve. "Present company excluded, of course."

That made Kate smile.

Clara hustled back to the table then. "Carol never went outside. She left about ten minutes after Kate, so Kate was long gone by then. She said she didn't see anything suspicious either. I haven't been out back since I got here this morning."

"Thanks, Clara," Steve said. "My deputy is checking the neighborhood behind the café."

"Anybody could walk behind the café and nobody would probably notice. Kids go through there all the time." Kate doubted Steve's deputy would find a witness.

"I guess my advice is to lock your car doors from now on." Steve didn't look happy when he said that. "And Clara, it probably wouldn't be a bad idea to keep the back door locked here. For awhile anyway."

Once again a heavy silence settled around the table.

※　※　※

Kate hit the save button on her computer, then shut it down for the night. Steve must have found something interesting to watch because the TV was still on. She stood up, rolled her necks a few times to loosen the kinks.

Her nerves and emotions on high gear, wanting to avoid Steve, she'd suggested to him to get comfortable and watch TV when he had arrived. He hadn't argued the point with her.

When she wandered out to the living room she found him asleep. His stocking feet were propped up on her coffee table, his head against the couch back. The remote was still in his left hand. The dogs were dreaming near the wood stove.

Kate watched him for a while. At least in sleep his lean face was relaxed. She wanted to make love with him again, to feel his tall, lean body wrapped around hers. Against her better judgment.

Her life had been turned upside down when Harley had been murdered. Now the murderer was after her. Kate tamped down the fear that was always near the surface the past few days.

When she had moved back Windy Creek after so many years, she'd put down roots again, settled into a routine, allowing herself to get comfortable in her new life. Now Harley was gone. Now Steve had entered her life, for better or for worse. Confusion knitted her brows together.

Kate angled over to Steve, reaching for the remote. She couldn't leave him there all night. He'd wake up with a stiff neck and sore back. As she attempted to tug the remote out of his hand, his other hand grabbed her arm.

He sat up with a start. "What's going on?" He blinked a couple of times.

"You fell asleep watching TV." His hand loosened slightly on her arm.

He blinked again, staring hard at her.

The next thing Kate knew she was bounced down to Steve's lap. Then his arms were around her and his lips were everywhere. On her mouth, her cheek, her neck, the opening in her shirt. His tongue followed the line of her bra cups.

And suddenly she was as hot as a one hundred degree, scorching July day. Ripping at each other's clothes until they were both naked. Kate skimmed her fingers through the dark mat of hair on Steve's broad chest. Steve pinned her down on the couch, his lips closing around her aching nipple. Kate arched her back, tangling her hands into his hair. His hand slipped between her legs, while he raised his head. His hungry lips sought out hers. The taste of his tongue forcing into her mouth provoked an insatiable need growing inside of her.

When Steve plunged inside of her, Kate wrapped her arms and legs around him, her body pulsating with burning heat.

"Kate."

She found his lips, forcing her tongue inside his mouth, hearing Steve groan. Craving his rough passion, she tightened her hold on him.

Kate shut off every scary, grieving, frustrating thought. She needed this, she needed him.

Steve had the ability to make her forget and only focus on him. To only feel him. To only want him.

After Kate climaxed, eyes still closed, she reveled in Steve's release moments later. Then he was a heavy, hot weight on top of her. They stayed like that for a while before Steve propped himself up on his elbows, taking some of his weight off her.

"What are we going to do about this, Kate?"

His voice was hoarse, his eyes a combination of satisfied and bewildered.

"You started it." How lame did that sound?

His jaw worked. "You're avoiding the issue."

Her defenses prickled, forcing her out of her relaxed state. "That was a broad question. Are we going to get up and go to bed and get more comfortable? Are we going to keep having out-of-this-world sex? Let's see..." she paused. "Are you going to take me on real date soon?"

"Can it, Kate." Then Steve kissed her, his tongue thrusting into her mouth, bringing her heat back to the surface.

Kate's bed seemed miles away.

⚬ ⚬ ⚬

Friday when she got off work, Kate commandeered more boxes to take out to Harley's the following day. When she turned the knob on the canopy, she remembered she had locked it. Kate had to carry the stack of cardboard boxes back into the storage room, get her purse and dig out her keys. Since she had moved back to Windy Creek she couldn't recall one time that she'd locked her truck or canopy door.

Since the threatening note she locked it at work and at home. The necessity of locking everything behind her was annoying as hell as she made her way back outside through the fresh snow that had piled up since early this morning. After the boxes were loaded into her truck, she walked back inside to get her purse, which she had forgotten.

After Kate stopped at the supermarket and picked up some groceries, she headed toward home. About a half mile from her house, she felt her front passenger tire start to wobble.

Terrific. It felt suspiciously like a flat tire. Kate pulled over to the side of the road, got out to check her tire. She crouched down next to the front driver's side tire, noticing a long nail sticking out, heard the slow leak of air from the tire. Kate stood, kicked the tire, cursing under her breath. Why couldn't she have noticed the tire while she was still in town?

She stopped using her cell a few months after moving back to Windy Creek, because frankly she didn't get that many calls anymore. It had seemed like a waste of money and effort to maintain the cell phone.

Kate reached inside her truck for her purse and gun. Turning her collar up against the chilly air, she started hiking down the road.

A few minutes later, she heard the rumble of an older truck approaching behind her. Kate glanced over her shoulder to see if she knew the driver. It was an older, white Dodge truck. Her radar beeped instantly remembering the Dodge truck that had been parked on Elk Creek Road the day her house had been trashed.

The county road was empty except for her and the truck. She unzipped her purse, wrapped her hand around her gun. Since it was only two o'clock most people were at work, and the kids were still in school. The county snowplow had already been through and done its job.

Heart pounding, Kate stood by the side of the road, afraid to keep walking with her back to the truck. The truck stopped beside her, the old engine struggling to idle.

"Need a ride?"

It was Jack Daniel and as usual he looked as grubby as ever. The outside of the old truck was coated with dirt. She shuddered to think what the inside was like.

"No thanks, I'm almost home."

"See you got a flat."

"Yeah." Her hand gripped her gun tighter.

"I can give you a lift to your place."

Kate couldn't read his expression. But she wasn't about to get into Jack Daniel's dirty old truck. And why was he out here anyway? "What brings you out to this neck of the woods?" Kate struggled to keep her voice casual, but her heart kept racing faster and faster. Steve considered Jack Daniel a suspect in Harley's murder. As far as she knew Steve hadn't completely ruled him out yet.

His eyes narrowed a fraction. "Just out for a ride."

It wasn't that uncommon for people to get cabin fever around this time of year as the long winter dragged on. "Enjoy your ride. Sometimes it's good to get out. You know, cabin fever and all."

Jack Daniel's eyes narrowed more before he looked away from her, gassed the truck and continued down the road. At an extremely slow pace, Kate realized. She started walking again, but slowed her pace, too. Better to have him in front of her.

She took her gun out of her purse, transferring her purse to her other shoulder. She slipped the gun inside her jacket pocket. Kate was certain she saw him glance in his rearview mirror a couple of times.

She just wanted to get home, lock the door, have Sunny and Ranger near her. Jack Daniel disappeared down the road. Kate hurried, trying to run, but the road was too slick for that. She walked as fast as could without falling on her fanny, finally arriving at her driveway.

The dogs ran toward her, tails wagging. When they reached her, she bent down on one knee, not caring if she got her jeans wet and soggy, grabbed each one around the neck and hugged them close to her. "Oh, it's good to see you two." Sunny licked her cheek while Ranger's tail thumped against the snow packed driveway.

Kate stood. "Come on, let's go." The dogs flanked her as she hiked toward her house, her adrenaline still pumping on high.

She supposed it could have been coincidence that Jack Daniel had been cruising down her road. The problem was she wasn't sure about anything anymore. Paranoia was her constant companion lately. She considered calling Steve.

Inside her house, Kate added a log to the fire. She called Red's Towing Company in town. Red, the owner, came into the café every other day for lunch. When he answered, Kate said. "Red, this is Kate Madison. I had a flat on my way home."

"Where are you?" he asked.

"I walked home. My truck is about a half mile south of my place."

"I know where you're at. I'll be there in fifteen."

"Um...Red, could you come pick me up first so I can ride back with you?"

"Hard day at work. The old feet hurting?"

She probably would have walked back to her truck if it wasn't for Jack Daniel cruising the road. Kate decided she was too vulnerable on the empty road by herself. She lied like a pro. "That's for sure. Real hard day."

"I'll get you, don't worry."

"Thanks, Red."

Kate shut off the phone, still clutching it in her hand. She chewed on her bottom lip, wondering if she should call Steve. When the phone rang startling her, she jumped.

She punched the on button. "Hello."

"Let sleeping dogs lie."

CHAPTER EIGHTEEN

The man's voice was muffled again, the line going dead after delivering the threat. Fear skated down her spine like an Olympic skater gliding over ice.

Hand shaking, she called Steve.

Lucky for her he was in the office. Jenny passed her right through to him.

"I just got another threatening call."

There was a lengthy silence before he asked. "Are you okay?"

She was about as far from okay as a person could get.

"Kate, talk to me. Dammit."

She sucked in an unsteady breath. "He said, 'Let sleeping dogs lie.' The voice was muffled again."

"I'm on my way."

"Wait." She caught Steve before he could hang up on her. "Red is coming out to fix a flat I had on the side of the road. He's going to pick me up at home."

There was a heavy silence. "How far did you have to walk?"

"Not that far."

"Stay inside until one of us gets there."

※　※　※

Steve followed Red Brown's brand new Black Chevy king cab truck down Kate's driveway. When he pulled to a stop next to Red's truck, Red climbed out, angled around the front of the

195

Sheriff's truck. He wore a frown, a navy blue stocking hat pulled down over his ears. Red Brown was mid-fifties, husky, and had owned his mechanics and towing shop for over thirty years. Steve knew this because the Sheriff's truck had overheated last summer. Red had rescued him five miles out of town and proceeded to tell him his life story.

"Hey, Sheriff, what's up? I know I wasn't speeding. The truck's brand new."

Steve climbed out. "Relax, Red. I had to stop in and talk to Kate." He glanced over at the Black Chevy. "Damn nice truck."

Red grinned. "I got it last weekend down in Kalispell. Course, the wife said we didn't need a new truck. The old one was only four years old, but I can use it as a tax write-off. So I figured why the hell not."

Steve saw Kate walk out on the porch. The dogs rushed passed her, started barking.

"Easy guys," Kate called. The dogs bounded over to Red and Steve for some attention with Kate following.

Red scratched Ranger's head. "This Harley's dog?"

"Yeah, I'm taking care of him. Well...forever."

"Good girl, Kate. Sheriff said he had to talk to you. I can go change your tire, then come back and get you."

"I'll drive her down, Red," Steve said. "No need for you to go to all that trouble."

"Hell, it's no trouble. It's a slow day."

Steve noticed Kate's feeble attempt at a smile, but he could tell it was an effort. Her face was pale while her eyes were filled with wariness.

"Thanks, Red. Steve will give me a ride. Sorry I had you come clear to my house."

Red started toward his truck. "Like I said, it's a slow day."

"We'll meet you down there in a few," Steve said.

Red nodded before he climbed inside his new truck and drove off.

After Red was out of sight, Steve walked over to Kate, cupping her face with his hands. "Reassure me that you're okay." Her bottom lip started to quiver.

She wrapped her arms around him, pressed herself against him. Steve hugged her tight.

He pulled back from her, searching her face. She didn't look like she was going to cry. "I know this is rough, but repeat the call to me."

Kate swallowed. "Let sleeping dogs lie."

"And you're positive you didn't recognize the voice?"

Kate shook her head. "He muffled it again."

Steve's jaw tightened. "I'll take you to your truck and follow you back to Red's so you can get the tire fixed. After that I'll follow you home."

"I can get the tire fixed tomorrow. My spare is good."

"The tire needs to be fixed today. It's too dangerous to be driving around without a spare."

Kate moved out of his arms. "I have to get my purse. I'll be right back."

Steve noticed a slight slump to her shoulders as she trudged back to her house. Usually Kate had excellent posture. And an attitude. Up until now, she'd had an attitude that had driven him crazy, but an attitude was good in a situation like this. He didn't like the fear he'd seen in her eyes.

The dogs followed Kate from her house to his truck.

"Stay," she said before she climbed inside.

Kate's silence bothered him as he turned left onto the county road. He glanced at her from the corner of his eye as she stared straight ahead.

"Jack Daniel drove by when I was walking home."

Steve hit the brake so hard his truck slid sideways on the deserted road. He didn't give a damn that he was blocking the road, shifting on his seat to look at her. "Why in the hell didn't you tell me this sooner?"

"This was the first chance." She didn't look at him as she tugged on her gloves.

Steve felt like he was ready to blow a gasket. "Did he stop? What the hell happened?"

Kate nodded. "He offered me a ride, which of course, I refused."

Steve fought to stay calm. It was getting way too personal with Kate. His radar would have been flashing for John Q. Public, but this was Kate. His emotions revved up to overdrive whenever he found out she'd been in the path of danger. Keep your cool. Think like a cop, not a man drowning in unexpected emotions for a woman. "Have you seen him out here before?"

"No." Kate looked at him then. "I have too many trees that block my view of the road. I can't see who drives by. I do know the sound of my neighbors' cars and trucks."

"So you've never seen him out here before?" He had ruled out Jack Daniel out as a suspect, but now...

"Not that I can remember. You're blocking the road. And Red is expecting us."

Steve swore, kicked the truck in reverse, straightened it out. "I'll have to talk to him again."

"He said he was just out for a cruise. I asked him if he had cabin fever."

"Cabin fever, my ass." Steve rolled to a stop behind Red's truck. "He has plenty of shoveling and snow blowing to keep him out of his house."

Kate shrugged, giving him a look that said she felt the same way.

※　※　※

Kate climbed back up the step stool, arranged canned vegetables and fruits on the top shelf in her kitchen. Steve hadn't been able to follow her home after Red fixed her tire, because he'd been called out on a domestic disturbance in town. She had assured him she could make it home just fine. She had been in her house less than thirty seconds when he'd called to check on her.

Turned out it was a brand new nail stuck in her tire. She wondered about it being new. When Red handed the nail to Steve, he'd eyed it like it was a bullet just back from ballistics. Then he'd pocketed it.

Two accidents in town in less than an hour had him working late, so Kate had decided to be constructive by rearranging her cupboards. She'd made a stab at writing, but in the end had wanted to bash her hand through her computer screen.

She glanced out the window, watching the snowflakes float to the ground. The snow had started two hours ago and hadn't let up. She'd be shoveling a good foot or more of snow off her driveway tomorrow. But tomorrow they were going out to Harley's. Maybe she should bring his plow truck back, learn how to use it.

A half hour later, standing by the living room window, sipping hot tea, Kate watched Steve's truck cruise into her driveway. The relief gushing through her made her feel slightly giddy. Kate realized she was getting too dependent on him. Counting on him to protect her from Harley's killer. Counting on him to bring to life long buried feelings when they made love.

They dogs were getting to know him, because they raced to the door, tails wagging. "What if it wasn't Steve, then what would you do," she asked as went to the door. Sunny and Ranger eyed her for a moment.

When she opened it, they rushed out to greet him.

"Hey, you two mellow out." He patted each one on the head.

"They like you."

Steve strode inside. "At least they don't bark, snarl or give me evil glares like the rest of the mutts in the county."

Kate waited for Sunny and Ranger to go outside, and relieve themselves before she closed the door. The dogs shook off the snowflakes clinging to their backs before they padded over to the wood stove and got comfortable.

"Want some cocoa?"

Steve took off his jacket and ball cap. "Sounds good. Where's a closet around here?"

"There isn't one out here. Just toss your stuff on the couch."

Kate went into the kitchen. The kettle was filled with steaming water, so it only took her a minute to make Steve's cocoa. She plopped four big marshmallows into the mug. When she spun around he was sitting at the table, watching her. She wondered what he was thinking.

She sat down, pushing the mug over to him.

"Four big marshmallows. What did I do to deserve this?"

"I went shopping today, and I happened to pass by the marshmallow section." Kate shrugged before sipping her tea.

Steve gave her that same look again, which was starting to make her uncomfortable. He had his cop face on. Neutral.

"So how was your day, dear?"

He scowled at her and picked up his mug. "Tomorrow will be worse if it keeps snowing this hard. For all I know, I might even get called back out tonight. You'd think by now the average Montanan would know how to drive in the snow."

Steve was in a mood. "You know the old saying, accidents happen."

"Shit happens."

Boy, was he in a mood.

"I caught up with Jack Daniel."

Kate lowered her mug.

"He threatened to charge me with harassment if I didn't stop bothering him."

"Can he do that?"

"He's probably just blowing smoke. But I need more than asking him why he's driving on a county road, and if he bought any nails lately at the hardware store."

"Nails get dropped on the road all the time. It's not the first nail I've ever run over."

Kate noticed Steve rubbing his temples, wondering if he had a headache. If he didn't have one, by the looks of him, he would have one soon because of the tension carved deep across his face.

"How far were you from home when Jack Daniel stopped?"

"Maybe a quarter of a mile. After that I hot-footed it home. I called Red as soon as I got in the house. Then the s.o.b. called right after that."

"Did you notice if he had a cell phone?"

Kate shook her head. "No. I kept my distance. But he was driving an older, white Dodge truck."

Steve nodded. "I knew he had one. It popped up when I ran a check through motor vehicles."

He scowled at his mug, while shoving a hand through his short hair.

Kate tried not to stare at him. He was sexy even when irritated. She glanced down at her mug, which was empty. After a moment, she started tapping the side of her mug with her forefinger. She glanced at Steve, caught him watching her.

"What?"

"My wife, Tess." Steve paused, rubbing his temple again. "She had an affair and divorced me so she could marry the guy."

He looked directly at her, waiting for her reply. Steve's wife had cheated on him and she had committed the same sin in her marriage. She struggled to keep eye contact with him, but it was hard. "Um...I'm sorry."

"I guess we were in the same boat there for awhile."

Kate looked away because pain still lingered deep in his eyes. She glanced across the room, out the window. Her heart felt like someone had sucker punched it.

"Kate, if it hurts to talk about it, I understand."

All the rumors that floated around Windy Creek when she had returned...She had let the rumors float like dust on the wind, never bothering to set anyone straight. She'd kept her secret close to her heart, letting everyone believe what they wanted to believe.

"Kate?"

She forced her gaze back to his.

"I can see I shouldn't have brought it up. I just wanted you to know. That's all."

Kate pushed back from the table, took her mug to the sink to rinse it. She stared out at the snow falling, piling up on the ground. Dragging in a deep breath, she circled around to face Steve.

"You probably won't want anything to do with me anymore."

Steve's brows puckered together in confusion. "What are you talking about?"

She jammed her hands in the front pocket of jeans, bit her bottom lip. "I cheated on my husband."

Steve's expression switched from one of confusion to outright shock. At least that's what it looked like to Kate. The truth was out. She remembered the old expression. The truth will set free you. She didn't feel free. She felt rotten.

"What the hell?" The tone of his voice indicated he was having a hard time processing her confession. "Come on, Kate. I don't believe that."

She leaned forward from the waist. "Believe it. It's true."

Still staring at her, Steve's jaw worked itself into a tight line. "Why didn't you marry the guy then? Or live with him or something?"

The can of worms were open. "It was a one night stand." She stared down at her old, comfortable leather moccasins because she couldn't handle looking into Steve's blue eyes filled with shock and betrayal.

"Kate..."

She brought her gaze back to meet his. "Like I said you probably or definitely won't want anything to do with me anymore."

Steve didn't answer, took his turn at staring down at the table, away from her.

He slept on Kate's couch that night.

Her bed had never been more lonely.

CHAPTER NINETEEN

Steve hightailed it out of Kate's house a little after six. He'd simply gotten up, dressed, locking the door behind him.

Standing under the hot spray of the shower, he scrubbed his face hard, so hard it stung. He never would have believed that Kate was capable of infidelity. Not the Kate of his fantasies. Not the Kate he made love to like a man possessed.

After he finished showering, he faced the steamy mirror that told him he looked like shit. He felt like shit. Dog-tired, because he hadn't slept last night, wondering about Kate in her bed. Alone. He'd almost gone to her, but some emotion had held him back.

After Steve was dressed and in his kitchen, waiting for the coffee to brew, he remembered it was Saturday. He'd promised Kate he would go out to Harley's house with her today.

"Shit." He glanced at his watch, saw that it was seven thirty. He figured Kate was up by now. Hell, she'd probably heard him leave.

Steve nabbed his cell phone off the counter and hit speed dial. He'd programmed her number in a couple of days ago.

"Hello."

Her voice sounded tired, small, almost beaten. He cursed under his breath. "Kate."

Her silence grated on his burned out nerves. "I'll be over in an hour so we can go out to Harley's."

"You're not obligated."

He set his teeth together. "I'll be at your house in an hour."

"I'll meet you at Harley's."

"No. I'll pick you up. You're not going out there alone." Steve ended the call as abruptly as he had started it.

The coffee was done and he realized he'd better eat something because it would be one long day with Kate.

※　※　※

While her truck warmed up, Kate shoveled her walkway, waiting for Steve to arrive. Sunny as usual tried to catch the fluff of a snow that she tossed to the side. Ranger was marking all the trees in her yard. She had decided she'd drive herself out to Harley's. That way they wouldn't have to be alone together.

And she wouldn't have to feel Steve's anger, see the disappointment in his eyes.

When she heard the purr of an engine turn up her driveway, apprehension blew through her. It would be easier if she never saw him again. No, it wouldn't.

Steve parked next to her truck. Kate barely glanced at him before she returned the snow shovel to her porch. When she went down the steps, he walked towards her.

"Why's your truck on?" Steve ignored Sunny and Ranger as they crowded around him wanting attention.

No good morning. How are you? I'll forgive you.

With tired eyes and his face strained with fatigue, he stared at her. Steve looked like she felt. Sleep had been impossible to slip into with him out in her living room. "I thought it would be easier if I drove myself. I want to bring some stuff back here and drop the rest at the thrift store in town."

"There's plenty of room in my truck."

They stood facing each other, the twenty-degree weather making their breath fog. "I'd just rather drive myself."

"I'll follow you." Steve wheeled around like a military man, ready to do battle, marching back to his truck.

Kate refused to look at him while she got in her truck, backed up, then headed down her driveway. The dull ache that had lodged in her heart last night intensified as she drove down the road. Deer darted across the road, in search of food buried under four feet of snow.

Life went on.

※　※　※

At noon, Kate loaded a box with pots and pans on the floor in Harley's kitchen. Steve was in Harley's bedroom, packing up his clothes. In an unspoken agreement, they had each picked separate rooms. Occasionally Steve had come looking for her to ask her about a particular thing of Harley's.

He had closed up to her, even his eyes.

Kate ignored the grumble of her stomach. She regretted not making a couple of sandwiches to bring. They were half a dozen cans of soup in the first box she packed. She stepped over a box, rummaging through the box for the soup. She made fresh coffee, turned the soup to simmer. She found Steve walking through the living room, balancing two large boxes in his arms.

"Um...I put some soup on. I figured you'd be hungry by now."

Steve eyed her over the top box. "Yeah, thanks." Then he walked to the door, trying to juggle the boxes and open it.

Kate angled around him, opened the door for him.

When he stepped outside, without a word or glance at her, something snapped inside of her.

As he made his way to his truck, Kate yelled at his back. "Are you so damn perfect you've never made a mistake?"

Steve slowly turned to face her, staring hard at her over the boxes. She stomped to the edge of the porch, fisting her hands on her hips.

She wasn't sure how long they faced off and stared at each other. At last, some emotion from him. Anger blazed in his dark eyes. Anger pulsated through her body, too. Steve wheeled around, rim rod straight back, hiked to his truck and dumped the boxes in the back.

With swift strides, he pinched off the distance to the house. In a flash, he was standing so close to her Kate wanted to step back. Oh yeah, his eyes were angry. His entire body was stiff, poised, ready to do what, Kate didn't know.

"Why did you sleep around on your husband?" Steve demanded.

The way he phrased the question felt like a hard slap to her face. If only he would have worded it differently. It made her feel cheap. An unexpected lump inched up her throat. She swallowed it back. "I guess because I'm human."

Steve's eyes reminded her of an out of control wild fire, stormy, clouded with anger. "Why, Kate?" His voice was hoarse.

Besides anger, raw emotion gleamed in his eyes. She shook her head, desperately searching for the right words. "Because," she hesitated. "I was lonely. I know that's not a good excuse. It's not an excuse at all. David and I had grown apart. He was always working overtime, not that he had to, we had plenty of money." She raked a hand through her hair, suddenly realizing how cold it was outside. She wanted the heat of Harley's wood stove, the heat of Steve's arms around her.

"It was one time. I was having a vulnerable moment, one too many drinks. I regretted it instantly. I still regret it. Hell, I'll always regret it. My son still hasn't forgiven me. Not all the way." She had confessed, bared her soul to this angry man who made her feel like a woman again when he made love to her. She had absolved herself of her sins. Funny, she didn't feel cleansed. She felt lousy, weak, cheap. Kate squared her shoulders, waiting for the axe to fall. For Steve to say it was over between them. Over before it had really started.

A few days ago she wasn't certain what direction she wanted her relationship with Steve to go. Now the definite possibility that he would walk away in a heartbeat had desperation clawing at her heart.

"Why did you let everyone believe you were the innocent one?"

Kate's lower lip trembled as she shrugged. "Everyone just assumed. I never set them straight. I didn't want to talk about what happened. Pride, I guess. I was ashamed of what I had done. I didn't feel like broadcasting it to the world. Would you?"

He didn't answer her. She couldn't handle the look on his face. One of censure. She spun around, stomping back inside the house, attempting to bang the door shut behind her. But Steve blocked it with his arm, following her inside.

She hurried into the kitchen.

"You dropped one helluva bomb on me."

Kate sidestepped boxes. She slowly turned to face him.

"Would you ever have told me?"

Steve's question made her pause. She had told her husband a week later. Would she ever have confided her crime of humanity to Steve? Kate believed at some point she would have come clean about her infidelity in her marriage.

Guilt slid through her, guilt at breaking her marriage vows. She had already paid the price. Her twenty year marriage gone faster than a flash of lightning. Her fragile relationship with her son could go either way. Everyday she prayed he would forgive her, so they could have the easy relationship they had always shared before her mistake of a lifetime.

"I don't like talking about it. It's over, done with. There's nothing I can do about it now except live with it."

Steve worked his jaw, glancing away from her.

Kate decided there was nothing else she could do. Steve had two choices, forgive her or hold it against her. A heavy hand of sadness gripped her heart. "There's soup and coffee for lunch."

"Okay," he said without looking at her.

A few minutes later, they sat down at the table across from each other and ate in silence.

CHAPTER TWENTY

Steve eased away from the curb, a good part of Harley's things deposited safely at the local thrift shop in town. Kate headed in the opposite direction toward her house. When they had left the store, he told her he'd be out later. She hadn't protested or agreed, just simply got in her truck and drove off.

He couldn't leave Kate alone, not with Harley's killer still running loose and threatening her. He picked up his cell, called into the office. The weekend dispatcher, Sherry answered.

"This is Steve. How are things going?"

"Just fine, boss," Sherry said. "Not even a deer hit, a slide off the road. I'm keeping my fingers crossed that it stays that way."

"Good. If you need me, call."

"Roger that."

Steve dropped his phone back on the seat. A few minutes later, he rolled into his driveway. His one story, light brown rancher sat at the edge of town on a dead end gravel street. He had a half-acre and enough privacy to suit his needs. His house was bordered by tall grand fir trees with a few lodgepole pines sprinkled in the mix.

Steve went inside, unhooked his gun from the holster, laid it on the counter, battling his emotions over Kate. His emotions where she was concerned were waging a mighty war inside of him.

Steve went back outside, snagging the snow shovel off the back porch. Even though he'd done physical work at Harley's, tension still throbbed inside his body. Steve started shoveling his walkway. After he finished the walkway, he tackled the driveway. A snow blower was parked in his shed, but he needed the physical release.

Anger, disappointment, betrayal all crashed together inside of him forming a solid knot of tension inside his guts.

Whoa, boy. Kate hadn't betrayed him. She'd betrayed her husband, her family. But for some damn reason he felt betrayed. Tess had betrayed him, not Kate. He was comparing the two women. One his ex-wife. One his lover.

The problem was he felt things for Kate he'd never felt for his wife of fifteen years. Kate stirred raw emotions inside of him. From the beginning, she'd churned up his emotions. His fantasies had been fulfilled the first time he'd been naked with Kate, been inside of her.

Steve shoveled harder and faster, trying to run from powerful feelings threatening to snatch his cool away from him. When he finally finished, he was sweating under his warm clothes and jacket. He strode toward his house, wondering if he could find it in himself to forgive Kate her infidelity to another man.

꼭   꼭   꼭

Three hours later, Steve stood on Kate's porch. When she opened the door, her eyes were red and swollen. Maybe she had finally succumbed to her grief over Harley. "What is it?"

She lifted her chin. "Nothing. Make yourself comfortable. I'll be working." She disappeared down the hallway.

"Damn," Steve muttered as he unzipped his jacket. The dogs were at his ankles, tails wagging, wanting his attention. He tossed his jacket on the couch. Bending down on one knee, he petted the dogs, scratched behind their ears. "Okay, enough."

He straightened up, jamming his hands in the front pockets of his jeans. What the hell had he expected from her? Steve took a step, then stopped. If he went to her...

His feet took him down the hallway to the spare bedroom. Not his heart, he told himself. His mother had taught him well, never ignore a crying woman. Kate was done crying, he reasoned. He scowled at the closed door. It was quiet in there. He didn't hear the click, click of the keyboard being pounded on.

Steve raised his hand to knock, then figured the hell with it as he opened the door. Kate wasn't sitting at her desk in front of her computer. She leaned against the window frame, arms crossed over her stomach.

She gave him a sideways glance.

Hand still on the doorknob, Steve said. "I thought you were working."

"How do you know I'm not?" She didn't look at him.

"You're staring out the window."

"Maybe that's how I get my inspiration."

"Why were you crying?" Why was he asking? Did he really want to know?

She turned. "I'd say that's none of your business, Sheriff Lambert."

Major annoyance bowled through him when she addressed him so formally. "Dammit, Kate," he said for lack of anything better to say.

Anger brewed in her eyes. "I don't think you should stay here anymore. In fact, you can turn around and leave right now."

Anger started a slow burn in Steve, too. "That's not going to happen. And you know it. Not until Harley's killer is behind bars."

"I have a gun. I have two guns. And two good watch dogs."

"You're not staying here alone at night and that's final. So live with it."

"Excuse me?" She started toward him, then stopped. "Live with it?"

"Yeah, live with it. I'm not leaving you here alone."

Kate strode over to him, poked her forefinger at his chest. "This is a free county. I didn't ask for police protection. I can take care of myself. Besides, this is all unofficial." She poked him again.

Steve looked down his nose at her finger still resting against his chest. Kate didn't paint her nails. They were natural, but still long and filed into a nice shape. He wrapped his hand around her finger. Kate's eyes widened when he touched her. Sexual desire shot through him like a bullet, but he didn't let go. "I'm the top dog in law enforcement around here. So what I say goes."

Kate made an unladylike sound, glaring at him, trying to wrestle her finger free. He should have let go, but he didn't. Instead he wrapped his hand around hers.

She took one step back. "Don't touch me unless you mean it."

Steve cursed out loud. They stared hard at each other. In the end, Steve released her hand, backed out of the room.

⚹ ⚹ ⚹

The next three days were quiet. So quiet that Kate stopped glancing over her shoulder. She even let her guard down enough to stop listening to men's voices in the café. The regulars came in everyday. Then there were the regulars that came a few times a week. But sometimes, the bi-weekly regulars would pop in unexpectedly.

The lunch rush was over. Kate filled salt and pepper shakers at the tables. When Jack Daniels walked into the café,

Kate's spine tingled. He headed to the counter, sat his grubby butt on a stool. He didn't so much as glance in her direction. Carol had the counter today. She came out from the kitchen, carrying a tray stacked with clean mugs.

Kate tightened the lid on a salt shaker, watching as Carol pulled her order pad from her apron pocket, scribbled down Jack Daniel's order.

Jack Daniel wasn't a regular, regular. He'd stop in occasionally for breakfast or lunch. Kate moved to the next table, observing Jack Daniel from the corner of her eye. She moved around the room, checking and filling the salt and pepper shakers.

She gathered the large containers of salt and pepper and started back across the café. When she was almost to him, she said, "Afternoon, Jack."

He barely glanced over his shoulder at her and made a sound she couldn't decipher.

Funny, he didn't ask her if she got her tire fixed. Kate hurried back to the kitchen area, nearly colliding head on with Carol, bringing another tray of steaming, clean mugs out to the café.

"Oh, sorry, Carol. I wasn't paying attention."

"If you're like me," Carol shifted the tray, "You're feeling a little spacey. I'm starving. Didn't get breakfast this morning."

Kate had been preoccupied over Jack Daniel sitting at the counter. "Yeah, no kidding." She held the swinging door open for her.

"Thanks, pardner." Carol sashayed out the door.

Before Kate let the door swing shut, she caught Jack Daniel glaring her. Again her spine tingled. She walked over to Ace, who was putting the finishing touches on a cheeseburger.

She leaned closed to him.

Ace looked sideways at her. "Come to get some loving, Katie girl?"

Normally Kate would have joked back with him. "How well do you know Jack Daniel?"

Ace paused, a large tomato slice hovering over the plate. "You put your head together with the sheriff?"

Kate frowned. "Why do you ask that?"

"Steve dropped by my place about a week ago, asking questions about Jack Daniel." Ace plopped the tomato slice on the lettuce leaves.

Steve had never mentioned that to her. Any conversation between them now was strained, about boring things like the weather. She watched Ace remove the sizzling burger from the grill, sliding it onto the bun. He dumped a pile of french fries on the plate.

"Hold on, Katie," Ace said as he dropped a large dill pickle chunk on the plate. He wheeled around, took two steps, and hollered. "Order up, Carol."

Carol's head popped up in the opening that separated the kitchen from the back counter. "I'm right here, for crying out loud, Ace. One of these days you're going to chase off all the customers."

"Nah. That will never happen. My yelling is part of the ambience here."

Carol rolled her eyes. "Yeah, right." She snatched the plate and disappeared.

Ace stuck his head through the window area. "What do you want for lunch?"

"A grilled ham and cheese," was the reply.

Ace spun back around. "Sounds good. I think I'll have one myself. Want me to make it three, Katie?"

Kate still distracted, wondering why Steve hadn't told her about talking with Ace, said. "Excuse me?"

"You want a grilled ham and cheese for lunch?"

Kate shrugged. "Sure. Why not?"

She watched Ace pull six slices of bread from the bag on the counter. "You never answered my question. How well do you know Jack Daniel?"

Ace went to the fridge, gathered up the big slab of ham and a stack of cheddar cheese slices. He came back to the counter where Kate leaned her hips against it. "I don't really know him that well at all except to say howdy when he comes in here or I run into him around town."

Kate still held the large containers of salt and pepper. "Then why did Steve ask you about him?"

"I imagine 'cause he's following leads, asking questions of a lot of people around town concerning Harley."

"Okay, point taken."

Ace lowered his voice as he sliced the ham. "I told him about the time years ago, J.D. and I got shit faced together at the bar, how old Jack went on and on about some woman. Some lost love, I always figured. Ever since that night, he hardly gives me the time of day." Ace assembled the sandwiches, then slapped them on the grill. "He must have remembered more than I did about that night, 'cause I sure as hell don't. That was back in my hard drinking days."

"Maybe he confessed a deep, dark secret to you, Ace." She tried for humor, but in reality she was dead serious.

Ace watched the sandwiches cooking. "Might have. But I'll be damned if I can remember what it was."

"Why else would he stop talking to you? And for how many years?"

"Ten, twelve. Hell, I don't know. Maybe he's still embarrassed about crying in his beer."

Ace continued to speak in a low tone, so Jack Daniel wouldn't hear. But Kate knew it was almost impossible to hear conversation in the kitchen area unless Ace was yelling. "That's along time to be embarrassed."

Ace flipped the first sandwich over on the grill. "You know us men and our egos."

Kate wandered off to return the salt and pepper containers to the shelf. Ace didn't seem to care that Jack Daniel and he weren't buddies. She wandered back out to the café, sidled behind the counter. Carol was arranging mugs on the self so Kate went to help her.

Jack Daniel gave her a look over a half of his cheeseburger. "So how's the burger, Jack?"

She thought he mumbled fine before he stuffed three fries into his mouth. As usual he was grubby. "Enjoy your ride the other day?" Kate half-turned, started straightening mugs, watching him while she pretended to work. Carol seemed oblivious to Kate's unexpected friendliness with Jack Daniel.

"What's it to you?"

His hostility was obvious. "Just curious. You said you had cabin fever."

Jack Daniel scraped at his teeth with his tongue.

"Sandwiches are ready," Ace hollered.

Carol beamed. "I could eat a horse." She refilled Jack Daniel's mug. "Anything else?"

Jack Daniel shook he head, started in on the second half of his cheeseburger, completely ignoring Kate. Carol brushed past Kate to feed her appetite.

"That's the first time I've seen you out in my neck of the woods."

Jack Daniel paused, the cheeseburger almost to his mouth. He sneered over it at Kate.

"You're starting to sound like the sheriff. I already told him I'd nail him for harassment if he didn't back off."

Kate shrugged. "That's between you and Sheriff Lambert. I'm just a private citizen being friendly."

"I'd like to eat my meal in peace."

"Suit yourself."

She pushed through the swinging door, joining Carol and Ace at the table. A plate of French fries sat in the middle of the table.

Kate pulled out a chair, feeling the aftereffects of Jack Daniel's hostility.

"When's Clara getting back?" Carol asked as she grabbed a fry off the plate.

"Late this afternoon." Ace wolfed down his sandwich. "She had better remembered the dill pickles 'cause we're almost out."

"Clara never forgets anything when she goes shopping," Carol said.

Kate concentrated on the conversation. "Have you ever shopped with her?" Carol shook her head. "She slowly and methodically goes through the store, checks each item off her list, then circles the store again, putting another check by whatever. You need patience to shop with Clara."

Ace chuckled. "That's why I only went with her once, and refused to go again."

Carol laughed. "She asked me once, but I was busy. So thanks for the warning, guys."

"You ought to go at least once," Ace said. "It's an experience, not to mention her driving."

Carol rolled her eyes. "I know how she drives. Like a maniac. I've ridden with her."

Clara had a heavy foot on the gas pedal. She was a native Montanan and knew how to handle herself in all kinds of weather. "I just hang on and pray." Kate tried to keep with the lighthearted mood, but Jack Daniel sitting out there at the counter bothered her. She wished she knew why.

The bells over the front door tinkled.

"Well darn, I was hoping I would get to finish my lunch." Carol made a face at the french fry she was ready to pop in her mouth.

Kate jumped up. "I got it."

"You're officially off," Carol said.

"Remember, I owe you." Kate wiped her hands on her jeans on her way out to the café.

Steve sat at the counter, a few stools down from Jack Daniel. If Jack had been annoyed before while Kate had talked to him, he really looked bent out of shape now.

She glanced at Steve. He apparently was in a similar frame of mind as Jack Daniel by the expression on his face.

Kate picked up the coffeepot and a clean mug. "Coffee?"

Steve eyed her, then looked sideways at Jack Daniel. "Yeah."

She filled the mug for him. Why did just the sight of him, make her pulse rev up? "Lunch?"

"I'll take a cheeseburger and fries." He slanted another glance at Jack Daniel.

Jack Daniel stared straight ahead, his jaw twitching.

"Okay." Steve was still giving Jack Daniel an evil glare from the corner of his eye.

When Kate got back to the kitchen, she found a stray order pad, jotting down Steve's order. "Ace, cheeseburger and fries."

Ace stuck his tongue out at her. "I need to let my food digest. Who's it for?"

"That's going to decide how soon you make it?" Carol asked.

"Damned straight."

"The sheriff of Windy Creek."

Ace whistled. "In that case, I better get right on it."

"How's Jack Daniel doing?" Carol looked at Kate over the rim of her mug.

"I'll take care of him."

"We'll split the tip."

That actually made Kate smile. "What's half of nothing?"

Carol giggled.

Jack Daniel wouldn't tip if his life depended on it. Kate pushed through the door again. Steve and Jack Daniel were both staring straight ahead, boring holes into back counter stocked with dishes, mugs, silverware.

She ignored Steve as she cruised by him. But her rebel heart didn't. "Anything else?" She picked up Jack Daniel's empty plate.

He narrowed his eyes at her, pulled out a five-dollar bill tossing it on the counter. "Keep the change." Then he stood up and walked out of the café.

Steve circled his stool around watching Jack stomp out of the café. Kate was still slightly dumfounded that he had actually left somewhat of a tip.

Steve turned back to face her. "He harass you?"

Carrying the empty plate and mug, she stopped in front of him. "According to him, you're the only one doing the harassing."

Steve swore out loud.

"But then he kind of accused me of it, too."

"What the hell did you do to provoke him, Kate?"

"He provokes easily. He's got a major chip on his shoulder. I was only being a friendly waitress."

"Don't mess with him, Kate. I'll handle him."

There was a combination of anger and she might even call it concern in Steve's gaze. "Why didn't you tell me you talked to Ace about him?"

Steve drank some coffee. "It must have slipped my mind. The information Ace shared with me didn't have much bearing on the case. I've thoroughly checked out Jack Daniel. He's clean."

"But you still don't like him."

Steve lowered his mug. "What's likable about the guy? But I still haven't ruled him out as a suspect. Just because he's got a clean record doesn't mean he's not guilty."

Jack Daniel was surly, antisocial, grubby. He'd seemed extra grubby today. The man that had attacked her at Harley's house had been grubby. But the man had been bigger, huskier. The voice didn't fit... She remembered the attacker yelling at her. That might have altered the tone of his voice.

"I can see the wheels turning in your head."

Kate blinked, focusing on Steve. Now she noticed regret and affection in his eyes, which wrenched at her heart. She shook her head.

"Are you okay?"

"Never better." She left him sitting there, wondering...

꒞   ꒞   ꒞

Kate hung around the café for another hour, busying herself with side work that was a never-ending chore at the café. She'd let Carol take care of Steve. It was hard to be around him now that he knew her dirty secret. She would have to deal with him later.

After she left the café, she took care of a few errands. When she left the outskirts of town, it started snowing. Hard.

Flipping on the wipers, she slowed down. The sky was filled with plump, grey clouds, which were now pouring out their overflow. Lost in thought, she didn't hear the loud whine of a snowmobile until it was right next to her truck.

CHAPTER TWENTY-ONE

Flinching Kate turned the wheel, headed toward the high snow berm to her right. The driver glanced over at her, but his face was covered by a full face-guard helmet. Then he gassed it, sailing down the road.

By that time, Kate's right fender collided with the snow berm. "Dammit!" She shifted to neutral and climbed out to inspect the damage. There was a dent near her headlight. "Idiot driver," she mumbled as she climbed back into her truck.

She ought to call the cops, which of course would be Steve. The road she lived on was county, no snowmobiles allowed. Private roads were a different story.

It wasn't until she was home and adding wood to her stove that it finally struck her. The snowmobile had been trying to run her off the road. He'd been within inches of her truck, speeding until he was flush with her. Then giving her a look before he had gassed it. It had been a newer black Polaris and the driver had been dressed all in black, including his helmet. The driver was big, husky.

A newer Polaris had been seen on the logging road behind her house. A raw chill settled inside of her. Tailed by the dogs, she went into the kitchen, put the teapot onto to boil. When she spun around, Sunny and Ranger sat side by side, staring up at her with soulful eyes. She knelt down between them, hugged them to her. They responded with thumping tails and licks on her cheeks.

"I think you two deserve a treat." When Sunny heard the word treat, her ears perked up.

She pulled out two rawhide chew bones from the cupboard. Ranger barked while Sunny started dancing back and forth. "I'll even let you chew them inside today since it's snowing so hard." She handed out the treats. The dogs raced to the living room, so they could each stake out a good chewing spot.

Kate dunked a tea bag in the boiling water deciding to call Steve on his cell, bypassing Jenny.

"Sheriff Lambert."

She'd always liked the sound of his masculine voice. When they had made love, it had been masculine, sexy, throaty. Pushing those bittersweet memories aside because it hurt too damn much to remember.

"Is anybody there?" Steve asked.

"Yeah, it's me."

"Kate, what's going on?"

She heard the alarm in his voice. "I don't know if I'm overreacting or not, but I thou—"

Steve interrupted her. "What happened?"

"A snowmobile tried to run me off the road on my way home. At least, I think that's what he was doing."

"Are you hurt?"

"I dinged up my front fender when I hit the berm."

"I said, are you hurt?"

"No. I was going slow because it was snowing so hard."

"You just got home? Maybe I can get out there."

"Wait. I've been home for a little while. I had to add wo—"

Steve interrupted her again. "Dammit, Kate. Why didn't you call me as soon as you got home? And why in the hell don't you have a cell phone?"

Kate moved the phone a few inches from her ear as Steve's voice grew louder with each word. Yes, he had a masculine voice, a very loud masculine voice.

"Lock the doors. I'll be there in a few."

Kate lowered the phone, stared at it. She'd managed to piss him off. She realized it didn't take much for her to provoke him. Still holding the phone, Kate locked the back door first, then hurried into the living room, having to step over Ranger parked next to the door, gnawing at his treat.

"I hate this." The dogs ignored her. "I hate having to keep my doors locked." She strode back into the kitchen, put the phone away, picked up the mug of tea. She brooded as she leaned back against the counter, sipping her tea.

Every once and awhile, she glanced over her shoulder, out the window to survey the yard. The snow had let up. While it had snowed so hard, a good three inches had been added to the snow already accumulated on the ground.

"Oh, Harley..." she murmured. Just thinking of him had her wanting to blubber like a baby. With Steve on his way, she'd didn't want to be an emotional wreck when he arrived.

Hatred, swift and hard, bowled through her, causing her to clench her teeth. Harley's killer was free, running around harassing her. Literally getting away with murder. Kate took a deep breath, to calm herself in a futile attempt to even out her mood.

Steve. Steve on her mind wasn't much of a consolation. Something good between Steve and her had ended before it even had a chance to begin. Her confession of infidelity had brought their relationship to a screeching halt.

Her jaw started to ache from clenching her teeth so tight together. She opened her mouth worked it, then rolled her head back and forth hoping to ease the tension. The phone rang. She slid the mug on the counter, hurried to answer it, pausing as her hand hovered over the phone. What if it was the killer? Adrenaline started pumping through her body. She let it ring, her senses on red alert.

When the answering machine came on, Steve's voice bellowed out at her. "Where the hell are you?"

She snatched up the phone. "I'm right here."

"Why didn't you answer?"

She ignored his question. "Where are you?"

"I'm almost to your place, but I'm going to cruise the road and see what I can find. I wanted to check on you first."

Steve sounded concerned, worried about her welfare. Dare she hope that he might find it in himself to forgive her? "Okay."

"I'll be there in awhile. Are the doors locked?"

"Yeah."

"Good."

He didn't say good-bye, just ended the connection.

Kate finished her tea, continued to brood, paced the house, waiting for Steve. She should be working on her novel. Her emotions were too raw, too scrambled. Her adrenaline still pumped. Add anger to the mix and she was a real piece of work.

The dogs had finished their chewing competition. Now they sniffed the spot where the other one had chewed the treat. First Sunny trotted to the door, followed by Ranger. She opened the front door so they could go out. As soon as they were off the porch, she locked the door, her anger intensifying because of that fact.

She watched them through the window. After they both relieved themselves in the fresh snow, they started chasing each other back and forth across the yard. Sunny took a break by flopping on her back and rolling in the fresh snow. Ranger stood a few feet away, waiting for Sunny to finish her snow angel.

When the shot rang out, Kate was too stunned to move. Ranger hit the ground. Sunny rolled onto her stomach, ears up.

"Shit!" Kate was at the door, fighting to get in unlocked. She nearly busted through it before she got it unlocked. "Sunny, Ranger! Come now!"

Had one of them been hit? She didn't see any blood. Fear rooted her to the spot, not wanting to go out in the open, but she didn't want her dogs killed. Tails tucked between their legs, they beelined for the porch, Ranger in the lead. Sunny had barely got her hind end up on the porch when another shot cracked overhead.

Kate grabbed them by their collars. "Inside, now." She dragged them into the house, locked the door. She saw the fear in two sets of canine eyes. They were good watchdogs, but they had their limits. Kate ran to her bedroom, grabbed Harley's shotgun, checking to make sure it was loaded.

The dogs were crowded together behind the wood stove, sitting next to the wall, when she jogged back to the living room.

High powered rifle shots and close. Oh, God, too close.

Kate crept around the house, making sure she stayed away from windows. Since the dogs were scared into submission, she wondered if they would bark if someone was hiding outside near the house.

She had to call Steve. She crouched down, made her way across the kitchen to the phone, which sat on a small table in front of a big window. Kate flattened herself on the floor, crawled on her belly the last two feet, then reached her hand up to grab the phone, expecting her hand to be blown off.

When she safely had it clutched in her hand, she hit speed dial.

"Sheriff Lambert."

"Someone is shooting at me."

Steve's silence was one hundred times louder than the two gunshots.

"Tell me you're okay."

"Just terrified."

"I'm turning around now and I'm on my way back. Did he hit the house? I have to call for backup. For God's sake, stay down."

"Steve." The word died on her lips as he cut their connection.

Less than a minute later, the phone rang again. She needed to hear Steve's voice like she needed air to breath. "Steve."

"I'm long gone. Your sheriff will never catch me."

Terror like a hard, cold metal clamp wrapped tight around her body. Frozen, she listened to the silence at the other end of the line. He tried to kill her, then he taunted her.

Thumb shaking like a tall reed in the wind, Kate managed to hit the off button.

The squeal of sirens racing down the road finally brought her out of the paralyzing fear. She stood up, knees shaking. She hit speed dial again. Steve answered after the first ring.

"He just called. The bastard just called."

From the corner of her eye, she saw Steve's truck come to a stop at least twenty feet past her driveway, in the middle of her yard. He'd locked up his brakes.

"What did the son of a bitch say?"

Kate dragged in a breath. "I'm long gone. Your sheriff will never catch me. He disguised his voice again."

She heard the curse words roll off Steve's lips like water tumbling over rocks in a river. It was a dull roar inside her head.

"Stay inside. Do you hear me? Ron's on his way."

She angled to the window, watching Steve bend down as he climbed out, staying low behind the cover of the truck's door. A few minutes later, Ron Wood, Steve's deputy, roared up her driveway, ended up passing Steve with locked up brakes, finally stopping a few feet from the porch steps.

He imitated Steve when he climbed out. Kate watched the two men like a dream unraveling in front of her. Steve sprinted over to the deputy's cruiser, wearing a black bullet proof vest.

She wouldn't mind one.

A bubble of hysterical laughter escaped her. She wondered if the sheriff's department would loan her a vest. She could serve hot sausage and eggs while wearing one. Maybe the vests came with pockets to stash her order pad.

Get a grip.

Kate shook her head, took a big breath, willing herself to keep her cool. But her cool wanted to dash like a rabbit with a mountain lion hot on its trail. She focused on the two men. They were both behind the deputy's driver door now. Every few seconds, one would raise his head. While Ron Wood's blonde hair covered by the sheriff's ball cap glanced around the yard, her phone rang.

She glanced down at her left hand, realized she still had it gripped tight in her palm. "Steve."

"How long since the first shots were fired?"

She racked her brain. "Um...not sure. Maybe ten minutes. Maybe less. Maybe more."

"Two shots, then the phone call?"

"Yeah."

"We're coming in the house."

Kate wasn't sure how she managed to get to the front door, unlock it and open it with her knees bending like rubber. While Steve and Ron sprinted inside, guns at the ready, she dropped the phone at her feet, didn't care if one of the men smashed it with his foot. She still had a death grip around the shotgun.

Steve slammed the door behind him. The dogs trotted over to the men, still wary, tails wagging low.

Kate leaned against the wall next to the door, slid to the floor, holding the gun in front of her.

"Kate, are you okay?" Ron crouched down beside her, his blue filled with concern.

She nodded.

"Ron, check out the house. I'll see to Kate."

Steve knelt in front of her, pried the gun out of her hands. The last time the killer had attacked her in Harley's house, her adrenaline had leaped off the scale. She had chased after him, Harley's gun in her hand. This time the fear was too real, too close. Gunshots whizzing past her house, dogs, and her head was too much too handle.

Steve leaned her gun against the wall. He took her hand, his 9mm pointed at the floor. "Talk to me, honey."

Honey. He had never used a term of endearment before. She wanted to grab him, have him hug her so close she wouldn't be able to breathe.

"Kate."

She nodded.

His big hand held hers tight. "What direction did the shots come from?"

With her free hand, she pointed toward the kitchen.

"The west?"

"Yeah."

"That's the direction of your neighbors."

When Kate thought about that, she knew it was true. "Nobody should be home. The school bus hasn't gone by yet."

She heard Ron come back into the room, but she didn't look up.

"Everything is secured. All windows. Nothing disturbed," he said.

"Okay." Steve kept watching Kate.

"You want me to check around outside?" Ron asked.

Steve didn't answer him. "Do you know your neighbor's number?"

Kate rattled it off. Steve handed Kate's phone to Ron. "Call them to see if anybody's home. That's the direction the shots came from."

Without a word, Ron did what he was told. He lowered the phone. "I got the answering machine."

Steve glanced up at him. "Check outside. Keep low. Keep a tight perimeter around the house."

"Got it."

Ron disappeared outside. In silence the dogs laid down next to her.

"Kate, do you need to go to the hospital? I think you might be in shock."

When she heard the word shock, something broke inside of her. She blinked her eyes several times, stared at Steve. His blue eyes were so blue, but she'd always known that. The color was deep, the emotions behind the color were deep.

"No. I'll be okay." She started to stand. Steve gripped her hand harder, keeping her in place. "I want to get up."

"Only if you think you can stand."

That comment made her even more determined. "I can get up." The adrenaline combined with fear had left her weak-kneed, shaky, but she'd be damned if she would let the bastard bring her to her knees, which he had done so to speak.

Steve hoisted her to her feet. She leaned into him, at the same time his arm wrapped around her waist. "You're sure you're okay?"

Kate nodded before she laid her head on his shoulder. She felt his lips brush her hair near her temple. She closed her eyes, savored the moment of Steve holding her.

"We'll get him. I swear we'll get the bastard."

Kate wrapped her arms around Steve, held on for dear life, wanting and needing to believe him.

Steve kissed her temple. "I need to go help Ron."

She leaned back and looked into his eyes. It was the life-affirming thing again. She dragged his head down for a kiss. A long, sensual kiss in which Steve fully participated. Kate's heart swelled while her body warmed being so close to Steve again. When she leaned back, she said, "Maybe someday you'll forgive me."

"Kate," he breathed.

His radio attached to his belt crackled. He reached for it. Kate let him slip out of her arms.

Over the static she heard Ron's voice, couldn't exactly make out the words.

"I'll be right there."

"Ron found something."

"What?"

"We'll talk when we get back." Steve reached around her for the door. "Lock the door behind me, keep your gun with you just to be on the safe side."

Kate nodded. Before Steve walked outside, he glanced back her, burned her with a long, level look before the door closed behind him.

Kate hugged herself, wishing it was Steve. She shouldn't have kissed him, considering he was holding her one night stand against her. She'd done it on impulse. Just like her one night fling. A fling she had regretted the instant she had come to her senses in the king-sized bed at the Comfort Inn in Butte.

She locked the door, caught a glimpse of Steve disappearing around the side of her house. Kate bent to get the gun, but before she picked it up, she patted both dogs on their heads, cooed some soft words to them. She leaned against the door, closing her eyes and prayed everything would be okay soon.

And that meant everything in her life.

※　※　※

As Steve tramped through the snow to Ron's location, he struggled to forget the touch of Kate's lips. He hadn't realized how much he had missed touching her, tasting her, until she'd dragged his head down and kissed him like there was no tomorrow.

No tomorrow was a damned, definite possibility for Kate, Ron, for anybody. Life was precious. As a cop, he'd learned that sad fact years ago.

He spotted Ron waving at him.

Steve cursed himself for not putting on his snow boots. All thoughts of practicality had vanished when Kate kissed him. By the time he reached his deputy, he was back into cop mode.

"What did you find?"

Ron turned and pointed. "There are two empty casings. Looks like 30-06 rounds to me. And lots of boot tracks."

Steve nodded. 30-06 shells. The same caliber that killed the sow grizzly. They had to be connected. Steve had believed that theory to a degree. But now...

"Let's see if we can get those shells and not disturb the tracks. We need to measure the tracks and take photos."

"My gear is back at my truck. I'll go get it."

Steve didn't look at his deputy. "Good." He was trying to figure a way to get those shells without disturbing the tracks. Hell, he was already soaked up the knees.

He trudged through the snow, ignoring his damp uniform trousers. When he was directly behind the two empty casings, he snapped off two thin twigs of the pine tree he was standing next to. The he crouched down, tried to pick up the first shell with the twig, but he couldn't get close enough. "Shit." Steve laid flat on his belly, feeling the snow soaking through his trousers. At least his jacket was waterproof. He pushed the first twig into the shell. Then carefully did the same for the second shell.

By the time he was standing, holding an empty casing by a twig in each hand, Ron reappeared.

"Damn, Steve, did you dive into the snow to get the casings?"

Steve scowled. "The snow has let up for now. I didn't want these getting wet."

Ron nodded, setting a large plastic toolbox on the snow. "The perp probably wore gloves."

"True. But if he loaded at home, hopefully he was careless enough to use his bare hands."

Ron nodded and pulled out two small plastic zip lock bags. Steve trudged back over to Ron, careful not to drop the shells. Ron held the bags open while Steve dropped a shell into each. It wasn't until Ron sealed the bags that Steve started to breathe easier.

"Let's measure the boot tracks first."

Ron dug out a tape measure, a small notepad and pencil from the toolbox. They worked in silence. Steve had always appreciated that particular characteristic in his deputy. Ron was thorough, seemed to know when to talk and when to keep quiet. He was young, late twenties, but had keen instincts.

After they measured the boot tracks, Ron snapped digital photos of them. Ron glanced at Steve. "I'd guess size eleven.

Weight approximately one seventy-five. Puts more weight on his left foot."

"Why do you think that?"

Ron pointed to one track. "Looks like more weight by the indentation."

Steve took a step, crouching down next to the track. "I do believe you're right." He looked up at his deputy. "How did you know that?"

Ron took one last picture before he answered, "Marine training. Know your enemy. That even means whether or not they had a bowel movement for the day."

Steve had never been in the military. "Impressive."

Ron grinned.

"Why would he put more weight on the left foot?"

Ron returned the camera to its case. "Hard to say. He doesn't have a limp. Everybody has one foot bigger than the other. He might have a back or leg problem. Maybe he never learned how to walk correctly."

Steve's lips twitched up at the corner. Even he knew how to spot a limp through mud or snow. "Watching this bastard walk, you might not notice there's a slight favor to his left foot."

"Slim chance."

A chill invaded Steve's body. Now he would have to either go home and change or go back to the station where he kept a spare uniform. "How much farther did you go?"

"I hightailed it up to the old skidder road. Saw lots of snowmobile tracks. Fresh."

"Kate said she thought it was a newer Polaris that tried to run her off the road."

"All the newer ones have identical tracks. Polaris is the most popular model around here, probably in the entire state of Montana."

"That's the problem."

"I didn't find any other evidence. I did a thorough search." Ron closed his toolbox. "Just tracks and those empty casings."

Big snowflakes drifted lazily from the sky. They had retrieved and recorded the evidence just in time. "Let's head back." Kate had been left alone long enough.

CHAPTER TWENTY-TWO

Kate paced around Steve's living room while he showered and changed into dry clothes. Bottled up nervous energy kept her on the move. By the time they had arrived at his house, he'd been shivering. Steve had refused to leave her alone.

She decided his house was nice, a bit on the Spartan side, definitely a bachelor place, but not a pad. A group of framed photographs hung on one wall. The photos were all of his daughter at various ages, ranging from a happy baby to high school graduation with her royal blue cap and gown and Steve with his arm around her. She resembled him. She was tall and slender with the same eyes only light brown hair instead of black.

There was an oil painting of a mountain range in spring, with two mountains goats perched on a ledge. A brown leather couch sat in the middle of the room. The couch had seen some wear, along with the matching leather recliner.

Masculine. Manly. Just like him.

Kate decided to make herself useful, strolled into the kitchen. The wood table was handmade with carvings of moose scattered across the top and carved on the chair backs, too. Kate figured the oblong table and four chairs had cost him a pretty penny. She rummaged around in his cupboards, saw that he must eat out more often than not, because his cupboards barely contained the basics.

She found a box with two packets of instant cocoa, put water onto boil, started scavenging for two mugs.

She had just finished making the cocoa when she heard Steve come into the kitchen. She glanced over her shoulder. He was fresh scrubbed, his hair slightly damp at the ends. It was late in the day so he must have decided the hell with his uniform. He wore new blue jeans, black and light blue checkered flannel shirt. Kate turned back to stirring the cocoa because he looked so good. She battled back a powerful urge to walk over to him, unbutton his clean shirt.

She picked up the two mugs. "I thought you might like some cocoa."

"Sure, thanks."

Kate carried the mugs to the table. They sat down across from each other. Steve seemed to be studying her. In fact, his gaze was so direct she started to feel uncomfortable. "Nice table set."

He glanced down at the tabletop like it was the first time he had seen it. "Ah, yeah." He picked up his mug, blowing at the steam rising from it.

Kate did the same. Suddenly she felt as awkward as a thirteen-year-old girl at her first school dance, leaning against the wall trying to not feel too much like a wallflower. She took a small sip, stole a peek at Steve, who was watching her again. She slowly put down her mug. "Would you mind telling me why you keep staring at me?"

"I like looking at you."

His answer had been so direct, so honest she felt her cheeks warm. "Oh."

"You're a very attractive woman, Kate. But I think I already told you that."

The first night they had made love. He had whispered in her ear how attractive she was, how hot. Kate cleared her throat, hoping her face hadn't turned redder. Then she realized this could be the brush off. Start off with a couple of positives to soften the blow. Their relationship had been hanging in the balance since her admission of infidelity.

She wrapped both hands around the heavy mug. "Is this the brush off?"

While Steve took his time drinking more cocoa, her heart pounded hard. A sick feeling pooled in her stomach.

He lowered his mug. "I don't know what to do about you."

Her heart still pounded, and her stomach still had the sick feeling. Kate didn't know how to answer that, so she shrugged.

"I should be down at the station following leads, searching for the bastard that tried to shoot you. Instead, I brought you to my house..."

Kate glanced down at her mug, realizing the hot cocoa had lost its appeal, but she held onto the warm mug for comfort.

"I know why my wife cheated. I neglected her. It goes with the territory when you're a cop. I took her for granted."

"Is that what you're asking me? If I was neglected, taken for granted so therefore, I was driven to cheat on my husband."

She noticed how Steve's jaw tightened, his lips pressing tight together. "That's it, isn't it?" Kate shook her head, disappointment washing through her. "You're hoping I have a valid reason for cheating, for breaking my marriage vows, or at least an understandable reason."

"Maybe."

She shoved the mug aside, spilling cocoa on Steve's expensive handmade table. Kate reached across the table, poked his hand with her forefinger, then held it up in front of him.

"One time. One lousy time. One time out of almost twenty years. One fucking time."

Steve grabbed her hand. "Stop it, Kate."

"You asked. Oh, not in so many words. You want to know the dirt, all the dirt. Why I cheated."

Kate tried to pull her hand free, but Steve tightened his grip. "David is full of himself, always has been, always will be. I worked hard so my kid wouldn't turn out like his father. But now my son barely talks to me. I know David has taken advantage of my mistake concerning my son." Kate paused, feeling the tears crowd her eyes. "David was hung up on appearances, money. I met him in college. He was a jock, good looking, and I got reeled in, so I married him. Sometimes I felt like he was the shallowest man on earth."

"And." She stopped, bit her lip, trying to free her hand, but Steve hung on.

"And what?"

"Never mind. And please let go of my hand."

"I'm not letting go of your hand. What else? You were going to tell me something else."

Anger rushed through her like an unexpected harsh windstorm. "You know something. I don't have to bare my soul to you. I already did. Look where it got me."

"I'm trying to understand here." Steve reached across the table for her other hand, but she snatched it away, stuck it under the table.

"Why can't you just understand I'm human?" She fisted her hand resting on her thigh.

"Kate, I'm sorry. I've had a thing for you since the first time I saw you. There's always been something about you."

He'd had a thing for her since he'd met her. Oh, she'd felt the attraction. But she figured it was just that. Sexual attraction. Now Steve made it sound like more, more than she had imagined. "Sorry to disappoint you."

"Don't."

"What the hell am I supposed to do?"

Steve shook his head and let go of her hand. He stood up, walked over to the window.

"I really loved my wife. When she told me she loved another man." He paused. "I felt like I had been ambushed. I didn't see it coming. Now I know I should have, but I didn't." Steve turned to face her. "You're not Tess. You two are as different as night and day."

Kate wondered if that was good or bad, the difference between Steve's ex-wife and herself.

"I want you," Steve said. His eyes locked on hers. "I want to make love to you. I want to drag you to my bed and devour you."

The heat of his gaze stretched across the room, burning her senses. Before she could answer, Steve's cell phone rang.

"Dammit." He scowled, let it ring.

"You have to answer it."

Steve cursed again before he went to the counter for his phone. "Yeah?"

While Steve listened, Kate shifted her gaze to the window, her heart swelling with emotions. He still wanted her. But had he forgiven her?

"That was Ron. He's fairly certain the shells we found today match the shell casings that killed the grizzly sow. Fish and Wildlife had bullets and casings tested, hoping for a match."

Kate glanced back at him digesting the significance of Steve's news. Harley had known who killed the bear, had most likely confronted him. That's why he had died. "How can he be so sure so soon?"

"Ron's not a hundred percent. He has to do more tests, but right now it's about as close as we can get. We'll get more information tomorrow."

Steve switched into cop mode. Kate knew in her heart it wouldn't have been necessary for him to drag her to his bedroom because she would have gone willingly. Like a lovesick fool.

✄   ✄   ✄

Agitation worked at Steve like a woodpecker hammering at a tree trunk. Kate was at her computer. He assumed she was working. He'd spent the last hour on the phone. First, a lengthy conversation with Ron, the next with Bob from Fish and Wildlife. He'd managed to get hold of a tech, working overtime, at the Kalispell lab. Windy Creek didn't have the technology to run extensive ballistic tests.

Ron had volunteered to take the bullet casings to the lab on his day off since he was going to Kalispell anyway. Since there hadn't been any other murders lately, the lab would give it top priority.

Bob at Fish and Wildlife took his job as seriously as Steve. He took it personally when a wild animal was shot. Grizzlies were on the endangered species list. The way Bob talked one would think every grizzly in the state of Montana was his pet. That was a good thing because he'd commissioned ballistic tests on the casings found at the grizzly kill three years ago.

Steve paced Kate's living room, still holding his phone. He caught the dogs staring at him from their cozy positions next to the wood stove. Sunny and Ranger kept their distance from him, probably because they had picked up on his agitated mood. He dropped his cell phone on the end table next to the couch when he paced by it.

Even if the shell casings were a perfect match to the ones found at the grizzly kill, it wouldn't necessarily bring him any closer to Harley's killer. The Kalispell lab hadn't been able to match the casings to a gun or an owner for the grizzly shooting. Guns were passed around like a bowl of popcorn at a party. People bought and sold them privately. People bought them at gun shows, which were regular events in Montana. And people stole guns all the time, never to be seen again.

Steve paused by the window, raking a hand through his hair. The frustration of knowing Harley's killer was still at large pounded him. He wanted Harley's killer so bad he could taste it.

The frustration level moved up a notch for Kate. He wanted her so damn bad he kept fighting back powerful urges to take her in her office.

"Jesus," he mumbled.

He spun around when he heard her come into the room. She stopped. Something about his expression had her watching him with suspicion. He plowed his hand through his hair again, struggling to tamp down his emotions. "Ron's going to drop the casings off in Kalispell tomorrow. The lab promised to get right on it."

Kate nodded, walked to the wood stove, adding another log to the fire. Her shoulders were stiff, her body rigid.

"How's your writing going?" They needed to talk about something other than Harley's killer and the stand off in their relationship.

Kate lifted a shoulder. "Okay. I'm not having my best writing moments lately."

"That's understandable."

She didn't answer.

"What's this book about?"

"Did you read my other books?"

He'd read each one twice. "Yeah, I did." It was the first time they had ever discussed her writing career. "I liked them."

Kate seemed surprised. "Thanks."

She pulled the pink plastic clip out of her thick dark hair, causing it to tumble around her face. She impatiently shoved it back. "Another mystery."

Steve wanted to go to her, comb her messy hair back from her face, then kiss her down to the floor. He shoved his hands into the front pockets of his jeans. He could see she wasn't in the mood to discuss her latest book. Then what the hell could they talk about? "Do you need to work at the café?"

Kate fiddled with the hair clip. "I like the extra money. I'm not on The New York's Times best seller list, probably never will be. Working at the café supplements my income. Not all writers are rolling in dough."

He'd found her novels engaging, suspenseful, and very good reads. Was that because he had the hots for her and hadn't been objective when he'd read her books? Or was she truly an outstanding writer that hadn't been given the acclaim she deserved? "I'm not a literary critic, that's for sure, but I thought your books were damn good." He wished like hell he saw some kind of appreciation in her eyes.

"Thanks."

He'd never told her before that he'd read her books. He'd bought her two books at the local store. Steve had wanted her to sign them for him, but he'd held back, not wanting her to know his true feelings. "Maybe you'll sign them for me sometime." He'd seen the locals bring them into the café to have Kate autograph her books for them.

"We don't do very good talking about normal stuff, do we?"

Steve frowned, realizing Kate was right. They were struggling to make normal conversation. If things were going better between the two of them, Kate would undoubtedly be pleased that he'd read her books. For the past year, they had chatted at the café about everyday things. Since Harley had been murdered, they'd been thrown together, but conversation had been mostly about Harley and the man stalking Kate.

"Would you like something to drink?"

"You don't have to go to any trouble."

"Usually you like your hot cocoa in the evening."

"Yeah, I do. I can make it. I'm not that bumble footed in the kitchen."

"Okay then, I'd like some, too."

She crossed her arms over her chest, studying him. Her face wasn't giving any thing away. Steve sauntered into the kitchen. He filled the kettle with water and turned on the burner. He started opening cupboard doors in search of mugs and the instant cocoa. He found the bag of marshmallows first. He heard Kate come up behind him.

"Cocoa is to the left, top shelf. Mugs are on the bottom shelf next to the sink." Steve found the mugs, the box of instant cocoa before he turned to face her. "I would have found them."

She merely arched a brow before she sat down at the table. Steve wasn't sure why Kate watching him made him edgy. The problem was he was already edgy. Now that they were in the same room together, his desire for her burned hotter. He concentrated on making the cocoa.

When he brought the mugs to the table, she was still watching him. Her eyes were full of anger, irritation, annoyance? He sat down across from her, locked eyes with her.

She poked at the marshmallows floating on top of the cocoa with her spoon. Steve did the same. "Stop looking at me that way, Kate."

Her hand stilled. "What way?"

"Like you want to punch me in the nose."

"How did you know that's what I wanted to do?"

Steve yanked a paper napkin out of the holder in the center of the table, laid his spoon on it. "Gut feeling."

"Big surprise." Her words were coated with sarcasm.

"I deserved that dig."

Anger colored her cheeks a pale shade of pink. "Yeah, you did."

He drank the cocoa, struggling not to grind his back molars together as he sipped. Anger sprouted inside of him, too. The damned thing was, he didn't know who he was pissed off at, Kate or himself. "Point taken."

Silence thick with agitation hung over the two of them as they drank their cocoa. Steve was good at waiting out a suspect, getting him to crack. With Kate, he was losing his patience, but then she wasn't a criminal. She was a woman he wanted more than was good for his peace of mind. He stood up so fast his chair fell over with a loud thud.

Surprised, Kate looked up at him. He wasn't even halfway around the small table when he reached for her arm, dragging her to her feet.

She pushed at his chest, but he ignored her protests as his lips crushed hard against hers.

Once his tongue bullied inside her mouth, she stopped protesting. Kate's moan of pleasure had the blood pounding in his veins. With his hands, he cupped her bottom, pressing her belly against his groin. Kate nipped at his bottom lip, did wondrous things with her tongue.

"Kate."

She nipped at his tongue again, unbuttoning his shirt. He peeled her black turtleneck sweater over her head, dropping it to the floor. After Steve freed her breasts from her black lace bra, he lowered his head, drawing her hard nipple into his mouth.

And as usual, they struggled and ripped at each other's clothing.

Steve lifted Kate's silky hot body, sitting her on the table. She reached him for as he plunged inside of her so hard and fast his head spun.

Steve caught one of her nipples between his teeth. Kate's nails raking down his back fueled his desire for her, his insatiable need for her. Steve sought out her lips, frenched her until he couldn't breathe, their tongues ravenous with greedy hunger. Covering her breasts with his hands, Steve's lips slid down to her neck.

Nipping at her soft flesh, he felt Kate's body release itself, a throaty scream tumbling from her. Steve couldn't hold back any longer. His teeth clenched together, he emptied himself inside of her heat.

Steve leaned his forehead on her soft shoulder, slick with sweat. When his breathing returned to normal, he looked her.

Her face was flushed. And her eyes were still flooded with anger.

CHAPTER TWENTY-THREE

Kate had refused to let Steve share her bed last night. As she dumped dirty dishes into a large grey tote, she was surprised they weren't all broken into jagged pieces. She'd gone to bed angry, had slept angry, and was still roiling with anger.

The chatter and laughter behind her from the few customers still lingering after the morning rush didn't register with her. She hefted up the tote full of dirty dishes, walking toward the kitchen. Her mind on Steve, she bumped into Hal Jackson.

"Why the hell don't you watch where you're going, Katie?"

Kate wanted to hiss at him like an incensed alley cat ready to attack. She maneuvered around him, not even bothering to apologize. She didn't give a damn if she had rammed into him or not.

She dumped the heavy tote on the counter, then stormed into Clara's office. In the top desk drawer, she found the pack of Marlboro's that Clara kept for emergencies. Clara quit smoking four years ago, but still had an occasional cigarette when the need arose. Kate had quit ten years ago, but followed Clara's pattern, too. On occasion she bummed a cigarette. She tipped the pack, slid one out, grabbing the red disposable lighter and headed out back.

"Where you going, Kate?" Clara called as she turned the doorknob.

"I stole one of your smokes," Kate said over her shoulder.

"Uh...oh."

Kate walked outside, lit the cigarette, inhaled deep. The temperature had risen up to the mid-thirties. The sky was dark, loaded with pregnant clouds. She knew it would either snow or rain before the day was over. If it rained, all the snow packed roads would turn into a nightmare. The packed down snow would absorb the water, turning the snow into the consistency of mud. Or it would rain just enough to freeze them over night, turning the roads into an ice skating rink.

Kate took another drag, blew out the smoke, listened to a dog barking a few blocks behind the café. She leaned back against the door, wishing last night with Steve had never happened. Their lovemaking had been too carnal, too...too...she wasn't sure what.

Kate felt someone pushing on the door, so she stepped out of the way, figuring it was Clara come to find out what was on her mind. She hadn't even had a cigarette when Harley died.

Instead, Steve walked outside. Kate glared at him, took another drag. Now he would have smoking to hold against her.

He closed the door behind him. Then reached for her cigarette. She snatched it away from him. "You're not taking it away from me. I used to smoke. I still have one on occasion."

"I used to smoke, too."

Surprised, Kate let him have the cigarette, watching him raise it to his lips and inhale. When Steve gave it back to her their fingers touched, zapping her with his electricity. Their eyes caught, Kate remembering last night, wondering if Steve was doing the same. "What's going on?"

Steve took off his ball cap, plowing his hand through his hair before settling the hat back on his head. "I just stopped by to see how you were doing."

Kate lifted her chin. "I'm doing just fine."

His expression said he didn't believe her. "I'm going down to Fish and Wildlife to see if I can dig up any leads there."

Kate nodded, savoring the last drag of the cigarette before she dropped it, grinding it out with her shoe. She bent down to pick up the butt. "Okay," she said.

"Okay." Steve opened the door, waited for her to go through first.

They didn't speak as they wound their way back to the kitchen.

><   ><   ><

Steve spent an hour at the Fish and Wildlife headquarters, a mile north of town. Bob loaned him an empty office with a computer. The one thing Steve had learned was that some poachers kept poaching until all hunting rights were revoked. Just like a street criminal, they kept breaking the law, believing they could get away with it. Steve leaned back in his chair, scrubbed a hand down his face, then rolled his shoulders a couple of times to loosen the tension.

Fatigue rolled through him like a mist over a mountain lake. He had laid on the hide-a-bed, burning with a need so strong for Kate that he figured the bed might ignite from spontaneous combustion. That's how damn bad he wanted her. After their wild, hard, lovemaking on her kitchen table, she had gathered up her clothes, stomped out of the room without so much as a backward glance.

Steve cursed under his breath.

Bob strolled into the room with a mug in one hand and a Styrofoam cup in the other. "I figured you could use some coffee by now." He handed the Styrofoam cup to Steve.

"Thanks," Steve said.

Bob sat down across the desk from him. "You've been in here a long time. Have you found anything?"

Steve shook his head, sipping the bitter black brew. Bob was mid-forties, nearly bald, with twinkling green eyes, a weathered face, a hard, compact body.

"A heck of a lot of poachers manage to stay under the radar," Bob said. "There are too many unsolved cases to count."

Steve realized Bob was right. It had been a long shot to sift through the old computer files, but he needed any crumb he could dig up. "You know Jack Danielson?"

"You mean Jack Daniel?"

Steve nodded.

"He's got a clean nose as far as I can tell," Bob said. "Doesn't mean he's not guilty of anything. Just means he's never been caught doing anything illegal."

"You hit a wall with the grizzly sow?"

Bob nodded. "Pretty much. Except for the empty bullet casings and the slugs we dug out of the bear, which were a match."

Both men were silent as they drank their coffee. Bob broke the silence first. "We're not CSI here. If we find shells and casings that we can match on our database, then we're in hog heaven. If there happens to be a witness, then we're in hog, hog heaven. Unless someone leaves a sign that said I did it, our hands our tied.

There was no evidence at the grizzly scene. We got lucky and found the empty shells. That was it. Nobody in the area saw or heard a thing. People come forward when we ask. The good guys will report any suspicious doings if they witness it. Our main concern back then was catching the cubs, taking care of them. It happened in late October. Hibernation wasn't that far around the corner."

"Do you think that particular bear kill was an accident?"

Bob shrugged. "Who knows? If a kill is self-defense, the person will usually report it. Grizzlies might be endangered, but you still have a right to protect yourself. If it's an accident, the hunter mistaking it for a black bear and they report it, we keep it to a minimum fine, a slap on the wrist. This was a big mistake. A sow with cubs. The cubs were born the winter before. It's against the law to shoot a black bear sow with cubs, let alone a grizzly sow with cubs. A responsible hunter will watch the bear for a good amount of time to determine there aren't any cubs near. Young cubs don't wander that far from their mama. Even yearlings stick close."

Steve finished his coffee, stared down at the empty cup.

"You think whoever killed that sow, killed Harley Wilson?"

"It's a possibility."

Bob thumped his mug on the desk, crossed his arms over his chest. "I knew Harley for years. I transferred here fifteen years ago. He was a good old guy, went by the book when it came to hunting. We bumped into each other at the café a few years ago, had lunch together. He didn't like poachers. Animals shot for no reason. He had damn strong opinions on that subject."

"Yeah, that's what I understand. I didn't know him that well."

"Harley was the type of guy that would have confronted the bastard that shot the sow."

"I've learned that, too."

"Why did you ask me about Jack Daniel?"

Steve stared at his empty cup again, wishing he had more. "I consider him a suspect, but I have no concrete evidence."

"He's a strange one for sure. I know he fills every tag he can fill every year. He undoubtedly needs the meat."

"How many tags can he get?" Since Steve didn't hunt, he wasn't up on the limits for each individual hunter.

"He can get a general buck tag, elk tag, and then he usually applies for a special doe permit in his area."

"So he can get two deer and an elk?"

"If he's lucky."

"Does he apply for bear tags?"

Bob leaned forward and picked up the phone on the desk. "Molly, I need you to check to see if Jack Danielson has ever applied for a bear hunt."

Molly, Bob's assistant, called back a few minutes later. "Thanks, Molly." Bob replaced the phone. "He's never applied for one."

"Thanks, I appreciate your help." Steve crumbled up the Styrofoam cup in his hand, out of frustration and a strong feeling of impotence because he was no closer to finding Harley's killer than he was when he walked inside the Fish and Wildlife building over an hour ago.

"I'll ask my people about Jack Daniel, see if they've ever got wind of any suspicious behavior from him."

"Anybody else that shows up on your radar, I would appreciate a holler," Steve said.

"Will do."

CHAPTER TWENTY-FOUR

"It's a match, Steve."

Steve swung his truck into the side parking lot of the sheriff's station. He pressed the phone closer to his ear, to make sure he'd heard Ron correctly. "You're positive?" He killed the engine.

"Jason down at the lab ran the tests for me as soon as I got there. By the time I finished my errands, he had the reports. Jason had a slow morning, so he ran the bullet casings through and nothing came up, no owner of the rifle, no previous owner. The gun has never been used in a crime. Kate's shooter is the same as the grizzly sow. Unless the gun has changed hands."

The same rifle used in two crimes. It didn't mean squat if he didn't know who owned the gun. "Thanks, Ron. Enjoy the rest of your day off."

"Will do."

Steve climbed out of his truck, trudged toward the building, feeling at least seventy years old with the weight of this case he carried on his shoulders.

※　※　※

When Kate's shift was finished at the café, she headed home, her .22 pistol on her lap. Harley's hunting rifle was on the floor, barrel propped against the passenger seat. Anger still festered inside of her. She had to drive to and from work armed per Steve's orders.

Kate kept glancing at her rear view mirror. The road was usually empty of traffic mid-afternoon on weekdays. The brown UPS trucking came rolling toward her. Tom, the driver, tooted his horn at her when he passed. She did the same. So far, so good, she reassured herself as she cruised down the road. She let up on the gas when she spotted two deer poised on the side of the road, ready to cross. The deer waited until she passed by them.

As she turned into her driveway, she let out a sigh of relief. When her house came into view, the dogs leaped off the porch, ran to meet her. She stopped her truck, studying her house. She glanced around the yard. Everything looked okay. Sunny started barking when she stayed inside her truck. She pushed open the door.

"Okay, okay, I'm coming."

After she gave Sunny and Ranger their due, she grabbed her purse, both guns, then locked the truck doors. That just added to her displeasure. She'd never locked her truck since she'd returned to Windy Creek.

Inside the house, the dogs at her heels, Kate inspected each and every room. Holding a gun in each hand she walked from room to room, even checked the closets. The last thing she checked was the back door to make sure it was still locked.

She expelled another breath, a combination of relief and frustration. After she put her things away, she put the kettle onto boil. She was rummaging through the bright red tin, with a jolly Santa Claus on the top for a pack of Irish Breakfast tea, when the phone rang. Ever since the two threatening calls from Harley's killer she cringed involuntarily at the sound of it.

She walked over to the phone, waiting for the answering machine to pick up.

"Kate, you should be home by now. I called the café. Clara said you were going straight home. Where the hell are you?"

She could have picked up as soon as she heard Steve at the other end. Instead, she listened to his angry voice. He'd been angry when he'd made love to her last night. She picked up the phone. "I'm here."

"What took you so damn long to answer?"

"I was in the bathroom," she lied.

Steve's answer sounded sort of like a grunt.

"Did anything happen on the drive home?" he asked.

"No."

"Good."

An awkward silence followed. They had talked briefly at the café. She was still surprised that Steve had a vice. He used to smoke. He still did on occasion. His worse vice seemed to be he cussed a lot, especially when he was pissed off. She, on the other hand, overflowed with the afflictions of humankind.

"The bullets we found at your place yesterday matched the ones that killed the grizzly."

Kate wasn't surprised. "Were you able to identity the gun?"

There was a long pause. "No. The gun has never been tracked for a previous crime."

Disappointment oozed through her like thick sludge. "Oh."

"Bob at Fish and Wildlife is going to talk to his people, see if any of his crew remember Jack Daniel doing anything suspicious over the past couple of years."

"What if we're barking up the wrong tree?"

There was another long pause from Steve's end. "It's possible. Hell, anything is possible. It wouldn't be the first time myself, or another cop, has taken the wrong road."

At least Steve admitted he could be wrong.

"There's nobody else in our sights," he said. "It could be someone riding under the radar."

When she didn't answer, Steve said. "Kate, are you still there?"

"Yeah, I'm here." She knew without a doubt Steve was doing his best. Tragically some crimes were never solved, which compounded her anger. If not caught and brought to justice, Harley's killer could continue to live in Windy Creek, go about his business, have his freedom. The killer had taken all those things away from Harley. Now the killer, threatening her, had taken away a good many of her freedoms. She would like nothing better than to take the dogs for a walk through the woods, feel the cold winter breeze on her face, listen to the chatter of the resident squirrels.

"Dammit, Kate. Talk to me."

"Sorry, I was lost in thought."

Another pause. "What were you thinking about?" Steve's voice lowered.

If she told Steve she wanted to go for a walk, he would burn her ear off with four letter words. "Oh, this and that." She heard the kettle whistling behind her so she hurried back to the stove. With the phone wedged between her ear and shoulder, she made her tea. "Thanks for calling, I have to go. I have some stuff I need to do."

"Is your stuff needing to be done inside the house?"

"Of course," she lied again.

"Why don't I believe you?"

"Because you're suspicious by nature." Her comment was good for three colorful words from Steve.

"Just behave yourself. I'll be over later."

Before she could answer, he clicked off. Kate carried her tea into the living room, sat down on the couch, starting going through her mail strewn on the coffee table. She had neglected her mail for the past week. She made three stacks on the table. One for junk, one for bills, and one for miscellaneous mail. After she sorted her mail, she got up and added a few logs to the fire. The dogs were lying on either side of the stove, both watching her, begging for a romp in the woods, if their canine expressions could be trusted.

"Why the heck not?" she asked Sunny. Her yellow and brown ears lifted.

"I'm tired of being a prisoner in my own house." She said this to Ranger. He thumped his tail twice on the floor in response.

Kate retrieved her tea from the coffee table, drank the last few sips, then hurried down to her room to change into her snow pants and boots.

Ten minutes later, they were strolling through the woods behind her house. She had the pistol strapped to her hip and carried the hunting rifle in her right hand. Her snowshoes slapped up and down with each step she took. When she reached the logging road, she hesitated. She whistled for the dogs. They were trotting down it where they could make better time. Sunny and Ranger turned, racing back to her.

She didn't want to be a moving target. The road would be easier to walk on because it was packed down from the snowmobile traffic. Since she had on her snowshoes, she could go just about anywhere. She crossed the road into the trees. The dogs followed, walking, leaping, pushing through the snow where it was too deep for them.

Kate lost track of time as she trekked through the woods. She saw a half dozen deer, heard numerous squirrels quarreling, listened to the call of a raven cruising low, barely skimming the treetops. She paused by a narrow creek that meandered through the woods, where the dogs stood at the edge, lapping water. She pulled the small bottle she had brought with her from her jacket pocket and drank, too.

"Time to head home."

The dogs rushed to get ahead of her. Her head was clearer, even her emotions to a point. Kate retraced her steps back toward the logging road. Her heart ached to think Harley's killer might go free, never be brought to justice. Life wasn't fair, she had learned. But there were certain things that needed to be fair. Like murderers caught and punished.

When she spotted the clearing for the road, the dogs started barking, barreling toward it. Kate whistled, called for them. "Sunny, Ranger, no!"

Goosebumps popped out on her warm flesh, because she had worked up a mild sweat trudging through the snow. She raised the rifle, flicked off the safety. She paused, her heart rate kicking up speed. Kate crept toward the road, knowing there was somebody there. At the edge of the trees, she spotted a man.

CHAPTER TWENTY-FIVE

When he turned and spotted her, Kate groaned out loud. She walked the last few feet to the road. Steve stood in the middle of it, hands on hips, his expression contorted into an angry glare. The dogs, oblivious to his foul temper, frolicked around him, excited to see him.

Kate locked the safety back into place. Lowering the gun, she walked over to him, refusing to break eye contact. "What are you doing out here?" She knew it was a stupid question, but she didn't have anything better.

She kept a slight distance from him, because his eyes felt like they were boring holes into her.

He moved close to her, leaned his head down and got right in her face. "A better question would be, what the hell are you doing out here?"

If he was trying for intimidation, it had worked. She'd seen Steve angry many times, but not quite to this level before. She pushed back the urge to step back, slink away like a naughty child. "I went for a walk."

"No shit," he growled.

"I needed a walk."

"You need to be safe."

She held up the rifle, the stock banging him in the chest. "I'm armed. I have two guns and two dogs."

Steve straightened up, took the gun out of her hands. Kate didn't try to stop him. She figured that wasn't a good idea. He continued to stare at her, his face ablaze with anger. "How about some hot cocoa?"

"You're not getting off that easy."

"Send me to my room without dinner. Okay."

The litany of words that followed was not pretty. Kate decided a lady shouldn't have to hear those words. But she knew them all, had used a few herself. She reached up, placing her hand over Steve's mouth. "Stop. Just stop it. I know it was a dumb thing to do, but I needed it."

Steve removed her hand from his face, but held it tight between them. He didn't curse anymore, just stared at her hard.

"I'm not going to apologize if that's what you're waiting for. I needed a break. You do too." Kate glanced down, saw that he was wearing a pair of black knee high gators and snow boots. At least this time he wasn't getting soaked to his skin. She looked back at him. "Let's walk for a while. It might release some of your pent up anger."

Steve turned, still holding her hand and started back across the road in the direction of her house. Oh, it was clear he wasn't in the mood for a leisurely stroll. Kate tried to tug her hand free, but Steve wouldn't let go. He wasn't actually dragging her, but she struggled to keep up.

When they reached her yard, all that way in stony silence, Kate figured he would release her hand, but he walked her to the porch, up the steps to the door. He leaned the rifle against the house, then tried the knob.

Kate dug her key out of her pocket, believing she deserved points for locking up her house. Without a word or a glance, Steve took the key from her hand, unlocked the door. She had barely unbuckled her snowshoes and stepped out of them when he grabbed the gun and pulled her inside. He locked it behind him, then still holding her hand, he started toward the hallway.

Kate's heart danced a crazy tango while heat surged through her body. Talk about macho, caveman. Inside her bedroom, he leaned down to kiss her. She leaned back. "You think because you're pissed off, you can have sex with me?"

"You got a better idea?" Steve's tone was low, guttural.

Kate didn't answer. Steve kissed her hard, then unzipped her jacket. Before she knew what happened they were on her bed, clothes half on, half off.

It was angry sex like the night before, but Kate couldn't help from losing herself in Steve's rough, passionate lovemaking. He hadn't forgiven her yet for her infidelity. But God help her, she responded to him with a passion she had never known she possessed.

⁔ ⁔ ⁔

Kate sat on the couch, legs hugged up to her knees. Steve was sleeping in her bed. She'd thrown a blanket over him before she had slipped from the room.

Her emotions were raw, bruised. She pushed her hair back from her face. It was still a tangled mess, she hadn't bothered to brush it. Steve made love to her like a madman. She stared out the window, knowing she had opened herself up to her own vulnerability. Several minutes later, Kate heard Steve behind her, but she didn't turn around.

Steve angled around the couch and sat down in front of her on her sturdy coffee table. He had on his uniform, but his shirt was unbuttoned hanging loose over his trousers. His bright, white tee shirt strained against his chest.

They looked at each other, but neither spoke.

After a moment, he reached over, taking her hand. He turned it over, studied her palm for a few seconds like he planned on predicting her destiny. "I'm sorry, Kate. I'm sorry for my behavior." He paused, cleared his throat. "I shouldn't have taken you like that. Tell me I didn't hurt you."

Only her emotions. She shook her head.

"You're sure?"

"Yes, I'm sure." Her body responded to his passionately rough lovemaking. Every nerve ending in her body had loved it, needed it, craved more. Her battered emotions were another matter.

"I lose all professionalism where you're concerned. Which is my fault, not yours."

Steve certainly didn't look professional with his black hair a mess and his uniform shirt unbuttoned.

"Are you taking out your anger on me because of what your wife did to you or because of what I did to my husband? Or just cheating women in general?"

Steve winced. "Kate, don't say things like that."

She tried to pull her hand free, but he wouldn't let her. "Why not? It's true."

"I got pissed off when I came out here and you were gone."

Kate shook her head in disagreement. "That wasn't the only thing you were pissed off about in my bedroom. You were last night, too. And...well...so was I."

Steve wrapped both of his hands around hers, stared at them like he could find an answer in their hands twined together.

"You haven't answered my question," Kate reminded him.

"Tess was a good woman like you. Attractive, smart, a good wife, good mother."

Kate didn't help him out. Steve had to work through this himself if their so-called relationship could go anywhere. Right now it was stuck on hold. It was a stunningly clear moment of truth for her. She realized she did want their relationship to progress. She'd always been attracted to him on the basic level.

It wasn't until she got to know him and made love with him that she understood how deep her feelings could go for this man. By knowing him, she discovered what kind of man Steve was.

She had closed herself off after she'd moved back to Windy Creek. Erecting a tall, solid barrier where her heart was concerned.

"I don't know if I know the answer to that question." His face was drawn in confusion. "All I know is if we stop being together, I'll feel like a dead man."

Unexpected tears crowded at the corners of her eyes. She swung her legs off the couch. Her feet landed on top of his. Then she pulled her hands free, wrapped her arms around his neck. Steve's arms slid around her back. "Kate."

She stopped whatever he was going to say with a slow, sweet, gentle kiss.

They paused only a moment before they kissed again. This time, Steve's tongue invaded her mouth. One heady kiss and she wanted him again. So simple, so elemental.

Steve pushed her back onto the couch. His mouth hovered a breath away from hers when a phone rang somewhere in the house. Kate struggled to clear her senses.

And naturally Steve started cussing. "Dammit. It's my cell." He was off of her and disappeared before she had time to blink. Kate sat up, combing her fingers through her hair. She knew it was for the best. She had to stop being so ready for him. It could very well be her undoing.

She didn't look at him when he came back into the living room, his boots in one hand, the phone pressed to his ear. He sat down next to her, started pulling on a boot.

"I'll be there in ten." Steve tossed the phone on the couch, finished putting on his boots. "There's been a break-in."

She remembered her own house being trashed. Whoever the innocent victims were she had major sympathy for them. "Where?"

"About a mile east of town. The Krentz place. You know them?" He barely glanced at her as he laced up his boots.

"The name sounds familiar."

"They were gone for the day and just returned home a while ago. Their brand new ATV, chain saw and a bunch of expensive tools are missing."

Steve was back in cop mode. Kate wondered if his emotions were that in control, too. Hers were twisting like a tornado. There was a firestorm blazing inside of her all because of him. "Mmm...must have broken into a garage or storage shed."

"Garage," Steve said as he stood up, started buttoning his shirt.

He left the living room, came back a few minutes later, all dressed and ready to go.

He walked over to the couch, sat right next to Kate, so close she felt like he was crowding her.

Steve wrapped his hand around her neck, drew her close for a long, erotic kiss. When he pulled back, his eyes were hooded. "Damn." Then he released her, stood up, started for the door. With his hand on the knob, he turned to face her. "Are you going to stay put?"

Kate nodded, battling with her out of control emotions.

※　※　※

Steve spent the next hour and a half at the Krentz place trying to calm down Frank Krentz. Having his brand new four-wheeler stolen, which he had only owned for two months, had the man in a snit. Steve asked him if he had insurance.

"Hell, yes, I have insurance." Frank Krentz glowered at Steve. "That's not the point."

Steve agreed. Getting ripped off was no fun. The thief or thieves had carted off things easy to pawn, with the exception of the four wheeler. Expensive power tools, chain saw, that sort of thing. All the perps had to do was take their stolen cache down to Kalispell to one of the many pawnshops and they would walk away with some decent money.

"Excuse me a minute, Mr. Krentz." Steve walked a feet few from Frank Krentz, dug his cell phone out of his jacket pocket and dialed the station. "Jenny, call down to the Kalispell police and have them run an alert to all the pawnshops." He read the list to Jenny.

"Got it," she said. "I'll call right now."

"Good, thanks." Steve ended the call, angled back over to Frank Krentz, who hissed and steamed like a pressure cooker.

"We're putting out an alert to the Kalispell pawnshops so if the guy or guys try to hock any of your things, the police will be right on it."

"Fine lot that will do," Frank grumbled.

"Actually it does work a good amount of the time," Steve said. "The pawn owners work closely with the local police. Besides they don't want to plunk down hard earned money for stolen goods."

Steve's assurances were lost on Frank Krentz by the look of frustration on his face.

"What about my ATV?" Frank asked. "No idiot is going to try to hock that. They don't have the title."

"The ATV is a different story. If it was a local job, they can't really ride it around here."

But Steve knew it could be painted, serial numbers changed, if the perpetrator knew what he was doing. A lost title could be filed for after some time passed, but he didn't tell Frank Krentz that. "I suggest you call your insurance agent, so that he can get right on it."

Frank Krentz glared at him before he wheeled around and stormed toward his house. His deputy, Mike Patterson came over to him. "I checked for prints, Steve. Checked the entire perimeter. There are too many tracks to tell who's who."

Steve nodded. "Yeah, I know." He circled around. Frank Krentz's place sat on a couple of acres, a mile east of town. There were neighbors, but none that close. The plots ranged from two to twenty acres in this area. "If we're done here, let's go knocking on doors."

"Yup, looks like dinner will be late tonight."

Steve lips twitched up at the corners. "Sara have something special planned tonight?"

"I don't know what she has planned for dinner, but whatever it is it will be good and hot."

Steve glanced at his watch. It was close to five. It would take a couple more hours to talk to the neighbors, then back to the station for paperwork. That means he wouldn't get back to Kate's until late.

He had a quick flash of the two of them tumbling to her bed, half dressed. He was in deep shit where Kate was concerned.

Steve and his deputy each got into their own trucks. While he was cruising down the road to the nearest neighbor, he brooded over what his true feelings were for Kate.

He'd had the hots for her since day one. Once he'd looked into her rich brown eyes that had been it. He supposed if he was honest with himself, he'd have to admit he'd always been a little in love with her. Other women in town had shown an interest in him. Attractive women, nice women, smart women. The problem was Kate had always rattled around in his brain, stopping him from getting involved with another woman.

There was just something about Kate that he couldn't explain if he tried. Steve swung his truck into Frank Krentz's neighbor's driveway. He had a job to do. But, Kate, her infidelity in her marriage, his ex-wife's infidelity all wound together into a tight ball that lodged in his stomach. He didn't want to go down that road again where a woman he loved confessed to being in love with another man.

Was he that insecure? When it came to his job and his manhood he wasn't. But his heart was another matter.

※   ※   ※

After Steve left, Kate showered, changed into clean clothes, faded jeans, sky blue turtleneck sweater. Trying to keep her mind off Steve, she rummaged through the kitchen cupboards, gathering all the ingredients to bake chocolate chip cookies. She needed something sweet, warm, and filling to calm her nerves.

As she mixed the batter, she heard the dogs barking outside. She also heard the rumble of a four-wheeler mixed with her barking dogs. Frowning, Kate headed toward the door. Several of her neighbors owned four wheelers.

When Kate opened the door, she saw Jack Daniel standing at the foot of her stairs, the dogs behind him carrying on like they had treed a mounain lion.

"Shut your damn mutts up, or I'll shut them up for you."

CHAPTER TWENTY-SIX

Fear churned through her like white water over rocks. "What do you want?" Her pistol was next to her purse on the kitchen counter. Harley's rifle was leaning against the wall in her bedroom.

"I'm warning you, shut the damn mutts up."

Jack Daniel was scruffy, dirty as usual, dressed in a rag tag black snowmobile suit. But there was something about his eyes. They had a wild look to them, like a drug addict in desperate need of his next fix. "Ranger, Sunny, no!"

It took close to a half minute for the dogs to obey her and quiet down. But the fur on their backs was still ruffled up. Kate kept her expression neutral, struggling to hide her fear. She glanced at the four wheeler parked in her driveway. It looked brand new. She wondered how Jack Daniel could afford a new ATV. They were expensive, cost thousands of dollars.

"I said, what do you want? I'm busy."

"I want your sheriff to back off. I want you to back off. Leave me the hell alone."

"Tell Sheriff Lambert yourself."

"He needs to solve old Harley's murder, so he'll look good, especially to you."

Kate glanced at the ATV again, remembering the break-in east of town. How could Jack Daniel steal it, then ride through town? "I'll give him the message. Now if you don't mind, I'm busy." She wanted to go back into the safety of her house, but she didn't dare turn her back on him. He had deep pockets in his black snowmobile suit. He could have a weapon hidden. Kate refused to even consider that Jack Daniel was armed. If she knew he had a weapon concealed in one of his pockets, she could very possibly faint right at his feet.

Sunny and Ranger leaped onto the porch from the left side. They crowded next to her. She heard Sunny's low guttural growl.

"If that's all you have to say, then be on your way."

Jack Daniel moved closer, his right foot on the bottom step. "I'm not done talking. This is your last chance to back off."

Kate had never seen him so aggressive. He'd always been standoffish, surly, but never aggressive. "I'll pass the message on to Sheriff Lambert." Her fear mushroomed at a rapid pace inside her body. Jack Daniel was threatening her. She could tell him to take a hike, but figured that wouldn't be the wisest thing to do under the circumstances. "Okay, you made your point."

He shook his head like he didn't believe her. "You think I was born yesterday? You and your sheriff will keep digging and digging until you find the truth."

Kate got the impression he wasn't really talking to her, but to himself. "I told you I'll tell the sheriff to leave you alone."

"You and your sheriff don't know what's it like." He looked past her, not really seeing her.

Fear, deep and chilling, seeped into her bones. Jack Daniel's behavior was becoming more irrational with each passing minute. She softened her tone. "What don't we understand, Jack?"

His eyes flashed back to her, then narrowed. He stared at her for a good minute, the entire time her heart beating like a war drum.

"Old Harley wouldn't let it go." Jack shook his head again. "Just wouldn't let it go."

Jack Daniel was all but admitting he'd killed Harley. Kate wanted to scream, lunge at him and claw his eyes out. Her hands fisted at her sides. "Did you kill Harley?"

Anger mottled his face, but he didn't answer.

It took everything she had and more, to stay put, to stand her ground. "I think you did."

His face contorted into an angry mass of emotions. "You need to go."

Kate swallowed a scream for help. There was no one here to help her. Steve was...she had no idea where Steve was.

"If you kill me, Sheriff Lambert will know you did it. He'll hunt you down."

"I got it all figured out. If there's no evidence, he can't pin it on me."

Kate did not want to know what Jack Daniel's plan was to kill her. Dredging up her willpower, she managed to keep herself calm. Her thoughts raced, struggling to find a way out of this life and death situation. If he shot her now, Jack Daniel would have evidence to clean up. Fear skittered up her spin, knowing it would be her blood.

⚒ ⚒ ⚒

When Steve returned to the station and read the fax from Bob at Fish and Wildlife, his adrenaline rush threatened to shoot off the chart. He was in his truck in less than ten seconds flat, siren screeching. He called Ron. "Get the hell out to Kate's house now. Jack Daniel's fiancé was mauled and killed by a grizzly sow twenty years ago. He shot five grizzlies before he moved down here. The Alberta wildlife guys have been looking for him for years."

"I'm on my way."

Steve tossed the phone down.

Bob had been busy digging up that information. One of his men, Harold Stevens, had migrated from Alberta ten years ago, remembered the story of Jack Daniels fiancé. But it was the first time he had ever put two and two together about Jack Daniel.

Cars and trucks swung to the side of the road to let Steve pass. As usual a few followed him. He didn't give a damn this time. He didn't have time to stop and tell them to not follow him.

✂ ✂ ✂

Kate watched in horror as Jack Daniel pulled a coil of white plastic cord from the left pocket of his snowmobile suit.

He was going to strangle her. No blood. There would be no blood. No blood evidence.

Fear, so primitive and real, spun inside her body like a hard and fast moving tornado.

A smirk spread across his face.

"Go fuck yourself!"

Sunny growled low and lethal beside her. Ranger snarled.

"You might as well make it easy on yourself." Jack Daniel's eyes were wild, feral.

Battling to keep her mind clear, she sucked in a breath, her eyes glued on the roll of white cord. Should she run inside the house, bolt the door? Or jump off the porch, run toward the road? She had two guns inside her house. Kate started inching backwards. Her elbow collided with the door. She had to be quick, quick as lightning.

As she slowly inched her way in reverse, she said. "The day you attacked me at Harley's house, you were bigger."

He paused while confusion fanned out across his face. Kate realized his confusion was real. Now confusion tumbled through her. What the hell was going on?

"You were bigger that day." As she crept backward, the back of her heel caught the doorjamb.

"I don't know what the blazes you're talking about."

"You came into Harley's house and attacked me."

Jack Daniel shook his head. "No."

Two men were trying to kill her? Kate struggled to comprehend the possibility of two men wanting to kill her. This was all about Harley. Who killed Harley?

"You tried to run me off the road with a snowmobile. You shot at my dogs, my house and at me." Kate paused, gulped in a breath. "You called and threatened me."

"Wait one goddamn minute!"

Kate shut up.

"Yeah, I shot at your house. But that's all I did."

An eerie feeling swept through her. She felt like she was in some kind of mind-boggling movie where nothing made sense until the end. "Then why do you want to kill me?"

"Because Harley told you what I did," Jack Daniel said in a matter of fact tone.

They were both frozen in place. Kate stopped moving backwards. Jack stopped on the bottom step. She hadn't sensed movement from Sunny and Ranger either. They, too, were frozen in place, but still snarling.

Kate had to the urge to slap herself out of this cockeyed scene. "Harley never told me anything about you. We never talked about you."

"You expect me to believe that?"

"I have no idea what you're talking about."

And then she heard the screech of the siren in the distance. Steve. What if it wasn't Steve? What if a neighbor's house was on fire or it was ambulance screaming down the road because someone's heart had given out?"

Jack Daniel heard the siren, too. He swung his head in the direction of the road. The road wasn't visible from where they stood, but Kate heard the siren growing closer. She prayed it was Steve. But how could he know Jack Daniel was here, wanting to kill her?

He couldn't.

This was her chance. She backed into the house, slammed the door. While she fumbled with the lock she heard Jack Daniel hollering her name, damning her. She ran down to her bedroom, grabbed the rifle. And then the blessed wail of the siren turned up her driveway.

※　※　※

Steve saw the stolen ATV parked next to Kate's truck. From the corner of his eye, he saw a man attempting to run through the deep snow behind Kate's house. Siren still blazing, lights still flashing, Steve leaped out of his truck. He took off in the direction of the man attempting to flee, knowing in his gut it was Jack Daniel.

Adrenaline pumping, he raised his 9mm pistol. "Halt! Sheriff!" Jack Daniel didn't stop. Steve saw him stumble, lose his balance, go face down in the snow. "Halt now!" Cussing under his breath, trying to make tracks in the deep snow, he watched Jack Daniel get up, start trudging through the snow again.

"Danielson! Halt now!" Steve bellowed.

Jack Daniel hesitated.

"Hands up in the air. Now!" Steve bullied his way through the deep snow, not knowing if Jack Daniel had a gun. He had stopped as ordered, but his hands were still at his sides.

"Raise your hands above your head."

Over the blare of his own siren, he heard another siren speeding toward Kate's place, meaning Ron wasn't far behind

273

him. He realized he didn't know where Kate was, if she was okay. Anger and fear butted heads inside his system.

Steve switched cop mode back on. "Danielson, raise your hands above your head. Now."

Jack Daniel didn't do as ordered. Instead, he dropped to his knees, starting blubbering. Steve heard Ron yelling out his name.

"Over here!" he shouted.

Steve's trousers were soaked to his knees as he stomped through the deep snow. He couldn't understand a word of Jack Daniel's blubbering. And he still had no idea where Kate was. He tamped down his fear, stopped two feet in front of Jack Daniel, his 9mm pointed at the blubbering man's chest. "Put your hands above your head."

Again Jack Daniel ignored him. "Dammit! Get your hands up now."

Jack Daniel's face was buried in his hands. Was he crying like a two year old because he'd hurt Kate? Steve shoved aside the fear again. "Where's Kate?"

Jack Daniel started shaking his head back and forth.

"Dammit, I said, where's Kate?"

Steve saw Ron semi-jogging through the snow, if that was possible, toward Jack Daniel and him. "Did you see Kate?"

"No." Ron stopped next to Steve, his own 9mm pointed at Jack Daniel, too.

"We need to get him cuffed and find Kate."

Ron frowned. "What's his problem?"

"Who the hell knows?"

Steve pulled the cuffs off his belt, nodded at Ron. While Steve holstered his gun, Ron moved closer, his 9mm leveled at the back of Jack Daniel's head. Steve had to wrench Jack Daniel's hands from his face to get the cuffs on him. He'd stopped blubbering, now he stared off into space like a zombie.

Steve's guts were clenched so tight he wondered why he didn't double over in pain. There was no way in hell he could be objective where Kate was concerned.

Kate. He had to find her.

After Steve cuffed Jack Daniel, he hauled him to his feet. He shoved him at the nearest pine tree so he could search him. He found a roll of plastic cord in his left pocket. A knife in a leather sheaf in the right pocket of his snowmobile suit. Cord and a knife. Steve yanked the knife out of the sheaf. When he didn't see fresh blood, a hint of tension disappeared. But that didn't mean shit.

Steve patted him down, from neck to feet, not finding any other weapons.

When Steve turned Jack Daniel around, he saw Kate snowshoeing toward them, holding Harley's rifle held in front of her. His heart literally leaped into his throat at the sight of her.

"Stay back, Kate."

She stopped about six feet behind Ron. Ron glanced over his shoulder at her.

"He didn't kill Harley. He was going to kill me, but he didn't kill Harley."

"What the hell?" Steve really looked at Kate then. Her face was flushed, but her eyes were huge pools of fear. "Did he hurt you?"

Kate shook her head.

"Get back to the house while Ron and I take care of Danielson."

She didn't argue, turned slowly because of her snowshoes. He glanced over at Ron, saw him arch a brow. What the hell was going on? "Let's get him into your truck and down to the station. I want to know what the hell's going on."

Ron nodded. Together they escorted Jack Daniel back through the woods while Ron read him his rights.

✄   ✄   ✄

After Ron left with Jack Daniel safely secured in the back of the patrol truck, Steve shouldered opened Kate's door. She stood at the window, watching Ron drive off.

She turned. They met each other halfway. And then Kate was in his arms. He hugged her so tight, he wondered if he was hurting her. She didn't protest, just buried her head in his chest.

"Are you sure you're okay?" Steve whispered.

"Yeah."

Steve kissed her head, the side of her cheek. Kate finally pulled back, looked at him. Then he kissed her with a raw and fierce passion. He groaned, she sighed. He battled back the urge to make love to her right on the spot. Not knowing if Jack Daniel had murdered Kate while he held the bastard at gunpoint had been a hard act for him to follow through on. He'd battled back a powerful urge to abandon Jack Daniel, race back to Kate's house and hold her in his arms, like he was doing now.

Her arms twined around his neck. They paused one second before their lips found each other's again. After the second kiss ended, Steve had to stop where they were going. "Kate." His voice sounded raw. "Kate, we have to stop."

She blinked her eyes twice while comprehension spread across her face. Steve framed her face with his hands. "I have to book Jack Daniel, I have to conduct an investigation." He paused. "I have to be a cop right now. Believe me, it's the last thing I want to be right at this moment."

CHAPTER TWENTY-SEVEN

Irritation shot through Steve as he abruptly stood up, left the interrogation room, leaving Jack Daniel in his wake.

Ron leaned against the wall near the door, guzzling down a can of Coca Cola. "He's a tough nut to crack."

Steve gritted his teeth, headed to the break room, grabbed a fresh cup of coffee. It was closing in on seven in the evening, and he was tired, cranky, frustrated and hungry. Jack Daniel had sworn he hadn't killed Harley. Criminals didn't admit their crimes. They could be locked up for years and still proclaim their innocence. And he wouldn't cop to threatening to kill Kate.

Steve walked over to Ron. He watched Ron crush the aluminum can between both palms. "Why don't you take a round with him?"

Surprise spread across Ron's face. "Me?"

Some of the tension eased out of him at Ron's expression. If he hadn't been so uptight, he probably would have laughed. "Yeah, you. You need the practice. And I can't get shit out of him."

Ron tossed the crumpled can in a nearby wastebasket, then rubbed his hands together. "You got it."

His deputy was inside the interrogation room before Steve could change his mind. He flipped on the sound to hear the conversation inside the room.

Thirty minutes later, Ron walked out of the interrogation room looking a little worse for the wear. "Jesus, the guy is friggin' weird. His eyes remind me of a rabid dog."

"Lock him up for the night. We have Kate's statement. He doesn't want a lawyer, so lock him up." And throw away the key, he wanted to add.

Ron nodded, went to fetch Bill Johnson, the night deputy on duty. Steve turned his back on Jack Daniel. He couldn't stand the sight of the man. He went into his office, called the café, waiting for somebody to pick up. Clara finally came on the line.

"Clara, this is Steve. Can I talk to Kate?"

"She just left. I told her to st—"

"What the hell? I told her to stay with you until I was finished."

Kate had insisted in driving herself to the station for her statement. She'd promised him she would stay at the café until she heard from him. "Did she go home?"

"Yes. I'm so worried about her I'm starting to feel sick."

Steve didn't feel sick, because he was too pissed off at Kate for pulling that stunt.

"Don't worry, Clara, I'm on way out there."

Kate believed Jack Daniel didn't kill Harley. On the other hand, she had believed he was going to kill her. Steve put on his and jacket and hat. He gave the night deputy instructions on where to contact him before he left the station.

Nothing made sense. Jack Daniel's fiancé had been mauled to death by a grizzly. The only crimes he'd admitted to were shooting the grizzly sow and maybe he shot a couple of other grizzlies over the years. He'd clamped his lips together when Steve had asked him if Harley had confronted him about shooting the grizzly sow. He'd sworn he'd just gone to visit Kate. He had never threatened her. Why would he do that?

Tension pounded at Steve's temples as he climbed inside his truck. And he still had Kate to deal with. The whole damn package. Her safety, his feelings for her. And his powerful need for her that had exploded after apprehending Jack Daniel behind her house today.

Jaw clenched, Steve turned on his truck ready to do battle with Kate for going home alone.

⁂   ⁂   ⁂

Kate half listened to the TV as Stone Phillips pontificated about an unsolved murder in Austin, Texas. Murder. Murder wasn't her favorite word today. She closed her eyes again, tried to snuggle deeper into the couch. At the café, she'd helped with the dinner rush, her adrenaline still pumping at high speed. There was no way she could have sat still, done nothing. Now fatigue wrapped around her like a wet, soggy blanket, weighing her down.

There was still an s.o.b. out there waiting to get her. Lurking somewhere in the shadows. Steve believed Jack Daniel killed Harley. She believed he didn't. But she hadn't figured out why Jack Daniel had been intent on killing her. Or the meaning of the wild look in his eyes.

Shivering she hugged the blanket closer to her.

When Sunny and Ranger started barking outside, she ignored them. She had no idea when Steve would get here or if he even would. In the soft, hidden place in her heart, she knew he would come whatever the time.

She figured there were deer wandering outside or maybe a coyote. She'd heard one yapping in the distance when she'd arrived home.

Kate wanted sleep, needing it to block out the terrifying events of the day.

Suddenly a loud crash echoed through the house. Kate sat up so fast dizziness swamped her body. It was the sound of wood splintering. She heard the dogs barking over the noise from the back of the house.

Kate leaped off the couch, tossing the blanket in the process. She stubbed her big toe on the leg of the coffee table. Ignoring the pain, she reached under the couch, fumbling for the rifle. Her hand closed around it just as a hulking figure stormed into the living room. Sunny and Ranger tailing him, fur ruffled, teeth bared.

Hal Jackson.

His face was blood red while his eyes were swimming with anger. He held a splitting maul in front of him like a rifle.

Stunned, Kate straightened slowly, her forefinger on the trigger.

"You bitch!"

Kate raised the gun, her instincts ready to do battle. "You killed Harley."

"Damn right I did. He was nothing but trouble, the old son of a bitch."

Anger surged through Kate. Anger so powerful and all consuming she wanted to point the rifle at Hal's ugly face and blow it to smithereens. "You bastard. You killed the only father I ever knew."

Hal stepped toward her, raising the maul. The maul that had killed Harley. She knew that for a fact. Kate raised the gun to her shoulder. "Stay back. I'll shoot you. I swear to God, I will." Her finger pressed against the trigger.

Hal swayed back on his feet. The bastard was drunk. "Stay back," she warned.

The dogs kept barking and snarling. Stone Phillips kept talking. Hal kept scowling at her. Kate's heart hammered against her ribs.

"Drop your weapon!"

When Hal wheeled his big beefy body around, she saw Steve then, in full uniform, his 9mm handgun poised in front of him. His face grim and determined.

Hal hurled the maul at Steve. A cry stuck in her throat. Steve ducked just in time as the heavy splitting maul sailed past him, slammed into her kitchen table. The dogs beat feet away from Steve and Hal.

"Hands in the air, Jackson. Now, dammit, now!"

"That no good, old s.o.b. deserved it. I hated him from the time I moved next to him." Hal Jackson wasn't talking, he was yelling. The sound of his angry, drunk voice echoing inside Kate's head.

Over Hal's yelling, she heard the sound of a siren approaching. Steve had called for backup.

"Put your hands in the air," Steve repeated.

"I cut two lousy trees on his property. Harley had a shit fit over it. Said he was going to call the cops." Hal shook his head. "I needed the firewood. He said if I would have asked if he would have let me have them. You bet, you bet, you bet. He hated me, too. He wouldn't have given me any wood, any more than he would have given me the time of day."

Harley had been murdered over firewood. It was beyond Kate's comprehension. To kill a man over a couple of felled trees. To kill Harley, her father, not by blood, but bound by love. The urge to blow the back of Hal's head off swept through her like wildfire.

She watched Hal sway back on his feet again. Why couldn't the drunk bastard just fall flat on his face?

Ron came rushing up behind Steve, his gun poised in front of him. He moved flush with Steve.

"Get out of the way, Kate," Steve ordered.

It was then she realized she was in the line of fire of both men's guns. She scooted around the coffee table, walked sideways to the window. Steve scowled at her, not liking her position. It was as far as she was going her expression told him.

It took another five minutes for Steve to talk Hal down. Then his husky shoulders slumped while his hands lifted half-heartedly over his head.

⚹   ⚹   ⚹

Kate and Steve laid together on his couch, still fully clothed, a blanket tossed over them. Their arms and legs all tangled together. Kate could see the digital clock on the small table at the end of the couch. It was two seventeen a.m..

Steve's forehead was pressed against her cheek. She wondered if he was sleeping, but she knew he wasn't.

"I can't believe he killed Harley over firewood." Aching for Harley, she closed her eyes.

Steve stirred, turned his head. "I know you need a good reason for Hal murdering Harley, but there isn't one, Kate. There won't ever be one. I'm sorry."

The harsh reality of his words stabbed deep into her heart. Tragically Steve was right, but nevertheless, it still hurt.

"He confessed." Steve rubbed the back of his hand across her check. "He was drunk when he went over to Harley's that day. He and Harley argued. Harley ordered Hal off his property, which pissed him off. He grabbed the splitting maul that was leaning against a tree when Harley turned away from him..."

Steve didn't elaborate. She hadn't been in the interrogation room with Steve and Hal Jackson. She had wanted to be. She'd wanted to listen, but Steve had forbidden it. Ron had driven her to Steve's house, since she'd refused to wake up Clara.

She'd settled on the couch with a blanket she'd found in Steve's closet. Thirty minutes ago, when he arrived at his house, he had simply scooted her over and taken her into his arms.

The dogs were asleep on the floor next to the couch. Ron had nailed a slab of plywood across the opening where Hal had destroyed her back door.

"I was going to wait until the morning to tell you, but Ron finally got Jack Daniel to open up. Harley figured out he shot the grizzly sow. He told Jack to turn himself in, but he wouldn't. Jack was afraid Harley knew the entire story, that's why he went after you."

In the darkness, she clutched Steve's hand. "What is the story?"

Steve sighed. "I can see we're not getting any sleep tonight. Jack's fiancé was mauled to death by a grizzly sow up in Alberta twenty some years ago. Jack took it personally. After that, he went after grizzly sows to vindicate his woman's death. When the authorities were onto him, he split and moved down here." Steve paused. "For quite a few years, he was able to control his urge for shooting grizzly sows. Turns out Harley and Jack had a few beers at the local bar one night about ten years ago, and Jack spilled his guts to Harley, only he was too drunk to remember. Harley obviously wasn't drunk because he did remember. When the sow was discovered, Harley must have put two and two together. He confronted Jack and told him to turn himself in."

"He was going to kill me."

Steve snugged her tighter against him if that was possible. "Yeah, I know."

"You're holding something back."

"Ah...Kate. You don't need to hear everything tonight."

Her hand gripped his. "Yes. I do."

Steve kissed her cheek. "Jack had planned on killing Harley, but Hal beat him to it. But then he figured since Harley and you were so close, Harley had probably confided in you."

Kate let out a long, slow breath. "I never in my wildest dreams thought Harley had so many enemies."

"These two men created their own troubles. I didn't know Harley that well, but he struck me as the type of man that would have given firewood to Hal so he wouldn't freeze his ass off over the winter. He didn't rat on Jack Daniel. Instead he told him to turn himself in, which would have lessened the penalty for Jack Daniel with the Fish and Wildlife."

Kate's body was beyond exhaustion. Two attempts on her life in a few short hours... She sorted through Steve's information. The lies, the truths, the assumptions. Harley didn't tell her about Jack Daniels because he'd wanted to protect her. For Harley, confronting Jack Daniels would have been a man-to-man thing.

"Who did what to me?" Kate asked.

"Kate."

"I need to know."

"Hal threatened you with the phones call and the note. He was the one that tried to run you off the road with his snowmobile. He attacked you at Harley's house. Hal was the one snooping around your house that night. Jack Daniel did the shooting. He stole Frank Krentz's four-wheeler because he didn't have one. Drove the damn thing right through town."

Two men trying to kill her. Kate shivered.

Steve's arms tightened around her. "You okay?"

She soaked in Steve's strength and warmth for a time before she said. "Yeah."

After awhile, the fatigue in her body started to drown her, pushing her toward much needed sleep. She didn't bother trying to see the clock. They were squashed together on Steve's couch. But she knew they were both too bone tired to get up and drag themselves to his bedroom.

"I don't care what happened in your marriage, Kate. I don't care anything about your past. I just care about now."

Kate's eyes flew open like being awakened by an old time wind up alarm clock. She laid her hand on Steve's cheek, which was bristled with a day's worth of new growth. "You really mean that?" Steve had found it in his heart to forgive her. She wasn't prepared for the sheer relief that washed through her. The vice of grief and sadness loosened around her heart.

And now it was time to forgive herself. David had divorced her so fast she realized he'd been looking for an out. She had provided an easy one for her ex-husband. It was time to move on. In a moment of weakness, she'd made a mistake. If Steve could forgive her, she needed to do the same.

"Yeah, I mean it." He raised her hand to his lips, kissing her fingertips. "I'm hopelessly in love with you."

Kate smiled in the darkness. "Hopelessly. I like that."

"I don't," Steve muttered. "It makes me vulnerable where you're concerned."

For a man to admit he was vulnerable was a major thing. A powerful feeling swelled inside her heart.

"Say something, Kate. Like you're in love with me, too."

Kate smiled again. "Maybe a little."

"Give me a break," he grumbled. "Every time you see me, you jump my bones."

"You have terrific bones."

"What's that supposed to mean?"

She angled her head, kissing him softly on his lips. "It means, Sheriff Lambert, I do believe I might be hopelessly in love with you, too."

Patricia Parkinson

Patricia Parkinson lives near the magnificent Rocky Mountains in western Montana. Her writing is inspired by nature, the unsurpassed beauty of her home state and various wildlife, which includes an occasional meandering bear through her yard. Her hardy, and many times, quirky neighbors and friends have inspired more than one character for her stories. She has been composing poetry, short stories and books since childhood. She lives in an all female household, which includes a rowdy, girl black lab and two very, moody girl cats

Coming Soon by Ms. Parkinson

Crazy Daze of Summer, *ebook Available September 2006*

Visit www.samhainpublishing.com for updates!

Samhain Publishing, Ltd.

It's all about the story...

Action/Adventure
Fantasy
Historical
Horror
Mainstream
Mystery/Suspense
Non-Fiction
Paranormal
Red Hots!
Romance
Science Fiction
Western
Young Adult

http://www.samhainpublishing.com

Printed in the United States
55221LVS00001BA/103-510